BOOKS BY CLAIRE COOK

PRAISE FOR MUST LOVE DOGS

"Reading about how life goes for this wacky
marvelously lovable family becomes addictive."
—*Pamela Kramer, Examiner*

"*Must Love Dogs* has already been a major motion
picture, and now *New York Times* bestselling
author Claire Cook's hilarious and heartwarming
series is begging to hit the screen again
as a miniseries or a sitcom."
—*Nancy Carty Lepri, New York Journal of Books*

"Wildly witty"—*USA Today*

"Cook dishes up plenty of charm."
—*San Francisco Chronicle*

"A hoot."—*The Boston Globe*

"Reading *Must Love Dogs* is like having lunch with
your best friend—fun, breezy, and full of laughs."
—*Lorna Landvik*

Must Love Dogs:

Who Let the Cats In? (#5)

Claire Cook

Marshbury Beach Books

Marshbury Beach Books
Book Layout: The Book Designer
Author Photo: Stuart Wilson
Cover photo: Tsomkaigor

Must Love Dogs: Who Let the Cats In? (#5)/Claire Cook
ISBN: 978-1-942671-18-3

CHAPTER

One

"In three years I'll be ten and I'll be your babysitter," five-year-old Millicent said from our designated class bench.

"In three years I'll be twentieth and I'll be *your* babysitter," five-year-old Violet, who was sitting next to Millicent, said.

"No." Millicent crossed her arms over her chest. "Way."

"Yes." Violet crossed her arms over her chest. "Way."

"Ah, to be twentieth again," my teaching assistant Polly whispered. "Or even twentyish."

"No thank you," I whispered back. "I'm barely functional at fortiethish."

Another school day was about to bite the dust. The full-day students were arranged on our wooden dismissal benches, which were backless, low to the ground, and surrounded by a thick layer of sustainably harvested pea stone. The teachers and assistants were taking turns watching the students and escorting them to their cars as they arrived.

At the start of every school year, parents were given strips of white poster board. They were instructed to print their child/children's names in big block letters, and then to lean the sign up against the passenger side of the windshield at pickup time to move things along.

Dismissal was orderly, ritualized, even soothing. The message being that if you have a plan, if you follow the rules, if you take things one step at a time, it all works out.

Now I just had to figure out how to apply that to the rest of my life.

I wrapped my autumn-weight sweater a little tighter and glanced up at the sky. When my mother was alive, one of her favorite old Irish sayings, passed down from her great-grandmother, or maybe it was my great-grandmother, was *I believe in the sun when it's not shining*. It was a lovely sentiment, but I had to admit that sometimes I had a hard time believing in the sun even when it was shining.

If I were a poet, I might think the sky was the hue of ocean-splashed denim right now. Or maybe, like Thoreau, I might imagine a bluebird carrying the sky on its back. If I were Jimi Hendrix, I might hallucinate some purple haze and break into a little *Excuse me while I kiss the sky.*

But I was none of the above. I was a teacher at Bayberry Preschool. And I had to admit that on this particular November day, the sky looked pretty damn gray to me.

The line of vehicles inched forward from the main road, where an inevitable backlog always caused a minor traffic jam. This had resulted in the town of Marshbury installing a yellow blinking traffic light a few years ago, which probably made the members of some committee feel better, but did absolutely nothing to help the traffic situation.

The pickup line snaked its way up the long entrance drive to the school. SUVs and minivans and sedans and hybrids. Plus a surprising number of sports cars driven by parents who were apparently still in denial about the fact that they were parents now. The vehicles crept past a totem pole made of brightly colored clay fish and a row of painted plywood cutouts of teddy bears.

The front three cars pulled into three generously sized fluorescent paint-outlined pickup/dropoff spots, just across from the row of boxwood sheared in the shape of ducks that edged the walkway to the Cape Cod shingled building.

Kate Stone, my bitch of a boss and the founding owner of Bayberry Preschool, adjusted her boysenberry batik tunic and squinted at the first car in line. The name on the poster board was written in cramped, illegible cursive tucked into one corner.

"Wolverine," my bitch of a boss yelled. Wolfie's teacher walked him over to his car.

The nanny driving the next vehicle dropped her sign and then jumped the curb slightly as she bent over to retrieve it. The sign in the car behind hers looked like it had been professionally designed, complete with custom fonts and a caricature of a preschool boy with a halo over his head.

I yawned. The sun dropped a little lower. Five-year-old Gulliver hurled himself backward off our classroom bench. He imitated a bomb, or perhaps a small vehicle exploding as he hit the bed of pea stones, backpack first.

Polly caught my eye, silently asking whether or not she should click into rescue mode.

I did a swift scan for blood and/or signs of concussion, then shook my head in a quick, almost imperceptible no. If Gulliver, weighted down by his backpack like a turtle flipped over on its shell, had to figure out how to get up on his own, he'd be far less likely to fling himself off the bench again.

"Kevin Junior and Nicole Junior," my bitch of a boss yelled.

I crouched down and pretended to tie one shoe. Since my shoes didn't have any laces, this may or may not have been one of my smoother moves.

Lorna, one of my favorite teaching colleagues and partners in crime, grabbed my former husband's twins by their hands and headed for his car.

"Any love letters you want me to pass along?" Lorna whispered as they passed me.

"Ha," I said. I was witty like that.

"Why one human being is attracted to another is one of the great mysteries of the world," my father had once said to me.

The truth was I couldn't even remember being attracted to my wasband. My ex. Kevin. What the hell I'd been doing married to him, for ten years no less, was the real mystery. He'd finally left me for another woman, Nikki, aka Nicole Senior, chatty as hell and ten years younger than me, and already pregnant with twins. Not only were my ex and his replacement wife narcissistic enough to name one twin after each of them, but they'd enrolled them both at Bayberry and had even had the nerve to request me as their teacher.

I'd dodged the placement, and the twins had been relocated to Lorna's class. The situation had gone from awkward to slightly less awkward, and without any encouragement on my part, Nikki Senior had even sold my house for me. But that didn't mean I wanted to spend one more millisecond dealing with my wasband and his new tribe than I had to.

When I looked up from fake tying my shoe, Kevin had rolled down the passenger window to give me a big wave.

I fought an unteacherly urge to flash him my most expressive finger.

As their benches emptied of preschoolers, teachers and assistants strolled back inside to wrap things up for the day.

For the third time this week, Polly and I were the last teachers standing. And it was only Wednesday.

Kate Stone headed back to her office. Gulliver, our final remaining student, hurled himself backward off the bench again.

Polly and I ignored him. I gestured to an empty bench, out of Gulliver's earshot, but close enough to keep an eye on him.

"Seat?" I said.

Polly shook her head. "Nah, I'm always afraid I'll get butt splinters if I sit on those things."

I considered this. "If that were a possibility, wouldn't the kids get butt splinters, too?"

"Not necessarily. The kids are a lot lighter."

"Hmm," I said. "I have to admit that in the planning of these benches, it's highly unlikely that the teachers were taken into consideration. But you might as well get used to it—teachers' butts are always on the line anyway, so basically they're expendable."

Polly grinned and squatted low to sit on the bench. I plopped down beside her. We talked through our plans for the next day, moved on to chatting about our lives.

The late afternoon sun broke through some clouds, lighting up the freckles that danced across Polly's nose and cheeks. When she ran her fingers through her auburn hair, strands of gray twinkled in a quick burst of sunlight.

I pulled my sweater a little tighter, tried to remember where I'd stashed my coats.

"So," Polly said, "basically you and your boyfriend and his dog are homeless, you've all moved in with your dad, and now you've got to figure out what to do about a litter of kittens under the porch. Wow, that's a lot, Sarah."

"Look who's talking," I said.

Polly rested one hand on her stomach. Her eyes teared up.

"Sorry." I started to put a hand on her shoulder, pulled it back.

Polly sniffed, shook her head. "No, I'm fine. It's just these stupid hormones. I cry at everything now. Sad songs on the radio. Dead worms on the sidewalk after it rains. Elimination rounds on *The Voice*."

I put my hand on her shoulder after all, just for a moment. I'd hired Polly right before the start of the school year, when Kate Stone pulled a last minute switcheroo. She'd sent June, the assistant I'd worked my fingers to the bone to train, off to work with Ethan, the new teacher, resident school hunk, and my bitch of a boss's godson.

Polly had been a total train wreck at the interview. She had absolutely no experience with preschools, or even children. But my heart went out to her because she'd left her husband, moved across the country to Marshbury, and found a tiny winter rental on the beach. She was trying to figure out what the next chapter of her life might be, and whether or not it would include having a child by herself.

So against my better judgment, as well as the objections of my boss, I chose Polly instead of a more qualified applicant. And she'd ended up being a great assistant.

Except for the fact that it turned out Polly was already pregnant and wouldn't quite make it to the end of the school year before her baby was born.

Gulliver maneuvered himself up to his feet and came over to sit on the bench with us.

I picked a piece of dried leaf out of his hair, pointed at a low cloud drifting across the sky. "I see a fluffy cat with a long tail and pointy ears."

Gulliver pointed up at another cloud. "I see a big monster jumping on a little monster."

"Holy Rorschach test," Polly said. She pointed. "I see a boat sailing back and forth across the water, rocking me to sleep."

Eventually a shiny platinum convertible came speeding up the driveway, straddled two pickup spots, stopped. Wordlessly, I stood and reached out a hand to Gulliver. I steered him over to the convertible.

As I opened the passenger door, Gulliver's mother was touching up her lipstick in the rearview mirror with one freshly manicured hand.

"Stop being last," Gulliver yelled as he hurled his backpack into the car.

"Well said," I said.

His mother flipped her hair, which was highlighted the exact same color as her convertible, out of her face. She checked her Fitbit.

"Did you dismiss them early today?" she said.

"*What?*" I said.

Two

Crushed mussel shells crunched under the tires of my trusty old Honda Civic as I rolled up the driveway to the 1890 Victorian I'd grown up in.

Something caught my eye.

I put my car into park, opened the door, looked up. A red-tailed hawk was circling overhead, swooping and gliding across the sky, which was now an undeniable battleship gray. The hawk plunged low and hovered just over the wraparound porch at the front of the house.

"Shoo," I yelled, as if that might work with a hawk.

The hawk circled high above the porch, around and around like one of those plastic planes attached to strings my brothers used to fly as kids.

"Go away," I screamed. "Right now."

The hawk circled some more, swooped lower.

"One . . . two . . . three . . ." I tried.

The hawk ignored me. Apparently counting worked a lot better with preschoolers than it did with birds of prey.

"Go find some road kill," I screamed. Without taking my eyes off it, I reached one hand into my Civic and leaned on the horn. Hard.

It kept circling.

I ran for the garden hose, turned the water on full blast, pointed it skyward in the direction of the hawk.

By the time John found me, I was drenched and shivering.

But at least the red-tailed hawk had high-tailed it out of there.

. . . . .

John followed me upstairs to my old bedroom. I peeled off my soaked clothes and looked around for my bathrobe.

He reached for me. As we kissed, John rubbed his hands up and down the goose bumps that traveled the length of my arms.

"We don't have time for this," I said. "The hawk—"

"I know," he said. We kissed some more.

"The architect. And we still don't have a contractor—"

"I know," he said. We kissed some more.

John's dog Horatio let out a low whine.

"Place," John said.

Horatio sighed and jumped up on the new king-sized bed we'd swapped for the twin beds my sister Christine and I used to sleep on. The low bed took up most of the available floor space in the room, its clean modern lines a bit jolting against the hot pink walls from the century before this one, and the elaborate crown molding from the century before that.

A small bureau was jammed up against each of the room's two windows. John's and my alarm clocks perched on piles of old books crammed in on either side of the low bed. A gooseneck floor lamp turned on with the switch just inside the door, which meant that somebody had to walk over to turn it off at night and then roam blindly back to the bed.

"Place," John said again.

Horatio jumped down. He found his monogrammed dog bed at the foot of our bed, clawed the plush fur a few times, circled around, plopped down.

"Good boy," John said.

Horatio was the product of a dalliance between a Yorkie that lived in John's building and a runaway greyhound, though he'd somehow come out looking more like a scruffy dachshund. That he and John were attached was an understatement the size of, say, Australia.

We'd come a long way, Horatio and I. He'd gone from wanting to tear me from limb to limb to reluctantly acknowledging my spot between John and him in the pecking order. I tried not to rub it in.

Horatio sighed.

John and I kissed some more. He started maneuvering me in the direction of the bed.

"Hell's bells," my father's voice said right outside my bedroom door.

John and I froze. A sideways glance confirmed that the old door hadn't quite clicked shut.

"Now where in tarnation did I put that thingamabobbie?" my father said.

The door creaked open.

I dove for my robe.

John took a step toward the door, his arms wide to shield me.

Horatio jumped up, tail wagging, and circled around John to get to the door first.

. . . . .

"I wouldn't mind some of that noodle juice myself," my father said from his seat at the kitchen table, even though I was already putting teabags in three mugs while John filled the kettle.

I checked the tie on my bathrobe, pulled it a little tighter. Added a double knot just to be on the safe side. Took a moment to remember John's hands traveling the length of my arms, replacing one kind of goose bump with another.

"Dad," I said. "Do you know what happened to those long brass keys to the bedroom doors? You know, the ones that could lock the doors from either the inside or the outside?"

My father slapped his knee. "Your mother and I hid them on you kiddos. I believe it was right after you and your sister ganged up on your other sister and locked her in her room."

"That was Carol." I turned to John. "She was such an arrogant little shit. She totally deserved it."

I turned back to my dad. "You don't happen to remember where you hid them, do you?"

"That was your mother's department." He put his hand over his heart, looked skyward. "But I still talk to her every night when I say my prayers, so I'll make a note to ask her."

I wondered how long it would be before I didn't have to blink back tears when a mention of my mother took me by surprise. Even though she'd been dead now for more years than I wanted to count, she was still the superglue that held our family together. Her spirit filled every inch of this house.

Which might partially excuse the insanity of moving in here.

The kettle whistled and I poured the tea. John grabbed a treat for Horatio, and the humans took our seats at the scarred pine trestle table.

I dunked my teabag. "Dad, I think we all need to start knocking on doors around here."

My father dunked his teabag. "I was gearing up to mention that myself, Christine."

"Sarah," I said.

"Just making sure you're awake, Sarry girl. You and your fella could knock, or perhaps I could hang a flag on my door. Just so you both know to give me a wide berth in case I have some babycakes in there and the two of us are busy watching the submarine races."

John smiled. I wondered if he'd still be smiling a month from now.

"Flags could work," I said. "Hey, Dad, you haven't seen a hawk flying over the front porch, have you?"

"No bafflegab or malarkey about it," my dad said. "That hawk's not the only thing Homer and I are worried about."

For some mysterious reason, my father had renamed John's dog. This was not without precedent, since he'd also tried to change John's name to Jack at one point, his rationale being that we already had one John in the family, my brother Johnny. Jack didn't stick, but so far John's dog didn't appear to have any objections to answering to both Horatio and Homer, especially if treats were involved.

My father pushed a lock of thick white hair out of his eyes and wiggled his eyebrows. "If I'd been spifflicated or even half seas over, I never would have believed it. But on the well-tended graves of my forefathers, not even a wee sip was involved. It was only half past a poached egg on toast in the morning."

My father's word choices could make him sound like one of his own forefathers, or even a time traveler. Sometimes it was charming. Right now it was aggravating.

I gave my forehead a quick massage with my fingertips. "It's been a long day, Dad. Plain English would really help me out."

"A coyote," my father said. "Plain as the nose on your face. Strolling down the street in broad daylight as if it hadn't a care in the world. But that rascal didn't fool Homer and me for one minute—we knew it was casing the joint because it caught wind of what we had under our porch."

"Whoa," I said. "I thought coyotes were nocturnal."

"Try telling that to Wiley E. Coyote," my father said. "All's Homer and I know is what we saw with our own four eyes."

A heartbreaking meow cut in. A young cat with intense green eyes appeared like a vision through the kitchen's single French door, lit from above by the patio light. Black and ginger spots dotted her fur like beach pebbles on pure white sand. She was beautiful, in that exhausted, unkempt way of a young mother.

"There's our Miss Pebbles," my father said as he pushed himself up from his chair. "Just you hold your horses now, sweet pea."

The cat moved to the cover of darkness while my father opened a can of cat food with the ancient avocado green can opener that had been attached to the wall for as long as I could remember. John led Horatio in to the other room so Horatio wouldn't frighten the mama cat away.

I headed for the front hallway closet. I slipped my father's flannel-lined L.L. Bean field coat over my bathrobe and stepped into a pair of his boat shoes. I grabbed a flashlight from the junk drawer in the entry table and scuffed my way out to the front porch.

The sky had gone from gray to squid ink flecked with stars. I aimed the beam of light between the porch boards. I thought I caught a blur of movement, but maybe I only imagined it.

"Your mom will be right back, kitties," I whispered. "Whatever you do, don't go anywhere when she's gone. Just stay right under there until we figure out what to do about you. You're going to be fine, I promise."

I hoped it was a promise I could keep.

Three

"Two full tins of cat grub washed down with a dainty drink of water, plus a Slim Jim for the road," my father said once we'd reconvened in the kitchen. "It doesn't appear our Miss Pebbles is one of those gals that needs to worry about her figure."

Whether my dad had named her after the markings on her fur or as a tribute to *The Flintstones*, we were all starting to think of the mama cat as Pebbles. Even though her kittens were nestled under the front porch, Pebbles never meowed for food at the more conveniently located front door. Instead she'd circle around to the kitchen door at the side of the house, chow down, and then loop back to feed her brood.

Horatio had given us the first clue that something was up. Every time he passed over the front porch, he

barked ferociously like the overcompensating small dog
he was, and tried to claw a hole through the porch
boards. As soon as John and I caught a glimpse of the
tiny balls of fur underneath the porch, we started
taking Horatio in and out by the kitchen door. In fact,
we'd all begun using the kitchen door instead of the
heavy oak front door. We didn't want to spook Pebbles,
so we just pretended we didn't know anything about
any kittens, and it was perfectly normal for a cat to
inhale endless cans of food for no particular reason.

"Oh, the poor thing," I said. "I fed her before I left
for school this morning."

"I fed her a time or three earlier in the day myself,"
my dad said.

"I fed her twice," John said. "I worked at the kitchen
table for most of the day to make sure I wouldn't miss
her when she showed up."

When I met John's Heath Bar eyes, I felt the same
jolt I always did. John's eyes were his best feature—a
circle of toffee surrounded by a larger circle of chocolate brown.

I knew exactly why I was attracted to John
Anderson. I loved his intelligence, his earnestness, his
kindness, his sense of humor, even the residual
dorkiness that gave me a glimpse of what he'd been like
in high school. I loved the understated swagger in his
shoulders when he walked. I loved that, while I had a
tendency to flounder, he always had a plan. I loved that
he was as worried about Pebbles and her kittens as I
was.

The big mystery was what the hell John was doing with me. Sometimes I thought I might be a walking female embodiment of that Yeats quote: *Being Irish, he had an abiding sense of tragedy, which sustained him through temporary periods of joy.* The truth was that a big part of me kept waiting for someone to take John aside and point out that surely he could do better than Sarah Hurlihy.

We'd been through a lot, John and I. Horatio had tried to keep us apart. One of John's coworkers had attempted to cut me out of the picture and manipulate her way into John's heart. A brief trip to canine camp had almost put an end to us.

John and I had survived all that and committed to building a life together. I'd realized I could never make it as a city mouse, so John had decided to become a country mouse, or a least a suburban mouse. John ran the accounting department at a digital game company called Necrogamiac, and his boss had agreed to let him work remote most days so he wouldn't have to deal with the ridiculous commute from Marshbury, Massachusetts into the city. We'd sold my house, rented his Boston condo through a short-term executive rental company.

And now we were facing what might be our biggest challenge yet. We were buying my family house. Creating a separate space for my father. A shared gathering place for family. A private oasis for John and me, preferably surrounded by a moat.

Just call us crazy. And in the midst of all this, we'd also come to terms with the fact that, even though it might be too late, John and I wanted to try to have a child together. And of course, the universe being the universe, when we'd dared to hope for a baby, a cat had given birth to kittens underneath the front porch instead.

"Bottoms up," my father said. He tipped his mug and took a long gulp of his tea.

"Do you think," I said, "we should cut some old sheets or towels into little strips and try to stuff them between the porch boards with a ruler? Or maybe we could shove them through the holes in the latticework on the sides of the porch? Just to help keep the kittens warm until we can get them out of there?"

"I believe we've got some old heating pads around here somewhere," my father said. "You kids could plug them into those extension cords we use to fire up the Christmas lights."

I shivered. "What if the kittens get tangled up in the cords? Or chew through them?"

"I'd be afraid getting that close to her kittens might frighten Pebbles away," John said. "Our best bet is to continue heaping on the food to keep her engine going. She's their heat."

John looked down at his phone. "But I think we're going to have to move fast here. My app says we've got good weather through the next few days followed by a hard frost coming in Saturday night. So how about we spend the next two days doing the research and getting a plan, and then we'll launch Operation Rescue at the crack of dawn on Saturday. That way we'll have the whole day."

"Aye-aye, chief," my dad said. "I'm slated to work Saturday, but the girls won't mind me calling in otherwise occupied just this once." My father had a part-time job driving an ice cream truck owned by a company called Bark & Roll Forever. He passed out dog treats attached to business cards for Bark & Roll Forever's dog walking and boarding services, and sold the occasional ice cream on the side. The three boomer women who owned the company paid him in casseroles. Given my pathetic cooking skills, this might also partially excuse the insanity of moving in here.

I pushed myself out of my chair and opened the freezer to check out the dinner possibilities.

"Actually, Billy," John was saying to my father. "I think the most helpful thing you could do might be to take Horatio to work with you."

"Now you're on the trolley," my father said. "You two just get those fluffballs all rescued up and dropped off at the animal shelter. And then give us a ringaling on the tingaling and we'll come back when the coast is clear. Homer and I don't mind felines visiting every once in a while, but we like our space."

. . . . .

When I hit my alarm clock Thursday morning, it tumbled off the pile of books on my side of the bed. I swore, rooted around for it, finally managed to shut it up. I remembered John and reached for him. Found an empty pillow instead, still warm from his head.

I took a quick shower and scanned the immediate vicinity for something to wear to work. Dirty clothes spilling out of a laundry basket reminded me that I seriously needed to do some laundry.

I opened the top drawer of my childhood bureau, where I'd stashed my underwear. Only one fairly pitiful bra remained, and apparently I was out of fresh underpants.

While I yanked open the rest of the drawers, I debated whether or not I was brave enough to go to work commando just this once. I hadn't really bought in to that old thing about always wearing your best underpants in case you get into an accident, but hearing it repeatedly during my formative years had instilled just enough fear in me that I generally felt compelled to wear at least *some* underpants.

In the very last drawer, tucked way in the back with some other long-forgotten relics, I found a pair of the Lollipop underpants my sisters and I had worn until we'd generated enough personal income that we could afford to buy something with a little more sex appeal. Until then we were stuck with high-waisted white cotton, cuffed bands at the legs, the Pictionary definition of *full coverage*.

Without thinking, I checked the label. There it was: the red hand-stitched X that marked these underpants as mine. In order to keep track of six kids' tidy whities, our mother had assigned us each a color. As the eldest daughter, Carol got the girliest color, pink, which I had to admit I still resented. I was red, Christine was yellow, Billy Jr. was blue, Johnny was orange, and

Michael was green. Or maybe Michael was orange and Johnny was green. Our mother had a wooden spool of thread for each of us, and whenever we got new undies, she'd cross-stitch a thick X in the appropriate color.

I flashed back to the mountain of laundry our family of eight had produced. A laundry chute was hidden under a square door on the floor of the linen cabinet in the upstairs bathroom. You opened the door and threw your dirty clothes in. One floor directly below, the washer and dryer were tucked behind shuttered doors in a corner of the kitchen. There was another door on the ceiling just beside the washer and dryer. A string was attached to that door, and when you pulled it, an avalanche of dirty clothes descended from above, landing on your head if you didn't jump back fast enough.

My brothers had been known to occasionally initiate a new friend to the Hurlihy household by asking him to pull that string. And "knock it off or I'll throw you down the laundry chute," was the big threat between siblings when somebody got on our nerves.

I shook my head to bring myself back to the present, then wiggled my way into my old Lollipops. The leg cuffs stuck for a minute and then eased over my thighs. Wow, those old Lollipops really held up. And I had to admit I'd held up better myself in the decades since high school than I would have thought—the waist was even a teensy bit loose.

After I unearthed my least wrinkled black pants from the laundry basket, I found a boring beige top still hanging in the tiny closet. With my dark hair, pale cool skin and hazel eyes, it wasn't the most horrific color on me, but a pop of peacock blue or turquoise or even red definitely would have been way better. I was old enough to know my colors—I just didn't always have enough clean clothes to wear them.

I untangled the longish taupe cardigan I'd worn Monday from the mess on top of my dresser and attempted to shake the wrinkles out as I slid into a pair of black flats.

I grabbed my laundry basket, ran to the hallway bathroom and dumped my dirty clothes down the laundry chute. Then I raced for the stairs. To save time, I was tempted to try sliding down the long mahogany banister, past the wall of framed family photos, the way we used to when we were kids and our parents weren't looking.

John looked up from his laptop when I blew into the kitchen. "Good morning, Mary Sunshine."

"Funny," I said. I gulped some fresh-brewed coffee and gave him a quick kiss on top of his head while I waited for the caffeine to kick in. Then I opened the fridge, shoveled some of last night's casserole into one of my mother's old Tupperware containers, spooned some more into my mouth.

"Do you want me to make you a quick breakfast?" John asked. Another thing I loved about John was that he could actually cook.

"No thanks," I mumbled through a mouthful of cold curried chicken and cauliflower. "I've already eaten."

I started the washer and dryer, added some detergent, pulled the string to the laundry chute, jumped back. "Do you mind throwing these in the dryer when they're done?" I yelled as I jammed my dirty clothes into the ancient Whirlpool.

"Not at all. FYI, Horatio bunked in with your dad again, I just fed Pebbles, and don't forget, we've got to sign the papers on the house at the lawyer's office at four. The architect is dropping off the updated plans today, and I'm working on a list of contractors to call. And we both need to do some cat rescue research."

"Got it. Thanks. Love you." I gave him another quick kiss, grabbed my purse and keys and the Tupperware, opened the kitchen door.

As I backed out of the driveway, I saw Pebbles slip into an impossibly narrow gap between one side of the front porch and the rough fieldstone foundation of the house.

"It's going to be okay," I whispered to both of us.

CHAPTER

Four

Polly and I stood side-by-side as we watched the kids find their places for circle time.

I took a moment to bemoan the fact that most of the three-, four- and five-year-olds in my class were substantially better dressed than I was. Not that I'd raised the bar all that high, especially since I'd temporarily packed up most of my clothes in cardboard boxes. I gave the hem of my sweater a little shake in an attempt to exorcise the final wrinkles.

Five-year-old Celine was wearing either a short dropped-waist dress or a long drop-waist tunic over leggings with a pair of hand-tooled cowboy boots. I'd probably fantasize about borrowing the boots if I thought I could find a way to cram my feet into them.

Three-year-old Josiah was wearing a Burberry plaid shirt over black jeans with matching Burberry plaid cuffs, the combined cost of which was possibly equal to a week's pay for me, and that was without factoring in Josiah's matching Burberry plaid slip-on shoes.

Polly looked great, too. She was wearing nice pants and a cute rust and beige-striped boat neck top that brought out the auburn in her hair and also hugged her baby bump. Of course she had every right to be single and pregnant, but that hadn't stopped the other teachers and I, and even our bitch of a boss, from banding together to make sure Polly was safely out and proud about her pregnancy.

Sure the new assistant teacher, who just happened to be single, was pregnant—wasn't it great! How lucky the students were to watch her baby grow! Our early intervention was geared to shut the parental rumor mill right down. There is nothing more vigorous than a preschool grapevine, so just to be on the safe side, Lorna had launched a rumor of her own—that Polly's husband was on a secret mission for the CIA. And for her own protection Polly had to pretend to be a single mom.

Gloria, another one of my favorite teachers, had given Polly all her old baby stuff. Ethan, our resident school hunk and Polly's new friend, had even gone with her to a prenatal check-up, although that didn't fly so well with the girlfriend he was trying to get back together with. Kate Stone had promised Polly she could work in Bayberry childcare next year and bring her baby with her.

I was genuinely happy for Polly that everyone at Bayberry was rallying around her and her baby-to-be. And yet sometimes when I looked at her, a jolt of sadness would hit me, hard enough to make me want to curl up on one of our classroom nap mats and suck my thumb. How was it that everyone else—my colleagues, my sisters, even Pebbles—managed to get pregnant like it was no big deal at all?

Four-year-old Julian stopped at the new helicopter sticker that marked his place on the circle.

"Where's the dumb fuck?" three-year-old Depp asked.

A couple of the older kids giggled.

"That's adorabibble," three-year-old Harper said.

It was slightly less adorabibble if you were the classroom teacher and the parents had your phone number. A mispronunciation like that had a tendency to go home with the kids and reemerge at the dinner table. So Polly and I had changed out Julian's dump truck sticker for a helicopter sticker, and made a few other strategic sticker replacements as well.

Depp looked around some more. "Where's my fire fuck?"

"It's been a while since I've had one of those," Polly whispered.

Polly had her teacher-whisper down already. Just like those whistles that only dogs can hear, there's a certain decibel and frequency that teachers the world over use so that only other teachers can catch what they're saying. The teacher-whisper is its own kind of superpower.

Eventually we got Depp settled down on his new airplane sticker and the rest of the kids found their places.

I grabbed a bandanna, and Polly and I joined the kids on the circle. The bandanna was orange and covered with brown and gold turkeys. I had to admit I'd found it in the dog section at Marshall's. But in my defense I'd learned that a good preschool teacher can find materials for her classroom everywhere. I'd also learned to sprinkle our holiday activities lightly over a longer stretch, instead of subjecting the kids to a single day of holiday overkill.

I crossed my legs.

The kids crossed their legs, too.

I held up the turkey-covered bandanna and gave it a shake. "This is our Thankerchief. Can you say Thankerchief?"

"Thankerchief," they repeated.

I waited to let the suspense build, then I shook the Thankerchief again.

"I'm thankful," I said, "for all of you, the wonderful students in this classroom who are kind to one another and love to learn new things."

I gave the Thankerchief another shake and passed it to my right.

Five-year-old Pandora shook the Thankerchief as if it was a pompom and she was a cheerleader in training. "I'm-thank-ful-for-my-Bar-bie-jee-eep," she said, giving each syllable its own shake.

"I want a Barbie jeep," four-year-old Juliette said.

"Maybe someday," Pandora said as if Juliette didn't have a chance in hell. Pandora passed the Thankerchief to her right.

Three-year-old Griffin let out a sound that I hoped was a fart and not more evidence that he was not quite as toilet trained as his parents had led us to believe he was. Then he started whipping the Thankerchief around like he was bringing a plane in for a landing. "Me thankful for gummy bears. Me thankful for gummy worms. Me thankful for . . ."

Polly got up and wiggled in next to Griffin to get things back on track. She held out her hand.

". . . gummy everything," Griffin finished. He passed Polly the Thankerchief.

The turkeys on the Thankerchief danced as Polly gave it a shake. "I'm thankful for the sun in the sky and the swings on the playground." She looked down. "And for this baby in my tummy that I hope will grow up to be just as incredible as all of you."

"Does your baby daddy live at your house?" Morgan asked.

Polly's eyes grazed mine and I gave her a little nod. "No," Polly said.

"Where does he live?" Ember asked.

"Far away," Polly said. "In his own house."

"Will you grow a new baby daddy?" Zoey asked.

"I don't think so," Polly said. "Sometimes babies have a mommy and a daddy. Sometimes they just have a mommy. Or just a daddy. And sometimes they have two mommies or two daddies."

"Duh," Pandora said. "I have two mommies *and* two daddies."

"I have two hamsters," Jaden said.

A chorus of *I have two mommies and two daddies and two puppies and two guppies* broke out. I flashed back to the year one of my students, just-turned-six, announced at circle time that her parents were getting a divorce. I gave the mom a call that night to ask how I could support them. It turned out she and her husband were still living happily ever after. Their daughter had created a faux divorce to raise the drama quotient in her life to keep up with her classmates. The uncertainty of divorce would always be rough on kids, but the stigma at preschool was long gone. Nontraditional families were fast becoming the new normal.

Whether Polly grew a new baby daddy or not, her baby was going to be just fine.

. . . . .

Transitions are the most challenging part of any school day, and a good teacher knows you've got to keep things moving. So as soon as the Thankerchief made it all the way around the circle, I leaned forward to push myself into a standing position so we could do a quick segue to the next part of our day. I heard a dry, brittle crunch.

At first I thought it might be my knees. Then I realized the elastic waistband of my Lollipops had given way. Or disintegrated. Or crumbled into dust. Apparently everything did have a shelf life after all.

By the time Polly and I got the kids settled with individual work—lacing cards and alphabet tracing and counting games—I'd found one more thing to be thankful for: that I wasn't wearing a skirt. Because if I had been wearing one, by now I'd be walking around with my high school undies looped around my ankles.

As it was, my underpants had worked their way down both sides of my legs and were hovering somewhere mid-thigh. I wasn't a student of physics, but I was pretty sure they'd stay suspended like this. Still, I didn't want to take any chances. And I was starting to waddle.

After I grabbed two rubber bands from the supply cabinet, I caught Polly's eye, pointed at the hallway, mouthed *bathroom.*

I stood in front of the big mirror over the sink in the women's room, fishing down my pant leg for my underpants. I grabbed one corner, worked it up past the waistband of my pants. I bunched the fabric together, wrapped one of the rubber bands around and around it. When I finished, white fabric stuck out from my side like a little wing. I started fishing for the other side.

Lorna pushed open the door to the women's room.

"Underwear malfunction," I said.

"Too much information," Lorna said as she walked by me.

"Nothing lasts forever," I said. "Especially your high school underpants."

"All those years of having change of clothing bags for the kids," Lorna said from the other side of one of the stalls. "Who knew we needed them for some of the teachers, too. Oh, wait, maybe you can call your boyfriend and ask him to bring you a fresh pair."

"Cute," I said. I bunched some more fabric and started wrapping the other rubber band around it.

"I don't want to tell you how to live your life," Lorna said to me in the mirror while she washed her hands. "But why don't you just run home at lunch and see if you can locate some underwear from this millennium."

CHAPTER

Five

One of those unseasonably warm bursts had come out of nowhere, the kind we used to call Indian summer back in the days before that became politically incorrect. The sun was shining in a cloudless sky. Dry leaves skittered across the parking lot. The rubber bands around my Lollipops were still holding up as I jogged to my car.

Before I sold my ranchburger, I used to be able to dash home from school and back in under ten minutes. My father's house was at least three minutes farther from Bayberry, a detail I was just now realizing I hadn't factored in when deciding to buy it. I only had a half hour for lunch, so I was really going to have to move.

I leaned the Tupperware container against my steering wheel and popped it open as I drove. Then I ate my lunch with my fingers. I had to admit that by the third meal in a row, two of them cold, curried chicken and cauliflower casserole was losing its luster.

As I turned into the driveway of the house I'd grown up in, I thought I caught a flash of something by the front porch. I rolled halfway up the driveway and stopped to get a better look.

Two tiny kittens, one ginger and white, one black and white, were stretched out just in front of the latticework, eyes closed, faces turned up to the sun.

"Aww," I said. I watched for a moment, my heart filling up.

An even tinier black and white kitten wiggled out from a miniscule gap under the porch. It toddled past its siblings and into the yard.

My heart skipped a beat.

"Don't," I said. I peered through my windshield for hawks, checked my rearview mirror for coyotes. I tried to decide whether or not to jump out of the car and see if I could scare the kittens back under the porch. Or maybe I could access my inner Wonder Woman and attempt an early rescue.

The ginger and white kitten sprang into action before I did. It caught up with the runaway kitten and head-butted it back in the direction of the porch. The tiny kitten nudged the tinier one under the porch. Then it head-butted the other black and white kitten under and followed.

"Good job," I heard myself say, as if the ginger and white kitten was one of my students.

. . . . .

When I sailed in through the kitchen door, John was working at the table. I grabbed a pair of clean underwear from the top of the dryer. One more thing to love about John: he actually folded laundry. In neat little piles, no less.

"What's up?" he said.

"I'll be right back." I took the stairs two at a time, bolted into the bedroom, kicked off my flats, yanked down my pants. I pulled the rubber bands off my Lollipops and they fell to the ground. I stepped out of them and held them up. My high school underpants, which had appeared so perfectly preserved when I'd put them on this morning, had somehow ballooned into the shape of a wide-mouth vase with leg holes.

When I pulled on the fresh undies, they felt lighter than air. If I'd had time to think about it, I might have found a metaphor in there somewhere. Maybe about how you can't go back or even something optimistic like how I'd come a long way, baby. I put my pants on again, stepped into my shoes, flew down the stairs.

"Listen," I said to John. "I have to get back to work, but I saw the kittens and—"

"How many teeth did they have?"

"Huh?"

"I was just taking a break to do some research, and it says here that a good way to figure out how old kittens are is to check their teeth. Kittens with no teeth are probably younger than two weeks. The first baby teeth pop through somewhere around two to three weeks of age." John looked down at his laptop. "Let's see, and the deciduous canines begin growing at three to four weeks of age. And then the premolars at around four to six weeks."

"I wasn't close enough to see teeth," I said. "I just saw three kittens out getting some sun. And the tiniest one made a run for it. Anything could have happened. But the ginger and white cat went after it. Exactly like one of the helper kids in my class—they become mini teachers and keep the other kids in line. I bet Pebbles puts that kitten in charge of the others whenever she has to go out."

I looked at the kitchen clock. "I have to go. Now. But do you think you could bring your laptop outside to work? And maybe we should both call in sick tomorrow so we can move the rescue up a day?"

John shook his head. "I can't do it tomorrow. I have to drive in to work for a staff meeting. Plus we still don't have a fully formulated rescue plan, and we've got to sign the papers on the house today, the architect is dropping off the final plans, and—"

"Gotta go," I said. I gave John a quick kiss and made a beeline for my car.

I was barely late when I screeched into Bayberry parking lot. I slammed the door of my Civic and clicked the lock over my shoulder as I ran.

My luck being my luck, my bitch of a boss was just heading out the door.

I slowed down to a more casual pace. "Beautiful day," I said.

"It's helpful, Sarah, when the teachers remain in the classroom *with* the students."

"Thanks for that," I said.

. . . . .

The pink Bark & Roll Forever ice cream truck was already parked in the Marshbury Savings & Trust parking lot when John and I pulled in. My father, wearing a matching pink Bark & Roll Forever T-shirt, was easy to spot behind the glass wall of one of the mini conference rooms.

My father's lawyer sat next to him on one side of the conference table. A beat-up leather briefcase was open on the table in front of the lawyer. My father, his lawyer, and the battered manila folders spilling out of his lawyer's briefcase all appeared to be approximately the same age.

There was a glass candy jar sitting in the center of the conference table. I noticed my father had topped off the red-and-white striped mints with dog treats attached by pink ribbons to Bark & Roll Forever business cards. Apparently my dad was still on the clock, and in his mind at least, this constituted working.

John held my chair as we took the seats across from my father and his lawyer. More to love about John: he held chairs. He also opened doors and never failed to let me walk through first.

"Perfect timing, kiddos," my father said. "I was just winding up for a joke."

My father put his elbows on the table and leaned forward, his shiny brown eyes twinkling, in full jokester mode. "So an ambulance chaser of a certain age has been diagnosed with a terminal illness and wants to prove that you can, in fact, take it with you after all. After some serious contemplation, the old bottom feeder—"

"Dad," I tried.

He ignored me. "So the old bottom feeder instructs the missus to go to the bank and take out enough dough to fill two pillowcases right to the tippity top with greenbacks and leave them in the attic. That way when the old jackleg finally bites the dust, he can swing by and grab them on his way up to heaven."

My father raked an errant clump of white hair from his forehead. "By and by, a few weeks after the funeral, the widowed missus is up cleanin' the attic and comes upon the pillowcases stuffed with moolah. 'Oh, that damn fool,' she says. 'I told him he should let me put the money in the basement.'"

My father threw back his head as he cracked himself up. The lawyer laughed politely, possibly consoled by the thought of my father's fee helping to fill his own pillowcases.

The mortgage guy from the bank sauntered in and took a seat at the head of the table. We introduced ourselves all around.

The lawyer cleared his throat, looked over his glasses at my father, then at John and me. "Is everyone present of sound body and mind?"

"Define your terms," my father said.

"Knock it off, Billy Boy," the lawyer said, "or this time around you'll be buying the drinks for a change."

"I do believe I'm feeling sounder already," my father said.

The lawyer cleared his throat again. "Are you all signing willingly and under your own power?"

We agreed that we were. So we signed the papers and the lawyer notarized them. And then the bank guy jumped in. John and I signed the mortgage papers to buy the house outright from my father. From the proceeds, our father deposited enough money to pay us rent for the next twenty years into a bank account set up to automatically transfer the rent to us on the first of the month. If my father was still alive and kicking after twenty years, he'd get to live with us rent-free from that point forward. If at any time he decided to move out, he got to keep whatever was left in the account. If he died, the remainder of the rent money went back into the pool with the rest of his assets.

My father and John and I signed our names and wrote the date beside our signatures about a gazillion times. Finally we made it to the last one.

"Done," I said. In my best teacher's voice, I added, "Pencils down."

John and I begged off on having a celebratory drink with my father and his lawyer. We watched them cross the street, my father's arm draped across his lawyer's shoulder, his beefy hand gesturing as he talked. They disappeared into The Grog Shoppe.

John and I kissed, right there on the sidewalk, where anyone could see us.

When we came up for air, his Heath Bar eyes met mine.

"Well," he said, "we did it."

"We sure did," I said. "We're officially bat shit crazy."

"Time will tell. But in the meantime, is there a restaurant around here that's not The Grog Shoppe? Somewhere perfect for a milestone celebration, maybe even a town or two away?"

"Are you kidding me?" I said. "We've got the house to ourselves."

CHAPTER

Six

"Okay," I said. "So how about you go across the
street to Maria's Sub Shop and grab us dinner—I'll
have a small turkey with cranberry sauce sub, please.
Wait, why don't you make it a large so I can take half
to school for lunch tomorrow."

I pointed. "And then if you walk down Main Street a
couple doors down that way to the packie—"

John tilted his head. "You mean the liquor store.
Where you buy liquor and pop."

"The package store," I said. "Where you buy booze
and tonic."

We smiled at each other.

"See," I said. "We'll never make it. We're from
completely different worlds."

He pulled me in for another kiss.

I pushed him away. "Come on, we need to stay focused. I'll grab a few things and meet you at the car."

I headed straight for the Marshbury Hardware Store. The musty smell of centuries-old wood greeted me as I pulled the door open. Ancient galvanized metal nail bins lined the center aisle. The noise from the Marshbury Bowlaway directly overhead rumbled like thunder. Growing up, our grandparents on both sides had told us we shouldn't be afraid of thunder because it was only the angels bowling up in heaven. Every time I walked into this hardware store I remembered that. I also pictured teams of angels above me wearing bowling shoes. And matching team shirts with extra holes for their wings.

It didn't take me long to find what I was looking for. I sifted through the options, made my choices, brought them up to the woman standing behind the old cash register.

I met up with John on the sidewalk.

He checked out the big paper bag I was carrying. "What's in there?"

"You'll find out," I said.

. . . . .

John and I were sprawled across our new king size bed, goofy après-sex grins on our faces.

He reached for his glasses, put them on again. "What's that?"

I followed his pointed finger to my Lollipops, which were still on the floor where they'd landed during my lunchtime dash home.

"Hard to say," I said. "Maybe an old parachute?"

Our stomachs growled in tandem.

"See, we are so in synch," I said. "Our stomachs even growl simultaneously."

John laughed. He leaned over for a kiss. Then he rolled out of bed and grabbed our subs from the top of my sister Christine's childhood dresser. When he tossed the brown paper bag in my direction, I caught it, no problem at all.

"Good hands," he said.

"Yours, too," I said in my sexiest voice as I wiggled my eyebrows. I was pretty sure it came out like a bad Groucho Marx impersonation.

John smiled. "Was that a lascivious look on your face, Ms. Hurlihy?"

"It was my best attempt, Mr. Anderson."

This is happy, I thought as John let Horatio back in and got him settled down in his dog bed with a fresh chew bone. I unwrapped our subs and flattened out the crinkly white paper to make us each a big square placemat. Had a fleeting urge to look for crayons so we could decorate our placemats while we ate. Decided to save placemat coloring for my classroom.

John held up the bottle of champagne. "Are you sure it's okay to open this, or shall we save it?"

If it turned out that miracles actually existed after all, and I somehow managed to get pregnant before my last egg was on its last leg, I knew I'd quit drinking immediately. But months had dragged into more months and still nothing. So what I'd started doing was switching back and forth between seltzer only and mostly seltzer plus the occasional glass of something stronger, depending on whether or not there was even a remote chance that I might be pregnant.

I'd been using a digital ovulation kit. The way it worked was that beginning on day five of my menstrual cycle, first thing in the morning I'd insert a new test stick into the plastic holder and pee on it. The digital display window would stay empty until somewhere around days eleven and twelve. At that point, when I peed on the stick a smiley face would appear in the display window to tell me to have sex fast, because these were my most fertile days, and God knows I didn't have many more of them on my horizon.

I hated that stupid smiley face. *Ha*, it taunted me. *Sure you're going to get pregnant. As if. Don't hold your breath, honey.*

Who do you think you are? my Irish ancestors chimed in. *What have you done to deserve this? Don't you know that happiness is for the next life?*

After a while the whole ovulation thing started to feel like too much math to deal with. Peeing on sticks got to be too depressing. My eggs and I had more than enough on our plates without it.

So when I packed up my ranchburger, I'd tossed my digital ovulation kit in one of the boxes. With my warm coats? With the rest of my bathroom stuff? As soon as I got organized, I was absolutely going to dig it up and start using it again.

John was still holding up the champagne bottle.

"Sure," I said. "The timing is perfect."

It had been a long day, so I probably would have used paper cups from the upstairs bathroom. But John was the kind of guy who insisted on running all the way downstairs for champagne flutes.

"To us," John said as we held up our glasses. "May the roof over our heads be as well thatched/As those inside are well matched."

"Holy pot of gold at the end of the rainbow," I said. "You just gave an Irish toast."

"Not bad for a Midwestern boy, huh? Especially one whose ancestors are either Scottish or Swedish, depending on which one of my parents you listen to."

"Do me a favor and don't mention that last part to my father, okay? He's a big believer in equality, but it really throws him for a loop when someone brings it to his attention that the whole world isn't Irish."

John got out of bed again and crossed the room. I stayed right where I was and enjoyed the view. Not that there weren't more important things in the world, but he looked pretty damn good from this angle.

John grabbed a pen off my sister's old dresser and brought it back to bed, picked up the champagne cork and wrote today's date on it.

HOME SWEET HOME, he wrote underneath the date in square block letters.

"Champagne cork journaling," I said. "I love it."

"I was thinking we could use wine corks, too. You know, mark the big milestones. I suppose we could even use water bottle caps if we had to, depending on the timing. Pick out a special bowl to keep them in. Go through them all once a year or so and take a stroll down memory lane."

"Totally romantic." I leaned over for a kiss. "Hmm, I wonder if I could turn it into an activity for the kids at school."

He looked at me.

"Sorry. I just popped the romance bubble, right? Okay, I'm officially not working. I don't think champagne corks would fly with the parents anyway."

We sipped champagne and woofed down our dinner.

"Cranberry sauce on a turkey sub," John said. "Who knew it was even a possibility."

"Maybe it's a local thing. Marshbury is part of the cranberry capitol of the world, after all."

"I thought you said Marshbury was part of the Irish Riviera?"

"Who says it can't be both." It took every ounce of willpower I had to re-wrap the second half of my sub for tomorrow's lunch.

John unrolled the plans for the renovation and spread them across our laps.

I stared at the first page. "Well, it certainly looks like the architect knows what he's doing. I just have a hard time reading these things—it's like I can't translate all those straight lines into actual rooms. Maybe a pair of 3D glasses would help."

"See." John traced one finger along the page. "This is where the existing wall will come down between this room and the one next door—"

"The boys' room."

"Right. And that will give us space for a walk-in closet here, and for an en suite bathroom that will back up to the existing bathroom. And these two other bedrooms will remain intact. One will become a shared office—see, with built-in storage and a double desk along that wall."

"Got it," I said. "And then the other room, my dad's bedroom, can be a guestroom, or you know, whatever."

John and I paused to sip some more champagne. Then we both leaned over to put the narrow champagne flutes down carefully on the stack of books on our sides of the bed.

"Okay," John said. "Where were we? So then this room at the end, the one that opens into the long screened-in balcony—"

"The sleeping porch."

"Right. The sleeping porch stays, but we'll put in new energy efficient double French doors leading out to it. And the room next to it will become our separate living space. The architect says that since the living room fireplace is directly below, we'll be able to open up the chimney behind the plaster and put in a vented gas fireplace, no problem."

John tapped his finger like it was a magic wand. "Mantel here. Television over it. Nice couch here. A couple of comfy chairs here and here. It'll be cozy, but we'll have a place to get away whenever we need it."

"Once we get it finished, let's never leave." I tried to imagine the cold blue lines on the paper turning into places where we actually lived and breathed. "Did we forget to tell the architect about the moat?"

"We can always add the moat after."

"Sure, maybe we should wait until there's a sale on crocodiles somewhere."

John tapped his finger again. "Well, it's not quite a moat, but our space will have this new door at the top of the main staircase. And when we build the new garage, we'll have a private staircase going up from that as well."

"The word private," I said, "does not exist in my family lexicon."

John turned the page, tucked it carefully behind the others. We reached for our champagne glasses.

"So," John continued, "here's your dad's space, which will take over the entire garage, as well the room above—"

"The secret room."

"Right. And the staircase will be relocated over to here, because that existing staircase is way too narrow and steep. The outside door to the mudroom will stay, as well as the door from the mudroom to the kitchen. When we add the new garage, your dad will have a direct entrance from there as well. And we'll have new locks put on so he has his privacy."

"Like my father has ever locked a door in his life."

I held John's glass so he could turn another page. "Okay, so the heart of the home will remain essentially the same. It'll be accessible from our space, your dad's space, and also to the rest of your family from both the front and the kitchen doors."

"Sounds like a plan," I said. "And now all we have to do is live through the construction."

Seven

I slid off the bed, grabbed the bag from the hardware store, got settled in next to John again. Then I pulled out a roll of canary yellow construction tape that said CAUTION KEEP OUT in black letters.

"This," I said, "is to block off the front porch until the kittens are safely rescued. And after that, we can use it wherever we need it. If things get bad, maybe we can even wrap it around the whole house."

I reached in again and pulled out a rectangular cardboard sign that said STOP! KEEP OUT! "And this is for our bedroom door."

"Subtle," John said.

I pulled out another sign: STAY ALIVE. STAY OUT. "Or this one. I couldn't decide. Maybe we can rotate them so they don't lose their effectiveness."

I pulled the third sign out of the bag. DANGER! DINOSAUR AREA! KEEP OUT! "And this one is for my dad's bedroom."

John shook his head. "In case he's in there with some babycakes watching the submarine races?"

"Exactly."

John reached for the bottle of champagne, poured us each another glass. We sipped silently, lost in our own thoughts.

"Holy stupid idea," I said. "This is never going to work, is it?"

John took his time answering. "Well, I know it's not going to be perfect, but I think as soon as we get some ground rules established, we have a fighting chance of making it work."

"Company!" my father's voice boomed from below.

"We might be a tad late on the signs," John said.

. . . . .

John and I didn't rush. We put our clothes back on while we drank the last of the champagne, enjoyed one more kiss for the road. We swung through the dining room where I opened the cabinet under the sideboard. We chose an antique carnival glass bowl—iridescent blues and greens with stippled rays of gold and ruffled edges that reminded me of the ocean on a sunny day— for our cork collection.

"Perfect," John said. "Great bowl. Do you know that carnival glass was actually used for prizes at carnivals back in the early 1900s?"

"Beats those long stuffed snakes," I said.

We left the bowl with the champagne cork in it on the kitchen counter, looped around to the family room. My father was stretched out on his battered old recliner in the family room like he still owned the place. Despite signed papers and some serious money in his bank account, he probably thought he *did* still own it.

Three women sat elbow-to-elbow across from him on the sofa. Even without their hot pink T-shirts, I recognized the Bark & Roll Forever ladies immediately. Tonight they were wearing jeans with retro-inspired tops and funky flat shoes with Velcro straps. Their hair was long and flowy, and it ranged in color from salt and pepper to sterling silver to snow white with a big pink streak down one side.

I'd read somewhere that the baby boomers were reinventing each new stage of life as they encountered it. These women made me think it might be true. It was like they'd invented a new kind of agelessness—neither young nor old, and definitely still awesome after all these years. I wanted their clothes, those shoes. I wanted that big pink streak in my hair. I wanted to be just like them when I grew up. If I grew up.

"Here's that research you ordered," my dad said. "Everything you need to know about rescuing those felines just happened to be sitting right there at a booth in The Grog Shoppe. So, no pussyfootin' around, I invited some good-looking walking instruction manuals home with me."

"And don't think for a moment we're not going to dock your pay by a casserole for malingering on the job, Billy," the middle woman said. None of the Bark & Roll Forever women cooked anymore, so they bartered with a friend for the casseroles and just pretended to my father that they'd slaved over a hot stove for him. It was interesting to note that life didn't necessarily become less complicated as you got older.

My father shook his head. "I already told you gals, I left a pile of those cards with the dog treats at the bank *and* The Grog Shoppe." He pushed out his chest and stretched his pink T-shirt so BARK & ROLL FOREVER was legible. "And let's not forget the value of having Billy Boy Hurlihy as a walking billboard. Per my calculation, that's a full casserole's worth of work and then some."

John and I were still standing in the doorway as if we were the visitors. Horatio had already jumped up on the couch, and all three of the Bark & Roll Forever ladies were petting him.

"Thanks for stopping by," I said. "We really appreciate it." Since it didn't look like my dad was going to reintroduce us, I added, "Just to refresh your memories, I'm Sarah and this is John."

"Doris, Betty Ann, Marilyn," the three women said from left to right, their voices overlapping slightly like a wave at a ballgame. I took a moment to wonder if my father still had the hots for Betty Ann, who appeared to be the leader of the pack. Hoped he hadn't broadened his interests to include the other two women, which might threaten his job security, not to mention my casserole security. My dad had a tendency to get overly ambitious when it came to his dating life.

"Well, don't let me stop you from getting educated," he said. "Homer and I will just mosey on into the kitchen and excavate us some beverages."

At the mention of one of his names, Horatio jumped down from the couch. The rest of us placed orders for water. John and I sat down in the remaining chairs.

"So," Betty Ann said. "We hear you've got a mother cat and some kittens under the porch. Is the queen a feral?"

"I don't think so," I said. "I'm pretty sure she's still in the palace in England."

John laughed, another thing to love about him. The Bark & Roll Forever ladies joined in.

"A cat giving birth is called queening," Marilyn said.

"And the cat is called a queen," Doris said.

"I don't think Pebbles—that's the mother cat—is a feral," John said. "She looks pretty normal. And I don't know, put together."

"It's like being homeless," Betty Ann said. "You don't necessarily have to look the part. Sometimes life just hits you hard."

"A female cat that is pregnant is more likely to be feral," Marilyn said. "Only about two percent of the feral cats in the United States have been neutered."

"A feral cat won't allow itself to be touched," Doris said, "even by a caregiver."

"A stray cat," Marilyn said, "has been socialized to people, but has lost her domestic home, either by choice or through abandonment. In time, as her human contact diminishes, a stray cat can become feral. By the same token, because she's once been a pet, with patience a stray cat can often be successfully re-socialized to a human home."

"It's not always black and white," Betty Ann said. "Stray cats can appear feral when they're afraid. Feral cats will sometimes approach a caregiver for food and even show signs of familiarity."

"So," I said, "it sounds like you're saying the whole stray/feral thing is a kind of continuum. If that's true, then it doesn't really matter which one Pebbles is, right?"

"Before you boss ladies get your knickers all in a knot again, I'm officially off the clock," my father said as he made his entrance. He handed out water bottles all around, then held up his bottle of Guinness. "Homer and I are relocating to the front parlor for a game or three of pinball. Why don't you ladies join us when you wrap things up."

John raised his eyebrows at the mention of his precious pinball machines. He'd hired professional movers who specialized in antiques to move them both, one an authentic The Addams Family model, and the other an Eight Ball Deluxe. He'd decided they were too valuable to leave in his Boston condo while it was being rented. We'd gone back and forth about whether it was safer to keep them in a locked storage unit, where anything might happen, or in my family's house, where anything could definitely happen.

In the end, John decided that if the pinball machines stayed with us, it would be easier to keep an eye on them. School was still out on whether or not that was actually true.

"Feel free to join us for a game, Johnno," my father said.

"Gee, thanks," John said.

"True feral cats," Doris said as my father and Horatio disappeared again, "are still very social animals. They often join feral cat colonies, but they can't be socialized to people. The best bet for ferals is to trap and neuter them and then return them to the outdoors to live out their lives."

"Female cats are baby-making machines," Marilyn said. "Yours could be pregnant again already. If not, it won't be long—queens can have as many as five litters in a single year. The important thing is to get her spayed."

"And the kittens?" John said.

"Kittens born to feral cats can be successfully adopted into homes," Betty Ann said. "The trick is to separate them from the mother as soon as possible—six to eight weeks is ideal—so that the feral behaviors they've picked up from the queen don't stick."

Betty Ann leaned forward. "And then you, or whoever ultimately fosters them until they find their forever homes, need to handle the kittens as much as possible so they become fully socialized to people."

"Separating a mother from her children is not an option," I heard myself say.

That stopped the conversation. When John looked at me, two vertical worry lines had sprouted between his eyebrows.

I crossed my arms over my chest.

"Okay then," Betty Ann finally said. "It will be what it will be. You're going to have to start by capturing the queen. If you take her kittens first, she'll head for the hills."

"You might want to borrow a Have A Heart trap from the Marshbury Animal Shelter," Marilyn said.

"Stock up on Fancy Feast," Doris said. "She won't be able to resist it. It's like cat crack."

"Or you could buy a cat carrier and try that," Marilyn said. "You can leave the garage door open a crack and start feeding the queen in there, and eventually move the food to the carrier. Once you get her locked in the cat carrier in the garage, eventually she should settle down a bit."

John rubbed an index finger back and forth across his worry lines.

"Let us know what you need," Betty Ann said. "And if you decide you don't want to foster them yourself, we can help you find someone else. People who foster animals are a special breed, and there's quite a network. Sometimes they shuttle strays from state to state all the way across the country, with a series of people meeting up with the driver of the next leg, to give the strays their best chance."

"It sounds like the Underground Railroad," John said. "You know, like the animal version of transporting slaves to safety."

"You do what you have to do," Marilyn said.

The Bark & Roll Forever ladies decided to join my father for a quick game of pinball before they hit the road. John escorted them to the front parlor.

I followed everyone partway down the hallway, then bailed out and headed for the kitchen. I opened two cans of cat food and found a Slim Jim. I pushed the kitchen door open and flipped on the patio light. Then I grabbed a patio chair and dragged it until it was just in front of the door.

I sat down, looked up at the sky. I wished on the first star I saw that Pebbles and her kittens would be okay. Then I wished on another star that living here would work out. Realized the second wish might weaken the first, so I took it back fast so I could save it for another time. Hoped that didn't break any wishing-on-a-star rules.

A cool breeze kept the last mosquitoes of the season away. The ping-ping-ping of John's pinball machines drifted out to me. Laughter followed, my father's booming over the rest. It probably wasn't even 9 PM yet, but it felt like the middle of the night.

Finally Pebbles showed. She stopped just short of the circle of light. Always before, we'd waited for her to appear and meow for food. She seemed to consider the change in routine, ready to run.

I waited for a bit. Then I stood up slowly and put the cat food and the Slim Jim down halfway between us.

When I looked up, Pebbles had disappeared.

I sat down in the chair again and waited. And waited some more.

Pebbles reappeared and walked halfway to the food. She stopped and watched me. I stayed motionless.

She closed the distance and began to chow down.

"I know we can make this work," I whispered. "We just have to want it enough."

Eight

I woke up early, turning everything over and over and over in my head. So many details. John had made arrangements with two contractors to come over in the late afternoon to look at the architect's plans and give us estimates. We had to go buy a cat carrier. We had to finalize our rescue plans. We needed to make sure my family didn't drop by and screw everything up.

My family showed up for Sunday dinner once or twice a month, in varying configurations, whenever it worked out. Sometimes we all brought food, sometimes we ordered takeout. If our dad wasn't here, we ate without him. For better or worse, when John and I bought the house, I knew we'd bought this tradition, too.

I tried to picture Saturday's cat rescue going so well that Pebbles and her kittens felt like entertaining visitors on Sunday. I stumbled out of bed and grabbed my phone. Sent a quick foggy-brained group text to my family: *Lots going on so Sunday dinner cancelled. See you a week from Sunday if you're around.*

I jumped in the shower, threw on an entire outfit made up of actual clean clothes. By the time I got downstairs, John had already left to avoid hitting the worst of the rush hour traffic on the way to his staff meeting. He'd brewed enough coffee for me. And left a note to say good morning and that Horatio had bunked in with my dad again.

I gulped down the coffee as I scanned the fridge for breakfast possibilities. I broke off a hunk of cheese, which probably would have tasted better with the rest of an omelet, but it did the trick. I opened some cat food, filled a clean bowl with water, grabbed a Slim Jim.

This time Pebbles appeared almost as soon as I sat down in the chair. I set her breakfast on the patio, just a little bit closer to me this time. The moment I sat back down in the chair, she went right for the food.

"See," I said. "We've totally got this."

. . . . .

I made it to school early for a change and went right to work. I poked tiny holes in the tops of paper cups with my sharp teacher scissors, found pipe cleaners, beads, brown construction paper, googly eyes, smaller paper cups. Polly arrived in plenty of time to help me with the finishing touches. We tucked everything out of sight on a shelf in the supply closet.

Morning took on its usual hum as the students trickled in. Jackets on hooks, backpacks in cubbies. Wooden puzzles and matching games spread across a table or on a mat rolled out on the floor. Some of the kids jumping right in to work, others wandering around as they finished waking up.

I did a headcount to make sure everyone had arrived. Then I walked around the room, both my hands making peace signs, our classroom signal to stop talking, pay attention.

"Circle time," I sang.

Name a famous person, past or present, and I'll tell you exactly what she or he would have been like as a preschooler. Miley Cyrus and Gene Simmons were the kids always running around with their tongues hanging out. Gilda Radner was the wild child dangling upside down from the monkey bars who didn't give a rat's ass whether or not anyone could see her underwear. Florence Nightingale? The five-year-old who just wouldn't quit until she made sure everybody's booboo had a Band-Aid. Napoleon? The three-year-old with delusions of grandeur climbing up on a tabletop to yell, "Why won't anybody play with me?"

It worked in the other direction, too. I had a theory that adult personality could be accurately predicted by the way a three-, four-, or five-year-old handles circle time. I wasn't the least bit psychic in any other area, but sometimes an extrasensory signal came through, clear and strong like good cable reception, pointing me to exactly who my students would become as adults.

The kids found their places on the circle without a single *dumb fuck* or *fire fuck*. When you're a preschool teacher, these are the things that keep you going.

Polly sat at her place on the circle. I handed her a paper cup with a brown construction paper body shape we'd pre-glued to one side. Just like we'd planned it, Polly turned the cup upside down and placed it on the floor in front of her, so the holes I'd poked in the bottom showed. Then she rested both hands on top of her head.

Everybody giggled. I passed out paper cups all around, and the kids imitated Polly perfectly. Flip the cup. Put it down. Hands on head. Another giggle.

I handed five pipe cleaners to Polly, each one a different color—orange, red, yellow, brown, green. Carefully, she poked the end of each pipe cleaner into one of the tiny holes in the bottom of her cup until they fanned out like tail feathers. Polly crossed her arms and put her hands on her shoulders.

Right around the circle, the kids followed suit, the older students helping the younger ones when they needed it.

I passed out googly eyes and a glue stick next, because half the fun of googly eyes is getting to glue them on all by yourself.

"Oh, look," I said when we finished, just in case it wasn't immediately obvious. "Turkeys!"

A couple of the kids looked doubtful, but they went along with it. I mean, if a turkey and a paper cup got together and had a baby, I thought this was pretty much what it would come out looking like.

I grabbed a single die from an oversized set of dice, as well as a tray of smaller paper cups, which Polly and I had already filled with pre-counted beads.

"And now we're going to do some turkey math," I said, "with our turkey beads." They were actually little plastic beads called pony beads, but all is fair in holiday tweaking.

Once everybody had a tiny cup filled with beads sitting next to their turkeys, I rolled the die. Three dots.

"Gobble, gobble, gobble," Polly said. She took three turkey beads from her tiny paper cup and worked them down over one of her pipe cleaners.

Turkey see, turkey do. "Gobble, gobble, gobble," the kids said as they reached for their own beads.

Some of the kids spaced their three beads evenly along their pipe cleaners. Others jammed the beads all together. Kiera cried when her pipe cleaner bent.

"Are these real jewels?" Pandora asked as she held a bead up to the light.

I looked over to see Depp quietly stuffing turkey beads up his nose. I grabbed a tissue. "Blow," I said as I handed it to him. I made a mental note to count his beads at the end of turkey math.

Jaden jumped up. "Can I roll the dice?"

"A single dice is called a die," I said.

"My grandpa died," Violet said.

"My bird died," Griffin said.

I don't want to die," Juliette said.

"Here you go, Jaden," I said before a full preschool death knell could rev up.

Jaden jumped up. He shook the die, blew on it, yelled, "Let's pick a winner!"

Avert your eyes! I almost yelled to myself. I didn't want to see Pandora as an adult with closets full of designer clothes, her finger encrusted in real jewels, bored out of her mind. Jaden at the Las Vegas airport, running back to play one more slot machine before his plane boarded. I didn't want to think about what Depp might be shoving up his nose when he got a little older.

I wished I could freeze them all so they'd stay preschoolers forever.

· · · · ·

"TGIF," I said as I walked into the teachers' room for lunch.

"You mean TGIFF," Lorna said.

"Huh?" I sat down at the table, unwrapped the white paper.

Lorna finished chewing a baby carrot. "Thank God it's freakin' Friday. Ooh, can I have some of that?"

"Get your eyes off my lunch," I said. "You know the way to Maria's Sub Shop."

Lorna crunched another carrot. "Fine. Be like that. I'll just tell our esteemed colleagues how your ancient underpants disintegrated in school yesterday."

Ethan ran a hand through his sun-streaked hair. "It's essentially molecular degeneration—the fibers in the elastic break down from age. The same thing happened to me once with an old pair of swim trunks. They seemed perfectly fine until I stood up on the surfboard and the elastic gave out."

Lorna and Gloria's eyes lit up at the image of our resident school hunk standing naked on his surfboard.

"You are such a surfer boy," I said.

"Not so much anymore." Ethan pushed himself up from the table, limped across the room to the coffeemaker.

"Sorry," I said. Ethan's life had recently crashed and burned. He'd destroyed his marriage as well as a fledgling indie film career, totaled his car, wrecked his leg. When he bottomed out, our bitch of a boss, who happened to be his godmother, was the only one who would take a chance on him. The good news was that Ethan was a natural born teacher and the kids were lucky to have him.

Ethan shrugged. "Nothing to be sorry about. You're not the one who did a number on my leg."

"How's June doing?" I asked. June was my former and his current assistant. I'd trained her well, and her only tragic flaw was that she had a tendency to wander off to meditate. But she always came back.

"June's great," Ethan said. "The kids love her and she's teaching me a lot. Hey, how are those kittens under your porch doing?"

"Oh, that's right," Gloria said. "How are those little tykes doing? Have you figured out how you're going to get them out from under there yet, honey?"

"John and I are working on a rescue scenario," I said.

"Keep the kinky stuff to yourself," Lorna said. "Some of us are trying to eat."

"You are so bizarre," I said. "I don't even know what that means."

"Right," Lorna said. "*Sure* you don't."

"Play nice, you two," Gloria said. I loved Gloria, but she was one of those preschool teachers who mothered everybody who crossed their paths. The biggest challenge of being around her was that you had to resist the urge to curl up on her lap with your blankie.

"So," Ethan said. "Do you have something to put the kittens in once you rescue them?"

I looked at him. I hadn't even thought about that. Maybe I wasn't up to this challenge after all.

"A cardboard box?" Lorna said.

"A bureau drawer?" Gloria said.

"Let me look around my storage unit," Ethan said. "I'll swing by your house with whatever I find."

At one point in his indie film career, Ethan had been a set designer. His own classroom looked like a set from a Disney movie. Before the school year started, he'd donated an entire small fiberglass boat and helped Polly create a reading boat for our classroom to surprise me. Nautical-striped pillows cushioned the bottom. The stern was fitted out with a low bookshelf, a smaller bookshelf tucked into the bow. READ READ

READ YOUR BOOKS GENTLY THROUGH YOUR LIFE was stenciled in big block letters on one side of the boat. The other side said MERRILY MERRILY MERRILY MERRILY READING IS A DREAM. The kids couldn't get enough of it.

I had to admit I had a little bit of a fantasy going that if I ever did manage to get pregnant, Ethan would help John and me design the baby's room.

"Are you sure?" I said as I wrote down my new/old address for Ethan.

"Absolutely," Ethan said.

Nine

"You were right," I teacher-whispered to Lorna as I passed her, the full day students following single file behind me like I was the Pied Piper, Polly bringing up the rear. "TGI*FF*."

"We're almost there," Lorna teacher-whispered back. "I hear a dirty martini calling my name. And an *Orange is the New Black* binge—after the week I've had, all those prison scenes will be positively uplifting."

Polly and I got the full day kids settled on our dismissal bench.

"There she is!" a familiar voice said behind me.

Despite my better judgment, I turned. Nikki, aka Nicole Senior, was heading in my direction.

My luck being my luck, my wasband's new wife was looking right at me. Once again I was reminded of my ex-husband's total lack of imagination when it came to finding my replacement. We could have stepped out of a Dr. Seuss book as Thing One and Thing Two. Same height and build. Medium length brown hair. Dark eyes. The only difference was that she was chatty as hell. Okay, and ten years younger. And pregnant once again. Like it wasn't enough that she already had a set of twins that might have been mine.

Nikki caught me checking out her stomach. She smiled and gave her baby-to-be a pat. "Twins are supposed to be the worst, but this time around is even more brutal. Morning sickness *and* hemorrhoids." She laughed. "And those are just Big Kevin's symptoms."

"Karma is a boomerang," I said sweetly.

I pointed at Lorna. "If you're looking for your children's teacher, she's right there."

"Ha-ha," my wasband's wife said. "She'll tell me I need to make an appointment to speak to her. The twins are crazy about her, but what a drill sergeant. Anyway, they're home with a babysitter, and I'm just running in because Kevin Junior had a little accident and forgot to bring his change of clothing bag home. I figured it would reek to high heavens by Monday."

"Well, I won't keep you." I took a step backward.

"I know you already know this, but Big Kevin didn't stay dry through the night until sixth grade. Runs in the family." She leaned a little closer. "Tiny bladder."

I tried to figure out which was more pathetic: that my wasband's wife was trying to bond with me over a bladder, or that I felt slightly one-upped that not once

in ten years of marriage had my ex mentioned his
bladder to me, tiny or otherwise.

I took another step away from her. "Okay, then.
Well, back to the grind for me. You know, a teacher's
work is never done and all that."

"Wait. Sarah." She took a step toward me, hell bent
on invading my personal space.

I pretended I didn't hear her, pivoted in the
direction of Polly and the kids.

Nikki looped around me until we were facing again.
"I was wondering if you and John need some contractor
referrals. You know, for the renovations on your dad's
house."

"What?" I said. When Nikki had sold my
ranchburger for me despite my objections, she'd
pushed hard to help John and me find a house to buy.
We'd blown her off—actually, John had done most of
the blowing off while I focused on avoiding her—by
saying we had no immediate plans to buy. I told John to
tell Nikki we'd already found a place to live, and even
suggested that he might want to float the idea that we
were considering leaving the area permanently once
the school year was over. Maybe even leaving the
country permanently. The last person in the world I
wanted to know our current location was my wasband's
new wife.

"I bet you're wondering how I found oww-out," she
sang.

I stared at her.

"We realtors have our way-ays. Actually, our
next-door neighbor met your dad at The Grog Shoppe

last night. He told her all about the in-law suite you and John are building for him so you can take over the rest of the house. Smart move, that's a great old house. Oh, our neighbor told me to tell you to tell your dad she had a very nice time chatting with him and she hopes he'll give her a call."

"You know where I live?" I said.

"Of course I do. Big Kevin has driven me by a few times." She started digging in her purse. "Let me pull up the contractors on my phone."

"We're all set," I said.

"No worries," Nikki said. "I'll just text them to John. And tell your dad if he lost our next-door neighbor's phone number, I can text that to John, too. Maybe we can all go out together some night."

I took a giant step in the direction of Polly and the kids.

. . . . .

Gulliver hurled himself off the bench and landed on his backpack. He grabbed two fistfuls of pea stones and threw them up in the air.

"I hate late," he said as pea stones rained down on his face. I watched, on standby to execute a quick Heimlich maneuver in case he swallowed one.

I checked my big analog preschool teacher-sized watch again. "I hate late, too," I whispered to Polly. Polly and I were now officially five for five as the last teachers standing at dismissal this week.

For a preschooler, being picked up even five minutes after all the other kids can seem like five days. For a preschool teacher on a Friday afternoon, it can feel even longer.

It's not like Bayberry didn't have dismissal rules in place. At the start of every school year, a letter went home to the parents:

Dear Bayberry Parents,

Please remember that half-day students are to be picked up promptly at 11:30 AM and full-day students at 3 PM, unless they are scheduled to go to Bayberry Childcare.

Exactly fifteen minutes after scheduled dismissal time, or whenever students have been placed in all waiting vehicles, all remaining students will be escorted to Bayberry Childcare. Parents will be assessed a late fee of $25. (twenty-five dollars), as well as $2. (two dollars) for each minute (yes, minute) they remain in Bayberry Childcare before being picked up by a parent or designated adult. You may pay this fee when you pick up your child, or it will be added to your next month's tuition bill.

Warmly,
Kate Stone, Principal

Drawing this kind of line in the preschool sand with the parents worked pretty well. But over the years I'd learned that parents who are chronically late are generally in denial. You could tell them during a conference that children feel undervalued and abandoned when their parents are late. They lose their trust. Their self-esteem takes a nosedive.

And the parents would nod their heads in full agreement, a sympathetic look on their faces for those poor children whose parents don't have the good sense to pick them up on time.

And then they'd be late again the next day.

If you thrived on confrontation, you'd probably pursue a career as a courtroom lawyer or a reality TV show star as opposed to becoming a preschool teacher. Teachers are usually nurturers, fixers—lovers not fighters. When parents who are in denial about being late are faced with a late fee, and one that increases by the minute, I'd learned the hard way that no matter how much money they had, they tended to get a bit prickly. And as the classroom teacher, I was the one they came after.

So I had to admit I'd developed a slight tendency to drag my feet. I should have taken Gulliver to childcare the first time his mother was late. Or at least the second time. And I definitely should have done it every day this week.

A part of me was hoping that his mom would turn over a new leaf and miraculously get her time-management act together. So yesterday, after I'd put Gulliver in the car, I'd handed her a fresh copy of the late dismissal-warning letter.

"So, um, Tiffany," I'd said. "Just to let you know that if you're late again, you can pick up Gulliver in childcare."

Gulliver's mom had given me a puzzled look. "I left in plenty of time. You should have seen the traffic."

And even though I knew better, I was still just kind of hoping to slide through this week so I didn't have to deal with one more thing until next week.

I looked over at Gulliver. He finished placing pea stones in a long line across our dismissal bench. "Take that," he yelled as he karate chopped them all off.

"Heads and shoulders, knees and toes, knees and toes," I sang, touching the appropriate body parts.

Polly jumped right in. "Eyes and ears and nose and mouth, nose and mouth," she sang.

"No more school," Gulliver yelled.

"Excellent call," I said.

"Listen, why don't you just go," Polly whispered. "I don't mind waiting with him."

I looked at my watch again. If I left now, I'd have time to feed Pebbles and talk to John before the first contractor arrived.

"Are you sure?" I said.

Polly nodded. "Absolutely. And if you need any help tomorrow with your cat rescue, my day is open. My whole life is pretty much open, for that matter."

"Thanks for offering," I said. "It's just that I have no idea what to expect."

She smiled. "I've been feeling a lot of that myself lately. I could swing by at some point to see how you're doing, and if you need me before that, you could call."

I hesitated. The more time I spent with Polly, the more I liked her. If we didn't work together, I would have loved to hang out with her. But I'd learned the hard way how important it is for a teacher to maintain boundaries with her assistant, especially when a big part of the job is to boss that assistant around.

I did a quick eeny-meeny-miny-moe between no and yes in my head, ended up on yes. "Thanks," I said. "I'd really appreciate that."

I jogged to my classroom, flipped our kiddie chairs over on the tables, refilled the filtered water pitcher and put it back in our tiny fridge. I wrote my new/old address down on a bright pink index card, grabbed Polly's and my big canvas teacher bags. I turned off the overhead lights and pulled the door closed behind me.

When I handed Polly her bag and the index card, I saw that Gulliver was on his back again, throwing pea stones up in the air.

I shook my head. "This is ridiculous. I'm being a complete wimp. I'm enabling his mother, and it's not good for Gulliver either. I'm going to take him to childcare."

Polly looped her bag over her shoulder. "Why don't you let me do it? I'll be working in childcare next year anyway—it'll be good practice."

I gave my watch another glance. "Okay. Thanks."

"See you next week, Gulliver," I said. And then I ran for my car.

I was almost to the end of the long school driveway when a platinum convertible came screeching around the corner and almost took me out.

I kept driving.

Ten

I decided to swing by the grocery store on my way home from work. If Operation Cat Rescue was going to happen tomorrow, John and I were running out of time to get the supplies we needed. I would have preferred a big pet store so I had more choices, but the nearest one was way out by the highway.

I lucked out and found everything we needed at the local grocery store, Marshbury Provisions. I even found a hard plastic cat carrier, which looked both sturdy and stylish. It was turquoise and brown, which I thought would be great colors for Pebbles. It also had a door on the top, as well as one in the front—I could only hope two doors would double the chances of actually getting her into it.

After I put the carrier in my grocery cart, I added about a gazillion cans of Fancy Feast, choosing an assortment of flavors since I couldn't find one specifically called cat crack. I added a bag of cat treats, a couple of feathery cat toys, plus a big litter box for Pebbles and a smaller one for the kittens.

Then I spent way too much time considering the kitty litter possibilities. Clumping or non-clumping? Clay? Recycled newspaper pellets? Pine? Beet pulp? Corn? Was a commitment to a type of kitty litter a forever thing, or could you play the field a bit until you found the perfect match? I finally went for the litter with the label that specifically stated it was safe for kittens.

By the time I got home, the first contractor had already arrived. I pulled way over to the side of the crushed mussel shell driveway so he'd be able to get past my Civic when he left.

I jumped out of my car, reached back in to grab two grocery bags. The contractor's van was white. *Hammerhead Construction* had been painted on one side in silvery gray letters outlined in blue. Smaller letters underneath said: *Break It Down*. Beneath that was a caricature that appeared to be a cross between a hammerhead shark and M.C. Hammer.

If we hired this guy, maybe we'd all go fishing. Either that or dance around the kitchen with him so he could teach us some fancy hip-hop moves.

"Can't touch this," I sang. "Oh-oh, oh-oh, oh-oh-oh-oh." I threw in a couple of hip circles and a discreet bump and grind simply because I couldn't help myself.

For a split second I thought the '90s had sent some accompaniment for my flashback dancing, but it was only the vaguely musical sound of my phone's text alert. I reached for my purse, which was hanging from one shoulder. Realized the sound was coming from the backseat of my car, where my phone was probably buried at the bottom of my teacher's bag.

The text alert ended. I shifted the bags in my arms, began walking to the kitchen door. Heard a new text alert trill behind me.

I started to turn around, realized my arms were going to fall off if I didn't put these grocery bags down fast. Decided I'd grab my teacher's bag on the next trip.

There was no sign of Pebbles as I crossed the patio and let myself in by the kitchen door. I could hear the muffled sounds of male voices and feet clomping on hardwood floors overhead as John gave the first contractor a tour of the house.

I dumped the bags on the counter, opened two cans of Fancy Feast and put them on opposite sides of a dinner plate. I took another look at the labels on the cans so I could remember which was which. I grabbed a fresh water bowl and a Slim Jim.

Pebbles was sitting on the edge of the patio waiting for me. I put everything on the patio about three feet or so from the chair, sat down.

"Think of it as a taste test," I said as Pebbles closed the distance and started to eat. "I'll buy more of whichever one you like the best."

She devoured one mound of cat food and then the other, licked the plate.

"Okay then. I'll stock up on both. Listen, take your time with the water and the Slim Jim. I've got to run."

Thanks, I imagined Pebbles saying. *Catch you later.* Realized I was not only talking to a cat, but answering for one. Decided it was the least of my problems.

I took the stairs two at a time. The attic stairs had been pulled down from the hallway ceiling, so I scooted around them and into my old/new bedroom.

It hadn't really occurred to me ahead of time that anyone giving us an estimate for the renovations on the house would actually have to look at the rooms in the house. I resisted the urge to kick my high school underpants under the bed, thinking it might only call attention to them.

Instead I leaned back against my bureau to block the bra that was draped across the top. Horatio was up on our bed, his head buried between his paws. The contractor looked like neither a hammerhead nor a Hammer.

But he was wielding a really big sledgehammer.

"I don't think so," John was saying.

The guy put the sledgehammer down headfirst on the floor and rubbed his hands on his jeans. "It's no problem, man, it's totally free. It'll cost you zilch, nada. It's part of the branding—I check to make sure it's not load bearing, and then I break through the first wall right on the spot. Get it? Break it down?"

"Catchy," I said. They both turned to look at me. I gave a little wave.

"Thanks," the guy said. "I've got a show pitch in to HGTV."

"Listen," John said. "At this point we're still getting estimates. We're not ready to commit to removing a wall."

"I'll give you a minute to rethink that," the guy said. "And just to be upfront, unless it happens today, I'm going to have to charge you for it."

. . . . .

We'd barely managed to get the first guy out to the driveway when the second guy pulled in behind my car.

The second contractor had a shiny black truck with what looked like an oversized toolbox taking up a big chunk of the truck bed. Shiny red letters on the side of his truck said, *Paul Jackson & Sons: We've Got It Nailed.*

I wondered if he had a show pitch in to HGTV, too.

He flung his truck door open and climbed out.

John held his hand out to the first contractor. "Well, thanks for stopping by. If you can work up those figures and email them to me, I'd appreciate it. We'll be making our decision soon."

The first contractor held his ground as the second contractor walked over.

They checked each other out. I imagined them racing over to pee on the house to see who could mark it as his territory first.

We all stood there awkwardly for a long moment.

"Come on in," John said to the new guy. Then he swung his arm over my shoulder and steered me in the direction of the house, hoping only the second guy would follow.

I started to giggle.

"Don't look back," he said. "You'll turn to dust."

"Are you sure?" I said. "Maybe we'll luck out and the first guy will turn to dust instead. But if he doesn't turn to dust today, he'll have to charge us for it."

John shook his head. "That was insane. He was like an old door-to-door encyclopedia salesman trying to jam his foot in the door so we couldn't get rid of him."

"Aww, encyclopedias. I loved encyclopedias. Ours came from the grocery store though."

"Ours, too," John said. "We were a Funk & Wagnalls family all the way."

I sighed. "I loved our Golden Book Encyclopedias. I used to read my favorite volumes over and over—Aardvark to Army, Ghosts to Houseplants. And I'd try to get my mother to buy whichever one was on sale that week at the grocery store even if we already had it, so I could cut out the pictures."

"I guess I missed the Golden Books. My parents were all about buying things my sister and I could grow into. Adult encyclopedias. Two-wheelers instead of tricycles. Shoes that I still can't fit into."

"Poor baby," I said. "At least you didn't have to wear your sister's hand-me-downs."

"You don't know that."

I leaned my head against John's shoulder. "Thank you so much for that image. Now I'm always going to picture you in pedal pushers and a midriff top trimmed with rickrack. And really big shoes."

John held the kitchen door open for me. As soon as we got inside, we turned around and peered through the glass panes of the door. Break It Down and We've Got It Nailed were both still on the premises.

Horatio screeched around the corner to greet us, his favorite stuffed squirrel in his mouth. He dropped the squirrel at John's feet. John threw it down the hallway and they played a few rounds of fetch.

I opened the refrigerator to check out the casserole possibilities. "So what are you up for?" I yelled. "Shepherd's pie with cauliflower crust or spinach meatball bake?"

A knock at the kitchen door made me jump.

Horatio erupted with a series of barks. John opened the door.

"I don't do dogs," the second contractor said. "You'll have to keep it leashed and out of my way at all times."

I waited to see if John would simply shut the door in his face.

John grabbed Horatio's leash off a hook beside the door, snapped it on. Horatio gave him a look that clearly said, *Seriously?*

John and Horatio stepped back. Ferocious animal contained, We've Got It Nailed deigned to cross our threshold.

We introduced ourselves. "So," I said, attempting to move things in a friendlier direction. "How old are your sons?"

He looked at me blankly.

"Paul Jackson *& Sons*?" I tried. Maybe he was one of the sons, whose name was also Paul. Or maybe he'd stolen the truck.

"It refers to the legacy I'm creating. You know, it's like a metaphor."

"Actually," I said before I thought it through. "Like would make it a simile."

John smiled. The contractor didn't.

"Okay, then," John said. "Moving right along. Let's do a walk through."

I took over Horatio's leash and the two of us brought up the rear. John explained the renovation and what we wanted to accomplish. A part of me could almost picture it now—another part of me wondered if we'd live through this.

Eventually we were back in the kitchen again.

"Let me give you a visual," the second contractor said.

"We already have a visual," John said. "Remember? The plans?" He pulled the rubber band off the architect's plans, held them out.

The second contractor unrolled the plans, glanced down at the first page.

"Right." He handed the plans back to John. "It's easy for these guys to say this stuff will work. And then they walk away and I'm the one who has to figure it out."

John and I made eye contact, looked away.

"Let me give you a visual," the second contractor said again. He pulled a fat carpenter pencil from his back pocket, grabbed one of the empty grocery bags from the counter, flattened it out.

He sketched a square house with a triangular roof on top and a small square garage attached to one side. It looked a little bit like something one of my students might have drawn. "Okay, so this is the house. You leave the existing garage, take out the wall between the room above it and the room next to it and, voilà, you've got that extra space you need."

"Which means my father is still in the next room," I said. "Only it's larger."

"No fuss, no muss," the second contractor said. "The other way to go is to tear down the existing house and start over from scratch. It'll be a lot less aggravation in the long run."

"Whew," John said after we'd finally gotten rid of the second guy. "And to think they both had pretty decent online reviews. Anyway, Nikki texted me a list of contractors earlier. Maybe—"

"No way," I said. "She's just trying to worm her way into our lives."

"What about asking your sister Christine's husband to give us an estimate after all?"

"Let me give you a visual," I said. "We give my family an inch, and they'll try to completely take over this renovation."

As if to prove my point, my sister Carol walked into the kitchen like she owned the place. "Jeez-Louise," she said as she placed two pizza boxes on the counter. "Check your texts once in a while, why don't you."

CHAPTER

Eleven

Leave it to my family to interpret the cancelling of this week's Sunday dinner as meaning they could just pick another day. Though I had to admit that at least when they dropped by without being invited, they brought food.

We all loaded our plates from the hodgepodge of pizza boxes and takeout salads that covered the kitchen counters, carried them to our seats in the dining room.

"Rub-a-dub-dub, thanks for the grub, amen," my niece Annie said.

"Yay, God," we all yelled.

Everybody held up their glasses—wine for adults, milk for kids.

"May the roof above us never fall in," our father said from the head of the table. "And the family gathered below it never fall out."

"Sláinte!" we roared.

"Good one, Dad," my brother Johnny said. "It's actually kind of amazing that the house is still standing. You know, given which one of us bought it."

"Knock it off," I said.

"Or you'll throw him down the laundry chute?" my brother Michael said.

"Don't think I can't," I said. "With one hand tied behind my back."

"Remember," my sister Carol said, "anytime he'd hear one of us threatening somebody with the laundry chute, Dad would say, 'If one of you falls down that thing and breaks both legs, don't come running to your mother and me.'"

We all cracked up.

"I meant it then and I mean it now," our dad said. "You kiddos all had plenty of brains when you were born, and I fully expect you to use your heads for as long as they hold up."

I took a bite of pizza. Horatio and Mother Teresa, my brother Michael's St. Bernard, were sprawled out next to each other on the floor near the kiddie section, which was made up of an assortment of card tables that formed a T with the dining room table. Both dogs were on full alert, waiting for the first kid to drop them a pizza crust.

Between the six grown Hurlihy kids plus their significant others and children, there were so many of us that it was impossible to tell who was here and who wasn't until we were all seated. I looked around, taking attendance.

"Hey," I said to my sister Christine. "Where's Joe?"

"Still working," Christine said. "Imagine that. People who aren't even related to his wife actually hire him as a contractor."

I sighed. "Come on, Chris. You know what they say about not mixing business and blood, which we all know includes blood by marriage."

"Says she who just bought the family house." Christine took a long sip of wine. "And I think the saying is actually 'blood is thicker than water.' Which, as you just pointed out, we all know includes blood by marriage."

The side conversations rolled to a stop as everybody tuned in.

"What about Liam Daniels," Carol said. "I think he's a contractor. Remember him from high school? He had a massive crush on me."

Carol's husband Dennis shook his head, reached for his wine glass.

"One of the guys I play golf with is a contractor," my brother Billy Junior said. "I can have him give you and John a call if you want."

Billy's wife Moira leaned back in her chair, mouthed *no*.

"Most of them are fulltime dewdroppers now, but I've still got a few friends who put in a day's work now and then," our dad said. "If it'll help you kids out, I can ask around and see if anybody wants to take on my man cavern."

I turned and looked at John, wondered if I could get away with calling a time out so we could discuss this privately. Knew my family would only talk about us while we were gone. Or worse, pick a contractor without us.

"Let me give you a visual," I said without moving my lips.

"There's always Nikki's list," John whispered.

"Hey," Carol said. "No fair. Speak up so we can hear you."

"Or we'll throw you down the laundry chute," Carol's three-year-old daughter Maeve said.

"Yeah," Christine's three year-old-daughter Sydney said.

I sighed. Christine was seventeen months younger than me, happily married with two perfect kids. As far as I could tell, Carol's position as family know-it-all was the only thing that Christine had ever wanted that she couldn't get. It drove her absolutely crazy that all family information filtered through Carol, the oldest sister, first.

If Joe did the work on our house, Christine would be in her glory, smack dab in the center of things, looped in on every bit of progress way before Carol. I weighed the aggravation of Christine driving me nuts against having to deal with my wasband's wife, whose irritating presence would surely be attached to any contractor we chose from her list.

Then I weighed both options against having to go back to square one. Murphy's Law in full play here, I tried to imagine the contractor John might find to follow Break It Down and We've Got It Nailed. I flashed on a big red contractor's truck pulling into the driveway—Oops, We Did It Again painted on one side.

"Fine," I said. "Why don't you tell Joe to stop by this weekend."

"I'll see if he can fit you in," Christine said.

. . . . .

My sister Carol's seventeen-year-old daughter Siobhan was seated at the exact intersection of the adult zone and the kiddie zone. Her plate spanned the crack between the dining room table and one of the card tables, teetering as she finished her salad. She picked up the plate and headed for the kitchen.

I picked up my own plate and followed her.

"Hey," I said. "How's it going?"

Siobhan added a few lettuce leaves to her plate, pulled a pepperoni off a pizza and popped it into her mouth, shrugged.

I tried again. "How are you feeling? Still crampy?"

When she looked up, her face was pale. "Not that much anymore."

"That's good." I poured two glasses of seltzer, just for something to do with my hands.

I gave one to Siobhan. "Thanks," she said.

"So, are you going out later? You know, Friday night and all that?"

Her eyes filled with tears. "Jeremy and his parents told the whole school it could have been anybody's baby. None of my friends are allowed to hang out with me anymore."

Carol was a great mom. She'd done all the right things. And it turned out that apparently you can lead a teenager to birth control, but you can't make her use it. Siobhan had gotten pregnant with her first boyfriend.

"Jeremy is a dick," I said.

Siobhan smiled a sad smile, twisted the retro ID bracelet I'd given her. I'd had ND, which stood for No Dicks, engraved on it as a reminder.

"Listen," I said. "The holidays are almost here. Once the New Year rolls in, everything will be fresh again. The whole school and their parents will move on to their next victim and forget all about you."

Siobhan didn't look like she was buying it.

I dug a little deeper. "Okay, here's the thing to hang on to. You're not supposed to be happy in high school. If you were happy, I'd be worried about you. Because the kids who are happy in high school—you know, the super popular kids—usually peak right there. And one day they're my age, or even Grandpa's age. And they're still stuck reliving their past—as the star athlete or prom queen or whatever—and they spend the rest of their lives looking back instead of living forward."

I knew this wasn't always technically true, but it certainly made me feel better about my own high school misery.

"Kelsey Jamison," Siobhan said. "She acts like she's the sweetest thing ever, but she's this total phony. And really mean unless she thinks you can do something for her."

"There are always going to be mean girls and bad boyfriends." I took a sip of seltzer. "And high school is supposed to suck—it's probably even in the rule book somewhere. That's what gives you the incentive to imagine a better life for yourself and the fire to go after it."

"I can't wait to get out of that hellhole."

"You will," I said. "Hey, can you keep a secret?"

Siobhan opened her eyes wide. "You're pregnant?"

Disappointment came out of nowhere and kicked me between the ribs.

When Siobhan had found out that she was pregnant, she'd made the choice to carry the baby and give it up for adoption. Long story short, she decided that John and I would be the perfect parents. Despite enough red flags to open a car dealership, eventually John got onboard. And I breathed a huge sigh of relief that even if it was too late to get pregnant myself, we'd end up with a baby after all.

And then it turned out that Siobhan had a tubal pregnancy, which needed to be terminated. She'd be fine, and I'd be fine, but I knew that every time we looked at each other, maybe forever, we'd both think of the baby that didn't make it.

"No," I said. "Not pregnant." I looked over my shoulder, lowered my voice to a whisper. "But we have kittens. Under the front porch."

"Kittens?" Siobhan's hazel eyes lit up. "How many?"

"I'm not sure. At least three. We're going to try to rescue them and their mom tomorrow. But we need to keep it a secret so the whole family doesn't show up and screw things up."

"I know how that goes," my niece said. "Don't worry, I won't say anything."

"If you're up for it, we'd love to have your help." If Siobhan had been willing to give John and me her baby, the least we could do was let her help us rescue the kittens.

"Yeah, totally up for it."

"I know it's the weekend, but do you think you can get over here really early?"

"For kittens? Definitely."

"Okay, I'll tell your mom that John and I need you for the day to move some stuff around for the renovation or something."

Twelve

Carol and I sat halfway up the center staircase, on the step that after much childhood trial and error we'd all discovered was low enough to spy on the floor below but high enough to keep the conversation relatively private.

Over the years the stairway wall had become a gallery of family photos. Wedding photos of my parents, my grandparents on both sides, my siblings. A barely noticeable gap where my wasband's and my wedding photo used to be, and where I kept meaning to put a photo of John and me. Candid photos, holiday photos, pictures of my nieces and nephews. A hodge-podge of frames, from elaborate gold gilt, to tarnished silver, to sleek modern, to handmade from painted Popsicle sticks.

"Don't you dare take these pictures down," Carol said.

I can if I want to, I started to say.

I took a deep breath. "Of course not. This is all going to be part of the shared space."

"Good."

"I might just rearrange it a little. You know, put the pictures of the siblings I like the most at the top and bury everybody else at the bottom."

"No problem," Carol said. "As long as I'm in the top row. And don't think I won't check."

Carol lowered her voice. "You do realize Christine is going to drive you insane if you hire Joe, right?"

"She'll drive me insane if we don't hire Joe. So the way I look at it, we might as well get the renovations done while she's driving me insane. Plus, you should have seen the two guys who came by earlier to give us estimates. Kevin and I never got around to doing much of anything on our house when we were together, so I had no idea how hard it would be to find someone good."

Carol leaned back, rested her elbows on the step above us. "Once, we hired a chimney sweep company called Ash Wipers. Their online reviews weren't even that great, but I just wanted to hear them say it when they answered the phone."

"Ha," I said. "How about that truck I always see driving around town: Screwed Up Drywall."

John and my brother Michael cut through the hallway in the direction of the pinball machines. "And let's not forget Dirty Hoe Landscaping," Michael said.

I laughed. "I'm pretty sure I went to high school with them."

Michael shook his head. "If I said that, it would be totally sexist."

"Life's tough," I said. I blew a kiss in John's direction. He smiled. Michael going off to play pinball with John was a good sign. If his marriage to Phoebe was in one of its rocky phases, he'd be glued to her side, trying to please her. I heard a burst of group laughter coming from the kitchen, picked out Phoebe's voice.

Carol took a sip of her wine. Once John and Michael were out of sight, she whispered, "I've got two words for you: Liam Daniels."

"Then I'd never get rid of *you*," I said. "Plus it was pukeworthy enough watching you act like a teenybopper the first time around."

Michael and Phoebe's daughters Annie and Lanie came running in. "Can we please use this for a rehearsal space?" Annie asked.

When my sisters and brothers and I were kids, the stairs had been stadium seating for all kinds of performances in the wide center hallway—air guitar concerts, handstand contests, plays. I loved that the tradition had continued to the next generation.

"Sure," Carol and I said at the same time.

"Owe me a Coke," we both said.

Ian and Trevor and Sean cut past us and clomped up the stairs, Maeve and Sydney hot on their heels.

"Hey," Carol yelled.

"It's okay," I said. "We'll have a locked door at the top of those stairs soon enough. At least theoretically."

So they might as well enjoy having the run of the place while they can."

"The stage is all yours," I said to Annie and Lanie.

Carol and I stood up, looked around for a place to relocate. The pinball version of The Addams Family theme song blasted from the front parlor. Carol and I took a moment to cross our wrists and snap our fingers along with it. *Duh-duh-duh-duh. Snap-snap. Duh-duh-duh-duh. Snap-snap.* Lanie and Annie joined in.

More loud laughter was spilling out of the kitchen. My father had cranked up his ancient stereo in the living room and Dean Martin was belting out "Memories Are Made of This."

"So," Carol said. "Show me what Liam Daniels is going to do to my old bedroom."

. . . . .

"You're going to keep my room intact?" Carol said. "How nice of you. Turning it into a shrine to me is a lovely tribute."

"Ha," I said. "It wasn't big enough to fit a walk-in closet and an en suite bathroom."

"It's the perfect size for a nursery."

"Stop," I said.

"I was just—"

"I mean it. Don't say anything. I don't want to talk about it."

"Fine."

We let a few beats of silence go by.

I swallowed. "So, Mom and Dad's room will stay intact, too. I haven't even set foot in there since we went through Mom's things after she died."

"I haven't either."

I wondered if my face looked as sad as my sister's.

"So maybe," I said, "that's the room we'll turn into a shrine." Visions of my parents' room flashed before my eyes. Crawling into their bed with our Christmas stockings, begging them to come downstairs with us so we could start ripping wrapping paper off our presents. Trying not to spill the orange juice all over the tray as we served breakfast in bed every Mother's Day and Father's Day, year after year. Spending a sick day in the vast expanse of that bed, the only child in the house for one of merely a handful of days in my entire life.

I looked up at the ceiling and blinked back the tears that had welled up. "What was I thinking buying this house? So many memories."

"It would have been worse," Carol said, "if you and John had bought another place, and then we all had to watch this house go to an outsider when Dad couldn't handle it anymore."

"Yeah, I guess. Damned if you do, damned if you don't."

"Once Dad moves into his man cave—"

"He prefers it to be referred to as his man cavern."

Carol shook her head. "Anyway, you can turn Mom and Dad's bedroom into a guestroom. Leave a few special things, but not so many that it feels like a mausoleum. I'll come over and help you."

"Thanks."

We stopped at Christine's and my old bedroom. The ancient door had creaked open a crack.

Carol peeked in. "Ohmigod, you and John are like Oscar and Felix."

"What are you talking about?"

"Gee, I don't know." Carol gave the door a push.

The top of Christine's old bureau was completely empty except for John's laptop and phone. The bureau drawers were all neatly pushed in.

Okay, so the top of my old bureau wasn't in quite the same pristine condition. And I had to admit that fully closing a drawer you were only going to open again later had never quite made sense to me.

"What, were you born in a barn?" Carol said.

"If I've told you once, I've told you a thousand times," I said.

"Do you think I'm made of money?" Carol said. "And don't think I haven't used every single one of those lines with my kids. It's like once you have kids of your own, they just come shooting out of your mouth."

I didn't say anything.

Carol burst out laughing. She pointed in the direction of my Lollipops, still sprawled across the floor. "Did Sarah try to put on her big girl panties?"

"Whatever you do," I said, "if you find any of yours, even if they still look good, don't wear them." I tried to think of the phrase Ethan had used for it, but I'd spent just enough time being taught by nuns that the only term that popped into my head was Immaculate Conception. "The elastic disintegrates," I said instead.

"I'll remember that," Carol said, "next time I have a bizarre urge to try on a pair of my high school underpants."

I picked up my Lollipops with two fingers. "But look. Remember the X's mom used to embroider on them so we could tell our undies apart? We had to share so much growing up, crazy as it sounds, I think my red X's were one of the few things that made me feel special."

Carol reached over, caught the red thread with a fingernail, pulled it back to reveal pink stitching underneath.

"Gross!" I threw my Lollipops across the room. "Ohmigod, we wore hand-me-down *underwear?*"

"Think about poor Christine," Carol said. "She had three layers of X's."

"I hate you," I said. "All that brand new underwear. And not only that, but you got to do everything before we did."

"I also put in a lot of hard work fighting for everything from permission to date to skirt length. By the time you and Chris stepped up to the plate, the rules were pretty much in place." Carol shrugged. "But yeah, basically it was good to be queen."

Queen made me think of Pebbles. "That reminds me," I said. "John and I want to hire Siobhan for the day tomorrow to help us with some things around here."

"You mean to help you rescue some cats?"

I opened my mouth, but no words came out. Carol really did know everything. After years of lapsed Catholicism, it was the one miracle I still believed in.

"Shut your mouth or you'll catch a fly," my big sister said.

I shut my mouth.

Carol shook her head. "There's a cat carrier in the backseat of your car, plus two bags of kitty litter and a large and a small kitty litter box. I didn't exactly have to call Nancy Drew in for a consult."

"Just don't tell anyone else, okay?" I said.

"I won't. As long as you promise me you won't let Siobhan come home with a kitten."

"Deal," I started to say. But I was interrupted by a series of screams coming from the upstairs bathroom.

CHAPTER

Thirteen

Carol and I were right on the kids' heels as they clomped down the stairs. The worn runner that covered the center of the old maple steps made us sound like a muffled herd of horses.

We found Maeve in the kitchen, sitting on a pile of my father's dirty clothes at the bottom of the laundry chute.

"Now there's a sight to worry an Irish grandmother," my father was saying.

"If you broke both your legs, don't come running to me," Carol screamed as everybody gathered around.

"I swear we didn't push her," Trevor said. "She jumped all by herself."

"My turn," Christine's daughter Sydney said.

"Don't even think about it," Christine said.

Maeve had a big grin on her face, but I could tell she was really working to keep it there. "I'm gonna throw you down the laundry chute," she said.

"Look at the way she's holding her right arm," I whispered to Carol.

When Carol's husband Dennis scooped Maeve up, she let out a whimper.

"Oh, boy," Carol said. "Another Friday night at the emergency room. Can't wait."

The troops rallied around. Christine would drop off Carol's other three kids at home, with Siobhan babysitting her brothers, so Carol and Dennis could take Maeve straight to the hospital. I grabbed a bag of frozen peas from the fridge, which years in the preschool trenches had taught me not only holds the cold but gently shapes itself to the injured area better than an actual icepack. Somebody else put some cold water bottles in a plastic bag in case Maeve and company had a long wait at the ER.

As everybody paraded toward the kitchen door, Carol gave Maeve a careful kiss on her forehead. "You're going to be fine, honey."

"You come from good peasant stock," Michael said.

"Strong like bull," Johnny said.

"You can milk this for lots of presents," Siobhan said.

"We didn't do it," Troy said. "She jumped."

. . . . .

"Well, that was one way to get rid of everybody," I said.

"Poor kid," John said. "I hope she didn't break anything."

My father came into the kitchen carrying his jacket. "Your mother always said that laundry chute was an accident waiting to happen. I'll tell her all about it when I talk to her tonight. Anyhoo, if you kiddos don't need me, I think I'll head out. I've got a lady to see about a drink."

I wondered if my father told my mother about his dates, too. Maybe she gave him tips from heaven, sort of like a celestial dating coach. I made a quick wish that the lady he had to see about a drink wasn't Nikki and Kevin's neighbor.

"Have fun, Dad. And don't forget you're taking Horatio to work with you tomorrow."

My father zipped up his jacket and grabbed his car keys off the kitchen counter. "Homer and I both have it on our calendars. If I forget, he'll remind me."

"Never a dull moment with your family," John said once my dad had hit the road.

"That's an understatement. Thanks for putting up with them."

"They're a lot more interesting than mine. I don't think there's anyone on my entire family tree that would have had the guts to jump down a laundry chute. Especially in a house with tall ceilings."

"Guts or insanity, it's hard to say with my family. Hey, are you sure you're all right with using Joe as the contractor?"

John shrugged. "I don't know. It's a toss up between him and . . . Break It Down." John put both hands behind his head, hopped sideways a few times, ended with a bump.

"Impressive," I said.

"Why thank you, ma'am. I had a few moves back in the '90s, if I do say so myself."

I pulled out a long sheet from a roll of aluminum foil. John started handing me the leftover slices from each pizza box, stacking the empty boxes until we had a towering pile. We put the pizza and the leftover salad in the fridge. Walked around the house picking up stray glasses and loading them in the dishwasher.

"We're going to have to make a rule," I said as I tossed a bunch of paper napkins into the trash. "Everybody puts his or her glasses and dishes in the dishwasher on the way out the door."

"It didn't take that long to clean up," John said. "Plus we have enough leftover pizza and salad to live on for at least a week, so I'd say we made out okay."

"Good point. The last thing we need is for them to start taking the leftovers home with them. Whoever hosts definitely deserves the leftovers. Especially when they didn't invite anybody over."

I found a waterproof marker in the drawer, wrote PIZZA CRASH and the date on one of the evening's wine corks, dropped it in the carnival glass bowl.

I yawned.

John yawned back.

Which made me yawn again. "I hope Maeve's okay. And we really need to figure out our strategy for tomorrow."

"How about this? We go to bed early, get up even earlier, brew a pot of coffee, and make our plans while we walk the beach and watch the sun rise."

"Sounds like a plan," I said. "You know, you always think you're going to walk the beach all the time when you live this close to the ocean, but the truth is you start to take it for granted."

"Not to worry," John said. "I'll set a beach walk reminder alert on my phone."

"Is there an app for that?"

"There's an app for everything."

I fed Pebbles one more time. Then I got ready for bed while John took Horatio out for a final pee.

I thought I'd toss and turn all night as I worried about what tomorrow would bring. But I conked out before John even climbed into bed.

. . . . .

Even before I was fully awake, the beach felt like home to me. The sharp smell of the salt air, the give of the sand beneath my feet, the swoosh of the waves.

"I think," I said, "the ocean teaches you that what goes around really does come around. Whatever it looks like, it's all different a few hours later, and then a few hours after that, it comes full circle."

"It's like a metaphor," John said.

"Ha. Exactly."

The predawn light illuminated the sky just enough for us to walk the beach without a flashlight. When the sun finally peeked over the horizon, there were no crazy fireworks of pink and red and purple. Just soft shades of white and yellow and gold and orange. It was a peaceful, elegant, quietly beautiful sunrise. I hoped it was a good omen for the day to come.

"See how the sun rises up and to the right," John said. "That's because of the earth's tilt. So unless you're south of the Tropic of Cancer, it will always do that. Which is how you can spot a faked sunrise in a movie. Movie people often film a sunset so they don't have to get up early. And then when they reverse the footage to make it look like a sunrise, the sun ends up rising to the left."

"Good to know," I said. "I'll never fall for it again."

Horatio frolicked ahead of us, stopped to pick up a piece of something at the high tide line, threw it up in the air.

I squinted in the gray light. "What do you think? Piece of driftwood or dead fish?"

John took a sip of his coffee. "I think there are some things we're better off not knowing."

A cold breeze hit our faces as we walked. "When the wind is blowing from the north," I recited, "no fisherman should set forth."

I wrapped my father's flannel-lined L.L. Bean field coat a little tighter, promised myself I'd look for my coats once the cats were all safe and sound.

"Red sky in morning, sailors' warning," John said.

"Hmm," I said. "There's no red in the sky at all, so we seem to be getting conflicting information. Unless fishermen and sailors are in two separate warning categories."

"I'm pretty sure a red sky at sunrise means that a high moisture concentration in the clouds will bring heavy rain. The red color has something to do with sunlight bouncing off water vapor in the atmosphere."

"Got it," I said. "So that means wind but no rain for our rescue."

"Not that I don't fully believe in weather predicting via rhyming folklore," John said, "but I checked the weather forecast just for backup. Clear all day, with that severe cold front still coming in tonight."

I stopped to take a sip of my coffee, held the covered mug to my cheeks to warm them up. "Okay, so Pebbles has been letting me sit on the patio while she eats, and I've been moving the cat food a little bit closer to me with each feeding. I'm thinking that if I leave the kitchen door open and just keep sliding the chair back until I'm actually in the house, and I also keep sliding the food back, eventually she'll be eating in the house."

John nodded. "And then?"

"I'll have the cat carrier set up in the kitchen with its door open a little ways, and eventually I'll start feeding her inside the cat carrier. And when she gets comfortable with that, I'll just gently shut the cat carrier door while she's focused on the food."

"Any thoughts on where I'll be during all this?"

"Well, I'm afraid two of us hovering might spook her. So what if you do something else, and then I'll let you know when I've got Pebbles and then we can move on to rescuing the kittens."

"How about if I find a rake and tackle some of the vast quantity of leaves in our new yard?"

"Just make sure you don't get too close to the patio or to the front porch, so you don't scare Pebbles."

"No problem. It's a big yard—I'll just rake somewhere else."

CHAPTER

Fourteen

My father saluted us with his coffee cup as we walked into the kitchen. "'There is a harmony in autumn and a luster in its sky.'"

"Yeats?" John said.

"Shelley," I said. "Right, Dad?"

"The apple doesn't fall far from the sauce, as I've been wont to say. Good girl, Christine."

"Sarah," I said. I took off my father's jacket and held it out to him.

He reached for his jacket. "Thanks for warming it up for me, Carol." He drained his coffee, put the mug in the sink. "Well then, unless you two need anything else from us, Homer and I are off to the races."

"I'm curious," John said as we listened to the pink ice cream truck crunch over the mussel shell driveway.

"Does your dad know that Shelley was English and not Irish?"

"Do not, under any circumstances, repeat that in front of him," I said.

I helped John find a rake in the garage, grabbed the cat carrier from my car.

We stood in the driveway, looking at each other as if we were about to be separated for a long time. My stomach was jittery, and the rest of me wasn't far behind.

"Okay," I said. "As soon as I have Pebbles safely in the carrier, I'll come out and let you know."

John nodded. "If I have to come back inside for anything in the meantime, I'll make sure I use the front door. And if you need me, yell."

I looked at the rake John was holding. "Are you sure you know how to use that thing, urban guy?"

"I'll Google up some instructions if I run into any problems."

We leaned in for a kiss.

I opened the front door of the cat carrier and placed it on the kitchen floor. Then I opened the kitchen's single French door as far as it would go, until it rested back against the house. A gust of cool wind blew in, so I turned the thermostat way down and went in search of a coat in the front closet. I grabbed an ancient orangey-brown fringed suede jacket, tried to remember which one of us had owned it a gazillion years ago.

I scooped half of a tiny can of Fancy Feast into a cereal bowl. Then I placed the bowl on the patio, sat down on the chair, wrapped the jacket around me tighter.

Pebbles showed up immediately. As she sat on the edge of the patio, she seemed to check out the fringed jacket.

"It's vintage," I said. "I found it buried in the closet. It's one of those teenage relics that could be either really cool to wear again or a serious fashion faux pas. I'm still trying to decide, so feel free to weigh in if you have a strong opinion either way."

Pebbles closed the distance and practically inhaled the food. Then she let out a pitiful meow, apparently objecting to the stingy portion of cat food.

"Don't worry," I said. "There's plenty more where that came from."

When I reached over to pick up the empty bowl, Pebbles darted off. I walked back into the kitchen, outside door still wide open, and put the other half of the Fancy Feast can in the cereal bowl. Then I put the bowl down a little closer to the kitchen door and slid my chair back before I sat on it.

Pebbles came out of the bushes and went right to the plate. As soon as she finished eating, she looked at me with her piercing green eyes and meowed again.

By the fourth go-around, I'd crossed the threshold with my chair, and the bowlful of cat food was getting closer to the kitchen. I forced myself to take my time, not to move too quickly.

I wished I'd thought to bring a good book so I had something to do besides feeding Pebbles and waiting to feed Pebbles. I tried to think of an appropriate song to

inspire us. I sang a snippet of "The Siamese Cat Song"
from *The Lady and The Tramp*: *We are sia-mee-eez if
you plee-eez. We are sia-mee-eez if you don't please.*
Then I remembered Rowlf the Dog singing "The Cat
Came Back" on *The Muppets*: *The cat came back, she
wouldn't stay away. She was sitting on the porch the
very next day.*

Pebbles looked up from her Fancy Feast and tilted
her head.

"I know," I said. "I like that one, too. But those are
the only words I remember. And I'm pretty sure that's
my entire cat song repertoire. So jump right in if
you've got something."

Pebbles finished eating. Took off. Came back. Ate
some more.

I stood up. Got a bowl of cat food. Put it on the
patio. Sat down.

Eventually I slid my chair back until it was well into
the kitchen and side-by-side with the cat carrier. I put
another half can of food in the bowl and placed it just
inside the kitchen door.

When Pebbles came back, she stopped, waited,
looked around. And then she walked right into the
kitchen and ate the food.

I held my breath until she turned and scooted off.
I'd lost track of time, lost track of the number of times
we'd repeated the intricate steps of our cat food dance.

I got another tiny serving of food ready. I waited. I
waited some more. Maybe Pebbles was finally full.
Maybe even cat crack had its limits and she was simply

over Fancy Feast. Maybe she'd gone off to nurse her kittens.

I was dying to take a quick bathroom break, but I was afraid to risk it. I rubbed my hands together to warm them up, pressed my palms against my cheeks. Sniffed a sleeve of the old suede jacket and wondered if I was only imagining the faint scent of patchouli.

A car crunched into the driveway, stopped halfway up. I hoped whoever it was wouldn't mind helping John rake for a while.

Finally Pebbles showed. She gave me a long, penetrating look with those green eyes. And then she stepped right into the house again.

I held my breath once more. Pebbles chowed down, sat on the old kitchen linoleum, meowed. And then she bolted.

I picked up the bowl, got a refill. I put the bowl down just inside the cat carrier and sat in the chair again. By my calculations, I'd have to feed Pebbles twice more in the carrier before I could move the food all the way to the back of it. At that point, I'd close the door carefully. And I'd have her.

The kitchen was cold and damp. A few crisp sugar maple leaves had blown in, skipping across the linoleum with every fresh gust of wind. I took a deep breath, tried not to shiver. Realized my butt was either numb with cold or had fallen asleep from too much sitting.

Pebbles appeared, looked at the food resting just inside the cat carrier.

I didn't need to speak cat to know that the look on her face clearly said, *How stupid do you think I am?*

For the first time ever, she took off without eating.

I watched her walk away, tri-colored tail flicking back and forth in disapproval, ears turned out to the side like little airplane wings, alert to danger.

That was it. I mean, that was my entire plan. Entice Pebbles into the cat carrier with food and then push the door shut.

Clearly Pebbles was smarter than I'd thought she was. Possibly even smarter than I was. I tried not to focus on how much time I'd wasted. I fought to regroup while I stood up and did some knee lifts, hoping my butt would either thaw out or wake up.

I put the cat carrier out of sight in the front parlor so it wouldn't make Pebbles more suspicious.

Plan B rolled in on little cat feet, like the Sandburg fog poem I'd had to memorize in elementary school. I found an old roll of thick twine in a kitchen drawer. I cut off a long piece and tied one end to the kitchen door handle with the square knot I'd learned in Girl Scouts—right over left around and through, left over right around and through. I pulled the knot tight.

After I opened a can of tuna, I plopped it on top of the serving of Fancy Feast Pebbles had rejected. I opened the pouch of cat treats and sprinkled some liberally on top. Unwrapped a Slim Jim and stuck it in the middle like a candle on a birthday cake.

I slid the plate a few inches farther into the house. Then I moved my chair back, so I wouldn't freak Pebbles out by lurking too close.

I reached for the other end of the twine. Then I sat down in the chair, nonchalantly, as if I just happened to be holding a thick piece of string in one hand.

I thought about calling John in for a quick brainstorming session, just in case he might be able to come up with a better Plan B than this one. I thought about calling the Bark & Roll Forever ladies, who had a lot more experience with this animal thing than I did. I even thought about calling 411. Or 911. Or the Marshbury Animal Shelter. Was there a 1-800-GET-CATS that made house calls? Or maybe I should call the Marshbury Fire Department. I mean, how much different was capturing a cat than rescuing one from a tree—it was probably even way easier since you didn't need one of those long bulky ladders.

My hands were trembling. My heart was racing. I could feel the adrenaline kicking in as my body went into fight or flight mode. I didn't want to fight. I wanted to run upstairs to my childhood room, jump into bed, pull the covers over my head. I wanted to turn this whole thing over to John. I mean, wasn't one of the perks of having a man in your life getting him to do things like this? Unclog a nasty drain, catch an invading spider, figure out what that sound was up in the attic, capture a cat.

I really, really didn't want to do this.

But I knew I had to.

I waited. My palms were sweating so much that I had to keep shifting the twine from hand to hand so I could wipe them on the thighs of my jeans.

It felt like days before Pebbles finally stepped over the threshold again, but it was probably just a few minutes. I bit my lower lip as she checked out the new arrangement of food, hoping the extras I'd added wouldn't make her more suspicious than she already was.

Pebbles stayed perfectly still except for a slight flick of her tail.

Then she walked over to the plate and started to eat.

I watched her, forcing myself to gulp down some air.

Yanking the twine I held in my hand to swing the kitchen door closed was one of the scariest things I'd ever done in my life.

But I did it.

Fifteen

The nanosecond the door slammed shut, Pebbles exploded. Instantaneously and completely, like that exact moment when the flame reaches the end of the fuse on a Fourth of July bottle rocket. She slammed into the windows on the kitchen's single French door with mind-boggling force. The ancient panes of glass rattled but held on.

Pebbles spun around and whooshed down the long hallway, a superfeline whirlwind powered by fear. She hit the beveled glass inset in the heavy oak front door and bounced off. I thought she'd crumple to the ground from the impact, but instead she leapt into the living room, climbed the full-length drapes, digging her claws in as the dusty drapes swung back and forth. She perched on the valance, looking around for an escape route.

I finally understood the meaning of the word *petrified*—I was frozen in terror, fossilized by fear. I had no idea how to deal with a panicked cat. More than anything, I wanted to open the nearest door. To say *Whoops, never mind. Hey, stop by again real soon— we'll do lunch.* But I knew if I let her out, Pebbles would head for the hills and we'd never see her again.

She jumped down from the valance, darted into the dining room, climbed the heavy wood blinds that covered the big bay window with such intensity that one of the slats snapped in half.

My heart was pounding so hard it felt like it was clogging my throat.

"It's okay," I said, even though we both knew it was anything but.

Pebbles dashed back out to the center hallway. Instead of climbing the stairs, she scaled the family photo gallery as if it were a rock-climbing wall. Picture after picture crashed to the steps, glass splintering, pieces flying everywhere.

My parents looked up at me from their shattered sepia wedding photo, shards of glass sparkling along with the tiny rhinestones on my mother's cat's eye glasses.

"Sorry," I whispered. "I'm really sorry."

Pebbles ran down the stairs, hot-footing it right over the trail of broken glass. I stepped out of her way, glass cracking into smaller pieces beneath the soles of my shoes. She flew into the front parlor, leapfrogged over the abandoned cat carrier, landed on The Addams Family pinball machine.

Frantically, Pebbles attempted to scratch her way through the horizontal shield of glass that covered the playfield, to join Wednesday and Pugslie, to get Lurch or Cousin Itt to protect her, maybe even to climb into Thing's box and hide out in the dark with him.

"Please," I said. "Not the pinball machine."

Pebbles hurdled to the top of the tall cabinet at the back of the pinball machine. I held my breath as she hovered over Morticia and Gomez, trying to scratch her way in through the vertical pane of glass.

"We are sia-mee-eez if you plee-eez," I sang. "We are sia-mee-eez if you don't please."

Pebbles stopped scratching. She jumped off John's prized pinball machine.

"Good girl," I said.

She sprinted down the hallway.

By the time I caught up to her in the family room, she was scaling one of the built-in bookcases, trying to hide herself behind the contents of the shelves. I made it just in time to get one last look at the hand-blown glass vase we'd bought for our mother on her final Mother's Day. Remembered that we'd filled it with a huge bouquet of purple lilacs we'd cut from the ancient bush right outside the kitchen door, their sugary springtime smell filling the room.

And then the vase crashed to the floor and splintered into a gazillion pieces.

. . . . .

I'd been singing nonstop for so long that my voice was almost gone. When "The Siamese Cat Song" and "The Cat Came Back" started getting old, I tweaked some of my students' favorite songs to make them cat appropriate. Old MacDonald had a cat. The kitty on the bus goes meow, meow, meow. Ten little kitties jumping on a bed.

Somewhere along the way Pebbles had stopped knocking things off the shelves. She finally hunkered down at the back of an almost empty shelf, facing out, all gigantic scared green cat eyes.

"It's going to be okay," I said in between songs. "I promise."

I backed out of the family room, hurried to the front door. I flashed the outside light a few times. I opened the front door a crack and yelled, "Ready," then pulled the door shut as quickly as I could. I made a speedy and long overdue detour to the bathroom. After that, I circled around to the kitchen, grabbed the food and treat-filled cereal bowl, a bowl of water, a broom and a dustpan, an empty paper bag.

Pebbles hadn't moved an inch. I squatted down low and relocated a mason jar filled with seashells, the sole survivor of the bottom shelf. I stayed low as I swept the rubble away from the bookcase. Then I tucked a faded purple chenille pillow from the couch onto one side of the bottom shelf. Put the food and the water down on the other side. Grabbed the crocheted afghan from my father's recliner, rolled it up, tucked it in front of the shelf like a crib bumper.

"Ninety-nine pieces of vase in the bag," I sang as I picked up what was left of my mother's vase and dropped the pieces into the paper bag. "Ninety-nine pieces of vase. Round them up and say giddy-yup, ninety-nine pieces of vase."

As a preschool teacher, I could pretty much tweak any song to suit the moment. This wasn't my best version of the ninety-nine bottles of beer on the wall song, but it wasn't bad. And singing it made me feel a little bit less heartbroken about my mother's vase.

I'd sung my way down to thirty-seven when I heard the front door open.

Siobhan and John came in together. John's arm was draped protectively across Siobhan's shoulder. Siobhan cradled a tiny, scared, filthy, ginger and white kitten. For a split second, I had the oddest feeling that they were bringing me Siobhan's baby.

"Aww," I said. My eyes filled with tears. "How did you catch it?"

"Magic kitty treats," John said.

"We finally decided to make a long trail like breadcrumbs," Siobhan said. "As soon as we pretended to walk away, the bravest kitty came right out."

Siobhan handed me the kitten. Dirt was caked in the corners of its eyes and nose. Its face was semi-flat, its head seemed too big for its body, its big scared baby blue eyes looked like they might pop out of its head. It was the sweetest thing I'd ever seen.

I squatted down and placed the kitten carefully in the center of the soft purple pillow.

John, Siobhan and I backed away and watched from the doorway. Pebbles worked her way down carefully and angled her back end into a corner of the bottom shelf, sitting on her haunches, alert and ready to run. The tiny kitten rolled off the pillow. It toddled right over to its mother and started to nurse.

"One down," John said. He held up his palm to Siobhan, and she humored him with a high five. "Okay, back to work for us."

It wasn't long before Polly and Ethan came through the doorway to the family room. Ethan was cradling a tiny black and white kitten.

"It came out looking for the first one," Polly said.

Ethan handed me the kitten. It was just as dirty and scared and sweet as the first kitten. I tiptoed over and placed it on the purple pillow, careful not to get too close to Pebbles, and then I backed away as quickly as I could.

The black and white kitten went right for its mother. And Pebbles seemed to relax a tiny bit, as if with the arrival of her second kitten, she'd realized she wasn't going to lose her babies.

I relaxed a tiny bit, too, as if I'd realized I might not screw this up after all.

Polly put her hand on her belly. "Since you're not supposed to change litter boxes when you're pregnant, Ethan and I thought it might be safer if he held the kitten."

"Good call," I said. "Those two look like they've been rolling around in their own poop since birth. I know they make unscented kitty wipes—I should have thought to buy some."

"I'll make a quick run to that big pet store out by the highway and get some," Polly said.

"I'll take a ride with you to keep you company," Ethan said casually.

"Okay," Polly said just as casually.

"Thanks," I said. "If you're sure you don't mind."

When I went out to check on John and Siobhan, they were on their hands and knees, holding flashlights and peering through the gaps between the floorboards on the front porch.

I shivered, wished I'd thought to put the fringed jacket on again. Noticed the towering pile of leaves John had raked. "How many more kittens do you think are under there?"

"It's hard to see much of anything," John said. "But there's definitely at least one."

"It must be so scared," Siobhan said. "Oh, wait. Look."

A tiny black and white kitten appeared in the gap between the porch and the stone foundation.

"I don't think my arm will fit," John said.

Siobhan grabbed a cat treat and stretched out on her stomach. She managed to wedge one arm through the gap. When she pulled her hand back up, she was clutching a wiggly kitten.

"Nice job," I said.

"Thanks," she said. She handed me the second black and white kitten. I brought it in to join everybody else, waited until it found its way to Pebbles.

"There is definitely another one under there," Siobhan was saying when I got back out to the porch. "See—right in the middle, back against the house, curled up in a little ball."

John looked at his watch. "It's getting colder by the minute and it'll be dark in an hour. Maybe we should think about taking the porch boards off one at a time. I'm pretty sure I remember seeing a chainsaw in the garage when we were looking for the rake."

"You don't think the sound of a chainsaw might freak out an already freaked-out kitten?" I said. "Not to mention how freaked out my father would be about us dismantling the front porch."

"If Maeve hadn't hurt herself jumping down the laundry chute," Siobhan said, "I bet she could have wiggled down there. But my mom would never go for it now."

"That's okay," I said. "How is Maeve anyway? Anything broken?"

Siobhan shook her head. "Dislocated shoulder. The doctor popped it right back in. She's pissed they gave her a sling instead of a cast, so she's making everybody sign the sling."

"I've got an idea," John said. He disappeared into the garage and came back carrying a big piece of cardboard and a small handsaw. We watched him cut the cardboard to fit between the studs supporting the porch. Painstakingly, he inserted the cardboard between the porch boards again and again, nudging the panicked ball of fur toward the gap until Siobhan could grab it.

Siobhan handed me the tiniest and dirtiest kitten of all. I hugged it close.

"Well done," I said. "Thanks."

"Don't thank me," Siobhan said. "John was the one who figured it out."

I leaned across the kitten to give him a kiss. "That's one of the things I love about you. You always have a plan."

Sixteen

We slid the family room furniture back carefully to give Pebbles and her kittens more space. Then we microwaved slices of leftover pizza in the kitchen, dug into the remaining salad, carried our plates to the family room.

And now we were completely mesmerized.

"I read somewhere," I said, "that when you see something that touches your heart, there's a biochemical reaction that makes you happier, and even a better person."

"One can only hope," Ethan said.

"The mother cat is so beautiful," Polly said.

"She's a tri-colored calico," I said. "I looked it up. They're almost always female, which I thought was interesting. Don't the black and ginger spots look like beach stones on all that sandy white fur? I think Pebbles is the perfect name for her."

"Her eyes are awesome," Siobhan said. "They look like jewels, or maybe like green sea glass."

"In some cultures," Ethan said, "cats are considered to be mystical creatures, and the fairy world is actually watching us through their eyes."

"It's so interesting," Polly said, "that two of the kittens are black and white, and two are ginger and white, as if they each got half of the mother's genes and none of the father's. It kind of gives me hope." She cleared her throat. "So, have you picked out names for the kittens yet?"

"We don't even know if they're girls or boys yet," I said. "Plus, I think we should wait to name them until they show us some more of their personalities." I turned to John. "Don't you?"

John half nodded, half shrugged.

"Do you have names picked out for your baby?" Siobhan asked Polly.

"Not yet," Polly said. "It seems like such a big responsibility. I mean, on the one hand, I can see playing it safe and giving it a strong classic name."

"Ethan's a strong classic name," Ethan said.

"Funny," Polly said. "But on the other hand, just going by the kids at school, it seems as though they often live up to their names, so maybe it's better to name it something original and creative."

"There's always Apple or Moon Unit," I said. "We haven't had either of those at Bayberry yet. Are you going to find out if it's a girl or a boy ahead of time?"

Polly shook her head. "I like not knowing. The rest of my life is a complete mystery, so basically it fits right in."

One of the black and white kittens rolled off the edge of the shelf and onto the afghan. It managed to get on its feet again, wobbled back and forth. Pebbles stood up, shook off the two nursing kittens, and head-butted the meandering kitten back to safety.

"It's like having a kitty cam," Siobhan said. "I could watch this all day."

I reached for my seltzer. "Your mom made me promise I wouldn't let you come home with a kitten. Just saying."

"I don't want one anyway," Siobhan said. "It's too much responsibility. I hate the way people get pets and then they get bored or the pet does something wrong, and then they just ignore it or give it away. Pets are supposed to be forever."

"Forever doesn't always happen," Ethan said.

"No kidding," Polly said.

I put my glass on the coffee table, reached for my pizza slice. "Yeah, well, people can usually find a way to fend for themselves when you're over them. Pets need you to figure out a way to make it work. And another thing I hate is when people let their cat out because they don't feel like changing a litter box."

"I read that in many areas the average life expectancy of outdoor cats is about a year," John said. "They end up getting hit by a car or being a quick snack for some coyote. An indoor cat can live into its twenties." He shook his head. "That's a long time."

"Look," Siobhan said.

Three of the kittens were nursing now. The smaller ginger and white kitten had fallen asleep. Its neck was resting on the edge of the food dish, and its head was suspended in the air over what was left of the cat food.

"Aww," the rest of us said.

"That's pretty much the cutest thing I've ever seen," Siobhan said, "but it doesn't look very comfortable."

"Maybe," Polly said, "it just wants to be in the right place when it's ready for solid food." Polly put her empty plate on the coffee table. "I cannot believe I ate three slices."

"You're eating for two now," I said. "Two slices for you and one for the baby. Completely reasonable."

I put my plate down, picked up the packet of kitty wipes. "Thanks again for getting these. I think I'll wait till tomorrow to clean them up—give them a chance to get used to it here first. And make sure Pebbles is okay with letting me get that close to her kittens."

"It's so weird to think they've lived their whole life in the dirt under the porch," Siobhan said. "And I thought my life sucked."

"Lucky cats," Ethan said. "They definitely picked the right porch to be born under."

"Thanks," I said. "And thanks so much for bringing over that box. It's beautiful."

We all looked at the intricately carved wooden box.

"And completely wrong for the job," Ethan said. "Form should always follow function. The bottom shelf functions much better as a kitten space."

I smiled. "But now they've got a gorgeous toy box to put all the kitty toys you guys couldn't resist buying along with the wipes. Or we can turn it over on one side and they can use it as a playhouse when they get a little bit older."

A text alert went off. We all looked at Ethan. He reached into his pocket, turned it off without looking. Finished his last bite of pizza.

"Well," he said. "I guess I should probably get going."

Polly put her glass on the coffee table. "I'll get out of your way, too. Do you need some help cleaning up the rest of the broken glass?"

"Thanks," I said, "but we've got it."

Siobhan and John started rounding up the dirty dishes and glasses, while I walked Polly and Ethan to the door.

I gave them each a hug. "Thanks so much for the help. And not to ruin the rest of your weekend, but I'll see you both on Monday."

"And not to bum you out," Polly said, "but Gulliver's mother showed up right after you left yesterday—"

"I know," I said. "She almost plowed right into me when she came around the corner."

"I just wanted to give you a heads up that she made a pretty big scene in childcare."

I shook my head. "I bet she did. And maybe next week she'll actually get there on time to pick up her son for a change."

I opened the door. Frigid air burst in as we said our final goodbyes. Dry leaves blew off John's leaf pile and twirled their way to the ground.

After I shut the door, I couldn't help watching Polly and Ethan through the beveled glass. Ethan walked Polly to her car and they stood there talking. Finally he looked at his watch, put his hands on her shoulders, leaned over and kissed her on the forehead. His hands stayed on her shoulders. I could see her baby bump even from here.

Siobhan came up beside me. "Are they a couple?"

"No," I said. "Polly's husband left her for someone else. And Ethan's trying to work things out with his former girlfriend."

"They're like totally into each other."

I shrugged. "Life can be complicated."

"No shit," my niece said. "Is Ethan a dick?"

"I don't think so. I think they both genuinely care for each other. But I'm not sure there's an easy category for whatever the thing is between them. Maybe they'll figure out a way to be in each other's lives. And maybe they won't."

We watched Ethan open the car door for Polly. We watched Polly climb in, Ethan shut the door. It was as if we'd gone from a kitty cam to a human cam. We watched Ethan cross the driveway to his own car—his limp, his surfer boy good looks. The two cars backed out of the driveway, one right behind the other, bumpers almost kissing.

"Well," Siobhan said, "I'm out of here. I have a term paper due Monday."

"What's the topic?"

Siobhan reached for the doorknob. "I'll let you know when I finish writing it."

Once Siobhan was gone, I slid into the fringed jacket and grabbed a flashlight from the table just inside the front door. I didn't think John and Siobhan had missed any kittens, but I needed to know for sure. I got down on my hands and knees, ran the flashlight over each and every space between the porch boards, slowly, methodically, looking for even a hint of something stirring underneath. I stopped moving and listened for faint, panicked mews. It was cold now, so cold that I didn't think an overlooked kitten could make it through the night, especially without its siblings and mother to keep it warm.

When I got back to the family room, John was sitting on the couch staring at Pebbles and the four kittens.

I curled up beside him, rested my head on his shoulder. "Well, we did it. They're all safe and sound. No matter how many mistakes we make, no matter how much we mess up from this point forward, we'll always know that we managed to save five lives."

John didn't say anything.

"What's wrong?"

"It's just that I'm trying to figure out how this is all going to play out."

"What do you mean?" I tried to look into his eyes, but he was staring straight ahead.

"Jesus, Mary, and Aloysius," my father said from the doorway. "Who let the cats in?"

Horatio started barking like a maniac.

CHAPTER

Seventeen

Pebbles hissed.

John and I jumped up fast, as if we were teenagers who'd been caught making out on the family room couch.

Horatio kept barking.

Pebbles hissed again. Then she growled, deep in her throat, like she was gargling beach stones.

John backed Horatio out into the hallway.

"That's not my favorite afghan on the floor, is it?" my father said as I pulled the family room door shut behind me.

"How about a treat, buddy?" John said. He headed for the kitchen, Horatio hot on his heels.

"How about a beer, Dad?" I looped my arm through
my father's and tried to steer him in the same
direction.

My father slid out from my grip and marched down
the hallway to the staircase. "And what, pray tell,
happened here, young lady?"

"It was an accident, Dad. I think it looks worse than
it actually is—I'm pretty sure the photos are all fine.
I'll clean it up. I'll buy new glass for the frames. I even
have the broom out already. We were just taking a
break to get some food first. John and I hadn't eaten
since . . ."

My father crossed his arms over his chest, raised his
bushy white eyebrows. "Don't you *ever* leave your
mother and me in a heap on the floor, covered in
broken glass, no less."

"Sorry," I said. I started to reach for them.

My father beat me to it. He scooped up his wedding
photo and tried unsuccessfully to shake off the glass
still wedged in the corners of the frame. Then he held
the photo to his chest, shards of glass and all, and
waltzed a few steps around the hallway with his bride.

· · · · ·

I could count the times in my life that my father had
been this angry on the fingers of both hands. Maybe
even on the fingers of one hand.

I'd finally managed to get him seated at the kitchen
table with a bottle of Guinness Extra Stout. When we
were kids, our dad always drank Narragansett or

Schlitz, always tall, bottles in the house, cans when he was out on the patio grilling hotdogs and hamburgers, or to tuck between his knees while he was driving.

The drinking while driving thing had stopped somewhere around the time that seatbelt use had begun, after most of a childhood spent as one of six kids rattling around untethered in the back of a station wagon. My father had upgraded his beer choices along the way, too. He drank less beer now and Irish whenever possible. O'Hara's Celtic Stout, Murphy's Irish Stout, Guinness any way he could get it. He still didn't use a glass, but he drank from a bottle now and never a can.

Without a word, John grabbed Horatio's leash and a flashlight and went out for a walk. I couldn't blame him.

I looked over at the wooden fanny paddle that had been hanging on the kitchen wall for as long as I could remember. It was probably a little over a foot long. The top said "A Fanny Paddle For All Occasions." The bottom said, "Use At Your Own Risk." Between the two, an unattributed poem was printed in black and red letters, and there were stick-like illustrations beside each verse.

For some odd reason, I'd felt compelled to memorize this poem at one point. At nine? Ten? During the same long, slow summer that my friends and I used to pick buttercups and hold them under people's chins to see if they liked butter?

I closed my eyes to find out if I still remembered it.

For angry moms
And burnt up teachers
For shooing toms
And likewise creatures

For small behinds
And little bottoms
For other kinds
That haven't got 'em

For little boys
Who tease the girls
Bust their toys
Or pull their curls

For little men
Or mean old ladies
Be they ten
Or in their eighties

For robbers, thugs
This board will do
For litterbugs
And fathers too.

I opened my eyes, checked my accuracy. How was it
that I could remember every single word of some silly
poem I hadn't looked at in decades, and yet I couldn't
remember where I'd put the box with my coats a couple
weeks ago?

To my knowledge, the Hurlihy family fanny paddle had never been used. As a teacher, I applauded that. Hitting doesn't work. Ever. It just teaches kids to look for someone less powerful to hit. Of course, washing kids' mouths out with soap, the preferred method of punishment for mouthing off in my family while we were growing up, doesn't work either, but that's another soapbox for another time.

While my siblings and I were threatening to throw one another down the laundry chute, my parents got their jollies by threatening to use the fanny paddle.

"Don't make your mother use the fanny paddle," our father would yell from the other room. "Keep it down to a dull roar out there."

"Your father wants to know," our mother would say, "whether you'd prefer his belt, a stick, or the fanny paddle."

We'd all call out our answers—*Fanny paddle! Big stick! Belt, please!*—knowing full well it would never happen.

Judging by the look on father's face right now, I wasn't so sure anymore.

I watched him drain the last of his beer.

"Another dead soldier," I said in my best little girl voice as I reached for the empty bottle, the way we used to when we were kids and it was time to fight over whose turn it was to get our dad another beer.

My father didn't say anything. Although I noticed he didn't stop me from getting him a beer either.

I opened another Guinness with the opener that had been screwed to the side of one of the lower cabinets for as long as I could remember. I put the bottle on the kitchen table in front of him. Considered pouring a glass of wine for myself. Decided that even a few sips might make me keel over from exhaustion. Poured myself a glass of seltzer instead.

"Jiggery-pokery or bafflegab, it doesn't matter," my father said. "The fact remains that a man shouldn't have to come home after a hard day's work and find out his castle been taken over by four-legged hooligans of the feline persuasion."

"Come on, Dad," I said as I sat down again. "You knew we were rescuing Pebbles and her kittens."

He took a long slow drink of beer. "I don't mind our Miss Pebbles and her brood stopping by now and then, but we've got enough going on around here without any more lollygaggers on the dole. There's a perfectly good animal shelter in town."

"But—"

"Homer and I like our space."

"Dad, listen—"

My father clunked his beer bottle down on the scarred pine trestle table. "What part of no don't you understand, young lady?"

"Sarah, Dad, my name is Sarah. You've only had over four decades to get it right. And I'm not a child anymore. I'm all grown up, or at least mostly grown up, so you don't get to boss me around anymore."

"Don't take that tone with me, young lady," my father said. "And don't think for one minute that you're too old to see the business side of a bar of Irish Spring."

I tried to stop right there. I gulped down some seltzer, too quickly. Bubbles burned as they escaped through my nose.

I blew out a puff of air. "John and I bought the house from you, Dad. We own it. We can have cats if we want to. We can have a giraffe, three monkeys, two elephants, and a partridge in a pear tree if we want to."

My father stood up.

Too late, I realized this wasn't the kind of thing I should have said *to* my father. It was the kind of thing I should have said behind his back to someone else.

In our family, we didn't have a lot of scenes. We complained about the little things, but we rarely talked about the big things. We swallowed them down, buried them alive. When in doubt, we made a stupid joke.

"Knock-knock," I tried.

My father poured the rest of his second beer down the sink. He picked up his wedding picture from the table.

The kitchen door opened. John and Horatio and my brother-in-law Joe came in. It took me a moment to process the extra person.

"I hope this isn't a bad time," Joe said.

"Homer and I were just on our way out," my father said. "You might as well make yourself at home. Everybody else has."

Eighteen

The leash exchange was so smooth that Horatio and my father were out the door before anybody else had time to say a word.

John gave me a look that clearly meant, *Did he just take my dog again?*

I shrugged. Remembered my sister Christine's husband.

"Thanks for coming over." I kissed Joe on the cheek.

"No problem." The dark circles under Joe's eyes said otherwise. His curly brown hair had flecks of sawdust in it. He glanced at the kitchen clock.

"Have you eaten?" I asked. "How about a piece of the pizza you missed last night?"

I nuked a slice for him while John unrolled the architect's plans.

"Beer, wine, seltzer, or water?" I said from the refrigerator.

"Water, thanks." Joe ate and looked over the plans at the same time. I walked out to the hallway, picked up the rest of the photos from the steps and the floor, managed to place them on the hallway table without getting cut on a fragment of glass. Tried to remember where I'd left the broom.

"So," John was saying when I walked back into the kitchen. "Sarah and I were thinking that it might make sense to get the existing garage space renovated first."

Joe nodded. "Yeah, three stages is definitely the best way to go if you're all planning to live here during the construction. Get Billy moved into his new place first. Do the rest of the house after that. Then add the new garage." He took a final bite of pizza.

"Another slice?" I asked.

Joe shook his head, rolled up the plans, tucked them under his arm. "Let's take a look at the garage and the room over it."

I opened the door from the kitchen to the mudroom. Once you were standing in the little square postage stamp of a mudroom, if you opened the door straight ahead you'd enter a two-car garage that was old enough to have once housed horses and a buggy. But if you looked to your right and unlatched a tongue-and-groove wooden door instead, you could climb a steep rickety staircase to an unfinished room over the garage we all called the secret room.

Every surface of the secret room was covered in the same century-old knotty pine planks, darkened by time to a deep caramel. Walls turned into ceiling and met in a point overhead, providing a small central area where you could stand up straight. The only electricity came from an old brown extension cord running through a hole cut in the ceiling of the garage.

"This is going to be a great space once you add the dormers," Joe said. "And windows on three sides will really brighten things up." He stepped down hard with one work boot, then gave a little jump. "We're definitely going to need to shore up this floor from below though, bring it up to code."

"It would be great if we could reuse some of this old shiplap on the walls," John said. "Not only would it add value, but it would be a nice way to preserve some of the original ambiance."

"I'm pretty sure my dad is less concerned with ambiance than with making sure he gets a 52-inch TV," I said.

"Not a problem," Joe said. "We can do both. And I might be able to cut down that old door that leads up here and use it as the bathroom door. Or at least reuse the original iron latch that opens it. The pine floor planks up here are in great shape, too, so we can keep those and insulate from below—you've got plenty of ceiling height in the garage."

We climbed down the stairs again, ducking to avoid hitting our heads where the stairs cut into the floor. We stood elbow-to-elbow in the tiny mudroom until John opened the door to the garage.

"Whew," I said. "I always forget how much crap is in here." I pulled two brooms out of a pile, stacked them against the wall so I'd be able to find them again. Checked out a massive grapevine wreath covered with dusty silk flowers that screamed '80s, a life-sized standup cardboard Superman, a badminton set, a bulls-eye target with a few arrows sticking out of it, an old wooden Radio Flyer sled, a pile of mismatched snow boots and ice skates, a buggy whip that was either original to the house or leftover from someone's Halloween costume, a random oxen yoke. Noticed what I hoped wasn't a real shark's jaw, complete with a mostly full set of teeth, hanging from a big nail hammered into one of the studs. Wondered which of my brothers would freak out if we got rid of it.

"Typical New England garage," Joe said. "You wouldn't believe how many people can't even fit a car in, which is crazy when you factor in how much snow we get here. But again, this is great space." He looked down at the plans again. "My only question is whether or not it would make more sense to put the bedroom on the first floor instead of the second. You know, in case your dad has a hard time navigating stairs when he gets older."

"We went through all that with him," I said. "He said if his legs give up the ghost, he'll get one of those chairs that gives you a free ride up the side of the staircase."

Joe nodded. "Cheaper than an elevator. And a lot less danger of getting stuck in it."

Joe stepped over a rotary lawnmower and a go-cart so he could get to the rest of the garage. He grabbed a big tape measure off the ancient workbench. John held one end while Joe took some measurements and wrote down the numbers on a notebook he pulled out of his back pocket.

I spotted another broom, worked my way over to it, as if putting all the brooms together might magically make the mess go away.

"Okay then," Joe said. "Here's what I think it'll cost you for this part of the reno." He gave us a number.

"That's in line with what we were expecting," John said.

"It's ballpark," Joe said. "Some of it will depend on choice of finishes and if we run into any problems along the way. You know these old houses."

"So when could you start?" I asked.

When Joe scratched his head, sawdust fell from his hair like dandruff. "If you can get everything out of here tomorrow morning—"

"Where are we going to put it all?" I looked around, completely overwhelmed by the detritus my family had managed to accumulate over the years.

"I'll have a storage pod delivered," Joe said. "And a dumpster. I send both companies a good amount of work so they'll deliver right away if I need them to. And then I'll come by at noon and start the demo. If the two of you want to pitch in, it'll save you some money, and I won't have to pay one of my guys time-and-a-half to work on a Sunday."

"Wow," John said. "That's fast."

Joe nodded. "I won't be able to pull the building permit until Monday, so it's a bit of a jump start. But if you want to get this done, that's my best offer."

I'd imagined spending a lazy Sunday sitting on the family room couch with John, watching Pebbles and the kittens. My father would show up at some point, probably as soon as he got hungry, and he'd pretend that it was his idea all along to let the cats in. I'd pretend my father and I had never had a fight. John would find a way to get Horatio to make friends with Pebbles and her babies, just like he'd eventually convinced Horatio to accept me.

John and I looked at each other.

"Okay, then," I said. "Let's do it."

. . . . .

I crouched low and put fresh bowls of Fancy Feast and water on the shelf. The smallest kitten was no longer using the old food bowl as a neck rest, but was sleeping beside it, which made it easier to grab the empty bowl. The other three kittens were squished together in a kitty pile next to their mom.

Pebbles watched my every move.

"Enjoy," I whispered as I backed away.

I carried the used bowls to the kitchen and put them in the sink.

John took the bowls out of the sink and placed them in the dishwasher. He had an irritating habit of lining up everything in the dishwasher neatly, as if the dishes would somehow get cleaner that way.

He shut the dishwasher door. I resisted the urge to open the door again and mess up all the dishes.

"So," John said. "I guess renovations start tomorrow."

"Who knew it could happen that quickly," I said. "Maybe if you want to get something done, asking family is the way to go after all."

"Apparently so," John said.

"Christine must be an even bigger control freak than I thought she was," I said. "Joe probably just wants to do the work right away to get her off his back."

John held up a bottle of red wine.

"Good idea," I said. "One glass and then right to bed. Otherwise I'll be arse over teakettle, as my grandmother used to say. What time do you think we should wake up? Six? Six-thirty?"

"I was thinking more like five-thirty. Give us time to have some breakfast, let the caffeine kick in." John finished opening the bottle, poured two glasses, handed me one.

I held up my glass. "May the hinges of our love never grow rusty. And may my father bring Horatio back before he gets all dusty."

"And she's a poet and I didn't even know it," John said as he tapped my glass with his.

"Exhaustion makes me creative, what can I say?"

We heard the sound of some kind of vehicle pulling into the driveway.

"Talk about speedy," I said. "Joe's only been gone for about a half hour."

John looked at his watch. "Twenty-three minutes."

I shook my head. "You're such an accountant. I wonder if it's the dumpster or the storage pod."

I flicked on the patio light and we peeked through the kitchen door as we drank our wine. The pink Bark & Roll Forever ice cream truck pulled in first, stopped behind my father's, John's, and my cars. My dad climbed out and waved a big silver truck past him and into the backyard.

Attached to a trailer hitch on the back of the truck was my father's friend Ernie's canned ham trailer.

It was a beautiful trailer, a fifteen-foot turquoise and white 1958 Shasta Airflyte with silver wings. I knew it had a rear gaucho bed, a fridge, a bathroom. And a vinyl dinette that converted to a surprisingly comfortable second bed. I'd spent a night in it once during a big stupid fight John and I'd had during our canine camp adventure.

"Uh-oh," I said. "My dad borrowed the trailer again."

"Which means?" John asked, as if my family was a foreign country and he didn't speak the language.

"Which means he's still mad at me because I pointed out that we owned the house now. Actually, in the scheme of things, I guess the trailer's not such a bad idea. It'll give us all a little bit of elbow room until my dad's man cavern is ready."

"Whatever works," John said. "As long as Horatio stays in here with us."

I took a sip of wine as I worked on my phrasing. "Or maybe Horatio can stay in the trailer with my father.

Just for a night or two. You know, to give Pebbles and the kittens some time to adjust."

John didn't say anything.

"I mean," I said, "it's not like Horatio doesn't end up sleeping in my dad's room most of the time anyway."

We watched my father and his friend Ernie put wooden blocks behind the trailer's wheels. Then they unfastened the trailer hitch. Ernie got back in the truck, pulled away from the trailer, made a U-turn through the yard. My father saluted. Ernie beeped and drove away.

My father let Horatio out of the ice cream truck. He circled him around by the leash until Horatio chose the perfect bush to pee on. Then he opened the door to the trailer and let Horatio in first. The interior lights flickered on.

"One night," John said. He drank the rest of his wine, put his glass carefully in the dishwasher. And then he went to bed without saying goodnight.

CHAPTER

Nineteen

I fed Pebbles one more time, and then I washed up and changed into a big sleeping T-shirt in the upstairs bathroom. I walked across the bedroom in the dark, stubbed my toe on the corner of the bed, swore softly.

As I crawled between the sheets, I could tell that John was way over on his side of the bed, asleep. Or pretending to be asleep. I pulled the covers to my chin and stared up at the ceiling by the digital light of my alarm clock.

I rolled over and dozed off, slept for an hour and a half or so. Woke up. Rolled to my back. Stared up at the ceiling some more.

I must have fallen asleep again because I was dreaming. Dark, terrifying dreams about trying to catch kittens. They were everywhere. Popping up from

holes in the yard. Tucked in the dishwasher between
rows of neatly lined up plates. Hanging out of the
louvered windows of a semi-circle of identical turquoise
and white canned ham trailers. As soon as I scooped up
an armful of kittens, I'd notice another bunch that
must have been there all along. Kittens who needed me.
If only I could get to them all.

When I woke up, my heart was pounding. I rolled
out of bed, pulled on a pair of yoga pants. I tiptoed into
my sister Carol's old room and grabbed the comforter
off her bed. It smelled like old house. And the hint of
mildew that just about everything absorbent eventually
took on this close to the ocean unless you were diligent
with sunshine or bleach.

Pebbles watched me through the narrow green slits
of her partially opened eyes as I walked into the family
room, navigating by the hallway light. The tiniest
kitten was sleeping on the food bowl again, its head
dangling over the smidgen of Fancy Feast left in the
bottom. The other kittens were curled up together so
tightly that it was hard to tell where one ball of fur
ended and another began.

I exchanged my father's afghan for Carol's
comforter, tucked it in close so everyone would stay
safe and sound.

"Sweet dreams," I said as I tiptoed away.

I opened the front closet, put the fringed suede
jacket on, slid my bare feet into an old pair of boiled
wool clogs. I grabbed a flashlight from the hallway
table, circled back through the house and opened the
kitchen door.

When I stepped out on the patio, the frosty air shocked me awake. I shivered my way across the yard, pointing the beam of the flashlight up so I could see the cloudlike puffs of my breath.

The lights were off inside the trailer. I opened the door carefully, tucked my father's afghan just inside, hoping Horatio wouldn't start barking like a maniac.

"Some watchdog you are," I whispered as I walked away.

I crossed back to the house and tiptoed up the stairs to the front porch, reached into the jacket pocket for the bag of cat treats.

I sat down on the porch with my back against the cold cedar shingles of the house. With one hand I shined the flashlight into the gap where the fieldstone foundation didn't quite meet the wood. With my other hand I dropped treat after treat slowly to the packed dirt underneath.

"Oh, please," I whispered. "If you're under there, just give me a sign."

I'd find a way to get the last kitten out from under the porch. I'd call the Bark & Roll Forever ladies or the fire department in the middle of the night. I'd find the chain saw and figure out how to use it and demo the whole porch by myself. I'd wake up John if I had to.

I sat there until I ran out of cat treats. I sat some more until the fingers on the hand that was holding the flashlight went numb. I switched the flashlight to the other hand and sat some more. My butt started to freeze, even though I was sitting on the bottom of the

suede jacket. My toes started to go numb, too, even
wearing boiled wool clogs.

Finally I pushed my way up to a standing position,
my joints cold and creaky. I bent forward and ran the
flashlight along the gaps in the floorboards again, all
the way across the porch, slowly, methodically.

"Okay, that's it," I said into the frigid air. "There
are no more kittens under here. No. More. Kittens. At
all. Definitely."

Gold stars twinkled in the cold dark sky. An owl
screeched in the distance.

"Black, white, and red on top, infinity," I added, like
we used to say when we were kids to make something
unquestionably, indisputably true.

I listened for tiny mews one more time, and then I
went back to bed.

. . . . .

My subconscious must have figured it out before the
rest of me did, because when I woke up again, I just
knew.

I tiptoed back downstairs again, turned on the
hallway light. I jogged quietly to the family room, hoping I wasn't too late.

Pebbles was stretched out on her side on the purple
chenille pillow, the bigger kittens lined up in a row—
black and white, ginger and white, black and white—
all nursing away. The smaller ginger and white kitten
was curled up on the shelf, its face pressed against the
side of the food dish.

Something was wrong with the tiniest kitten.

Pebbles met my ordinary hazel eyes with her mystical green ones. I imagined the fairy world looking out through them, watching me and waiting to see what I would do.

"Feel free to jump right in, fairies," I whispered, "if you've got any magic wands available."

I stretched out on my stomach and guerilla-wiggled my way over to the shelf. Pebbles watched but didn't appear to object to me getting this close.

I propped myself up on my elbows and slowly reached for the tiny kitten, stroking it carefully with one finger. Not that I was any kind of kitten expert, but its skin felt looser than it should have been. When it opened its eyes, they seemed dull and lifeless.

If there was a kitty version of failure to thrive, I was pretty sure I was looking at it.

While John and I were planning our cat rescue, we'd Googled everything about cats we could find. I knew it was possible to hand feed kittens whose mother had abandoned them or had been killed. I could call a vet first thing in the morning to find out exactly what to do and get whatever I needed. But I wasn't sure the tiniest kitten would make it that long.

I moved slowly and carefully into a sitting position, scooped up the bare handful of kitten. I held it against my chest, pressed over my heart, and ran my finger slowly from its forehead to its tail, again and again.

Its eyes were still open, but the kitten stayed motionless. I dipped one finger in the water bowl, held it in front of its mouth. The kitten didn't respond.

I dipped my finger into the water again, gently pushed it into the kitten's mouth.

I felt teeth, real kitten teeth.

I dipped my finger in the water again and again, fairly sure that some of the water had to be staying in the kitten's mouth.

"Come on, sweetie," I whispered. "Drink."

I looked at Pebbles, as if she might help me cheer on the runt of her litter, or even give me a few tips, or maybe a meow or two of encouragement. Pebbles stared back at me, calm, placid, at peace with the outcome, no matter which way it went.

I kept dipping my finger in the water. What if I was too late? How had I missed this tiny kitten that was too weak even to cry out for help? What was my problem? What was wrong with me that even when I shot for awesome I somehow managed to end up at flawsome?

I kept going, trying to will the tiny kitten to live. To fight, to drink, to eat, to thrive. I pictured it fat and healthy and rolling around on the bottom shelf with its siblings.

Somewhere along the way I began to sing. I started with a lullaby—*Hush little kitty, don't say a word.* I was afraid I might be sending the wrong message so I switched to a perkier *If you're thirsty and you know it, drink some water.*

Finally—Minutes later? More?—the kitten made a little movement with its mouth, as if it was gumming the water.

"That's it," I said. "You can do this." I dipped my finger in the water again, and the little kitten sucked on the end of my finger. We kept it up, our own little bucket brigade—finger to water to mouth.

After we took a short break, I tapped my finger in the remnants of the Fancy Feast, pushed my finger into the kitten's mouth.

Its mouth didn't move.

"It's okay," I whispered. "You're probably just not ready for cat food yet."

I cuddled the kitten close, then slowly lined it up next to its siblings. I lifted its head carefully and aimed it at an unoccupied teat. The kitten's head dropped to the pillow, inches away from the mother's milk that could save its life.

I looked at Pebbles. I didn't think she was rejecting her tiniest kitten. She was just letting the kitten decide. *Eat or don't eat*, Pebbles seemed to be saying. *Live or die. Because I'm still practically a kitten myself. And life is tough, even tougher when you've been homeless and faced starvation yourself.*

Bottom line, I imagined her telling me, *the harsh reality of the world is that in the end we all have to save ourselves.*

Tears poured down my cheeks, dripped off my chin and fell on my T-shirt. I stroked my finger from the kitten's impossibly small nose to its tiny tail, again and again. I looked through Pebbles' eyes to the fairy world beyond. "Please," I whispered.

Then I prayed with the fervor of a lapsed Catholic who would never be able to stop believing, at least deep down inside, especially during times of life and death. And star-crossed kittens.

"Come on, you guys," I whispered. To Pebbles, to the fairies, to the patron saint of lapsed Catholics, to the universe. "We can do this."

Pebbles might be too tired and overwhelmed to will one of her kittens to live, but teachers have to believe they can fix anything. I felt the energy of all the good teachers in the world behind me, cheering me on. I'd stay here all night if I had to. I'd stay here as long as it took to get the job done.

I lifted the kitten and aimed its mouth at the same teat, held it there. The kitten suckled weakly then stopped, suckled weakly, stopped.

"It's okay," I said. "There's no rush. Just take your time."

When the other kittens started rolling away from Pebbles and tumbling off the pillow to toddle around the bookshelf, I held the kitten for a private feeding. Then Pebbles stood up and walked away to lick the food bowl empty. She sat down and meowed.

"Coming right up," I said. I placed the tiniest kitten carefully in the center of the pillow, went to the kitchen for a refill.

I stayed low as I put the fresh food and water down, grabbed the empties. Pebbles dug right in as soon as I backed away.

"Now I get it," I said. "No wonder you're always so hungry."

I dozed when the smallest kitten slept, woke up and went back to work. Again and again.

Pebbles finished eating one more time and looked at me. She stepped off the shelf and walked over to use the big litter box. Then she sauntered out the door of the family room.

"Ohmigod," I said to the kittens. "She's letting me babysit you."

I picked up the tiniest kitten and cuddled it close. Then I reached into Ethan's carved wooden box and pulled out a wand, feathers dangling off a string attached to one end.

"This," I said as they all watched me with their big kitten eyes, "is from Aunt Polly and Uncle Ethan."

I dangled the feathery toy in front of the three kittens. They stalked the feathers across the shelf, moved in on them, batted at them with their little paws, one kitten overshooting and sliding across the shelf on its side.

I took a play break so I could pet the kitten I was holding some more. Then I turned my father's ancient record player on and I danced it around while Dean Martin belted out "Memories Are Made of This."

Pebbles came back and it all started again. Eat, sleep, cuddle, eat, sleep, cuddle. This motherhood stuff wasn't for sissies.

Just as the sun was coming up, the tiniest kitten wiggled away from me and toddled over to Pebbles to nurse on its own.

I named it Sunshine.

"Sarah," a voice was saying.

I jerked awake, my head crashing into the headboard, which somehow wasn't where it was supposed to be.

"Just another half hour, Mom," I said. "I barely slept at all."

I breathed in my sister's quilt, wondered how I'd ended up in her room instead of mine and who stole the pillow.

I opened my eyes. Realized I'd conked my head on the lowest shelf in the family room.

John was looking down at me.

"I saved Sunshine," I said.

"I'll be in the garage," John said.

I woke up again to the bitter, sludgy smell of coffee that had been sitting in the pot way too long. I dragged my stiff body from the family room to the kitchen and opened the cupboard to find the coffee so I could make a fresh pot. The coffee had disappeared. My eyes went to the space where Horatio's monogrammed stainless steel food and water dishes should have been on the kitchen floor. I opened the fridge: the beer was gone, too. All clearly the work of my father.

Since I couldn't think of another immediate option, I poured a cup of stale coffee, added extra cream to disguise the taste, gulped it down. Then I carried breakfast in to Pebbles. I waited around until she was ready to nurse and made sure Sunshine got in there with the other kittens for her own breakfast.

I brushed my teeth, threw on some clothes, and found the suede jacket again. I ate a slice of cold pizza as I circled around the house, past three cars and a pink ice cream truck. The turquoise canned ham trailer was still tucked into the backyard. A red and white storage pod and a sailor blue dumpster sat next to each other on the ground across from the garage door, the combination vaguely patriotic.

"Hey," I said. "You should have woken me up again."

John hurled a slightly unraveled webbed lawn chair into the dumpster.

"Wait," I said. "Somebody might want that."

I looked around. The garage was almost empty. The corrugated metal door to the storage pod had been rolled up until it was mostly hidden, and there were some neat piles of miscellaneous stuff inside. An extension ladder and a couple of stepladders leaned up against the outside of the storage pod, along with the two brooms I'd found yesterday. The hinged door at one end of the dumpster was closed, so I stood on my tiptoes, trying unsuccessfully to see inside.

"Is everything else in the dumpster?" I asked.

John shrugged. "It's almost noon. Joe will be here any minute."

"So you just threw everything away?" My voice sounded shrill, even to my ears. "I mean, I really appreciate all the work you've done and everything, but—"

"I did the best I could. Anything I wasn't sure about, I put right here." John pointed to a long row of assorted paint cans and used brushes, flanked by a hockey net and a couple of pucks, three sleds, a white meat grinder with a hand crank, a big wicker basket filled with pine cones, a wooden butter churner, a lobster pot with two buoys inside, a baton, two pogo sticks, a pair of stilts, a croquet set.

I took a step toward him, reached for a piece of what looked like spider web clinging to his sandy brown hair.

John took a step back. "Come on, let's just get this done."

. . . . .

My sister Christine held onto the top edge of the dumpster and jumped repeatedly, attempting to see what was inside.

"It's a good thing I came over with Joe to help you out," she said between jumps.

I certainly wasn't going to thank her until I found out how helpful she actually turned out to be.

Christine gave up and turned to look at me. "Is that my old jacket?"

"No way. It was definitely my jacket." I buttoned the top button, pulled the collar up, held out my arms and did a little shimmy to shake the fringe that traveled from the armpits to the insides of my wrists.

Just underneath the warmth of the sun, the air was somewhere between chilly and frigid. I had a moment of gratitude that Pebbles and the kittens were safe and sound inside, wondered if I should take another quick peek under the front porch in the daylight just to be absolutely, positively sure we'd found all the kittens.

"Don't be ridiculous," Christine was saying. "Johnny gave me that jacket when it didn't fit him any more. Or maybe it was Michael."

Christine worked just enough hours in retail to use her substantial discount to make sure she was the best-dressed sister in the family, like that was a big challenge. Getting my hands on the jacket she was wearing would definitely be a trade up.

"Fine," I said. "I'll give you this jacket if you give me yours."

Christine changed the subject. "I can't believe you let John throw everything in the garage away."

Two could play the change-the-subject game. "Where are Sean and Sydney anyway?"

"I dropped them off at Carol's so they could help entertain Maeve. Apparently keeping Maeve in a sling takes a village. So Carol's making infinity scarf slings for everyone who shows up and they're all wearing them to show their solidarity."

"Good idea," I said, "as long as Carol's not making everybody dislocate their shoulders, too, to entertain Maeve."

"Ha," Christine said. "I wouldn't put it past her."

Joe and John were pulling tools out of Joe's truck. Christine and I lugged the last few things out of the garage—an old beach chair with a broken umbrella attached to it, some sand toys, three tiki torches—and carried them right into the storage pod.

I found another broom and lined it up next to the three already leaning against the pod.

"What are you," Christine said, "a witch in training?"

"Better than a bitch in training," I said. "Present company intended."

"Ha-ha," she said. "So funny I forgot to laugh."

Joe started taking the door that went from the garage to the mudroom off its hinges. John began swinging a big mallet at the rickety old workbench. Even with safety glasses on over his regular glasses, he looked pretty sexy.

"Okay," Christine said. "What shall we do next? Wait, can I have that old hockey net and the pucks for the kids?"

She was already dragging the net to Joe's truck.

"Come on, Chris," Joe yelled. "We don't need any more junk."

"It's not junk," she yelled back. "It's a perfectly good hockey net."

"With a huge hole in it," Joe yelled.

"Like I can't fix it," Christine said under her breath as I helped her lift the hockey net into the truck.

"You'll never get around to fixing it," Joe yelled.

We tucked the hockey pucks in with the net and turned our attention to the long row of paint and brushes. I wasn't sure what year paint had been invented, but some of the paint cans looked like they'd been around almost as long as the 1890 house.

"I know exactly what to do," I said. "I saw it on HGTV once. We open each paint can one-by-one, and we put a dot of the paint on the lid so that we can see what color is inside without having to open it the next time. Then we find an empty notebook and put another dot of paint on a page in that. We walk around the house with the notebook to find out where that paint color is being used, and we write the room, along with the name of the paint color, next to the dot in the notebook. And then we go back to the paint can and write which room that color is used on across the lid of the can, too. That way, whenever we need to do a touch-up, we'll be able to find the right paint immediately." I took a deep breath. "And then we recycle any paint that isn't currently being used on either an exterior or interior wall."

Christine and I looked at each other.

"Or," Christine said, "we can just put it all in the storage pod and save ourselves about eight hours."

"Good point," I said. We walked all the paint into the pod, tried to imitate John's neat piles.

"What about the brushes?" I said. "Keep or toss?"

Christine shrugged. "You never know when you might need a good used paint brush."

We piled the brushes on top of the paint cans. Stood around on the driveway trying to decide what to tackle next. John and Joe had moved on to demolishing the wall to the narrow staircase.

"Need any help over there?" I yelled.

Nobody answered.

"Are you sure?" Christine yelled.

Nobody answered again.

"Well," Christine said. "It certainly looks like they have that under control. I think we should do a quick check of the dumpster to make sure John didn't throw away anything important. I still can't believe you let him clean out the garage without any supervision."

I started to tell Christine that I'd been up all night saving a kitten's life, but the more people in my family who found out about Pebbles and her babies, the sooner the whole family would show up. I wanted to give them a chance to adjust before they were mobbed by Hurlihys. And if I was really honest, I kind of wanted to keep them all to myself for a while.

"Long story," I said instead. "I was busy working on some other stuff."

We walked around to the end of the dumpster.

"I wonder why John didn't open the dumpster door," Christine said.

"Maybe he couldn't figure out how."

Christine reached for a big pin attached to a chain. "It can't be that hard. You probably just take this out and the door swings open."

We tried that. Nothing. We tried pulling a long blue lever. Then we tried pushing the same lever. Still nothing.

"Hey, Joe," Christine yelled. "How do you open the door to the dumpster?"

Joe didn't answer.

Christine shook her head. "He thinks if he doesn't answer me, I won't put any more stuff in his truck. I mean, come on, how long has he been married to me?"

"How about this," I said. "We lean the long ladder against the dumpster and drop the stepladder inside. Then you can climb down in there and hand me anything you think is worth keeping."

"Why should I be the one who has to get into the dumpster? John's the one who put everything in there, so you should have to climb down there."

I was already reaching for the long ladder. "Because you're the one who really wants all that stuff."

CHAPTER

Twenty-one

To avoid potential second-guessing from John and Joe, we carried the ladders to the side of the dumpster that was shielded from the garage. I held the long ladder against the dumpster while Christine climbed it. Then I held that ladder steady with one hand, worked the stepladder up to her with my other hand. Christine opened the stepladder carefully, leaned over the edge with it, lowered it into the dumpster.

"Okay, now what?" Christine turned to look at me.

The long ladder went with her. We both screamed. I leaned my weight into the ladder, got it balanced against the dumpster again.

"Don't you dare drop me," Christine said.

"Oh, ye of no faith," I said. "Okay, swing your legs over the edge of the dumpster and feel around until you find the top of the stepladder. Once you're down there, just take a look around and hand me anything you want to keep."

Christine teetered on the edge of the dumpster, facing me, then slowly lowered herself. I heard a thud followed by a scream.

"Now what?" Joe yelled.

"Don't dignify that with an answer," Christine yelled from the bottom of the dumpster. "Superman is down here if I need any help. I can't believe how well he's held up all these years—they sure don't make cardboard like they used to. We should definitely see who wants him."

"Okay," I said. "I'm climbing up now. Get Superman as high as you can and I'll reach over and grab him."

Just for a moment, I thought about asking John to hold the ladder for me. I knew he'd do it, but I didn't want to listen to him sigh, or feel the sigh he was holding back. Okay, so he'd done most of the work this morning. Love means not keeping score. Or at least giving the other person a chance to make it up to you.

Plus, what John didn't realize was that I *had* to give Christine an opportunity to save anything worth saving, or we'd be hearing about it for the rest of our lives. Technically, I'd already told my brothers and sisters they needed to get everything they wanted to keep out of the house. But complaining, at least in my family, wasn't necessarily a rational thing.

One simple dumpster rescue and my siblings would be off my back. We'd throw it all in Joe's truck, and Christine would get to be the center of attention, the thing she craved most, as she drove around and delivered it all as if she were Santa Claus.

I was almost to the top of the dumpster when the ladder started to tilt. I climbed another rung fast, grabbed the edge of the dumpster with both hands, straightened my elbows. The ladder kept tilting.

I screamed. I waited for John to come running around to make sure I was okay. Instead, I heard the sound of crowbars splintering wood.

I moved one leg. The ladder crashed to the ground.

"You look like you're doing a flying angel," Christine said as I teetered on the edge of the dumpster. As kids, we'd spent hours and hours making flying angels, one of us lying on our back, the other balancing stomach-first on the soles of our brother's or sister's feet, arms extended as if we were flying.

"I hate to admit it," I said, "but Carol's feet digging into my rib cage was a lot more comfortable than this."

"Okay," Christine said calmly, as if we'd planned it this way. "Now swing your legs over, then flip over to your stomach again and lower yourself down to the stepladder."

It's hard to think when your arms are shaking, so I didn't immediately realize that these were not the best directions I'd ever heard. I managed to get one leg over, then the other. I half-jumped, half-fell headfirst into the dumpster, arms out, knees bent, one leg in front of the other. I was pretty sure I looked less like a flying angel now and more like I was executing a life-saving dive.

"I can't believe you landed on Superman," Christine said beside me.

"Oh, shut up."

"You shut up."

I moved my arms slowly, hoping I wouldn't need to borrow Maeve's sling. "I thought this would be a fresh dumpster. Why didn't you tell me it smelled?"

Christine shrugged. "Um, because then you wouldn't have come down here?"

"Okay," I said. "You've got exactly three minutes. I'll hold the stepladder and you climb up and throw anything you want to save over the edge."

Christine grabbed the life-sized cardboard Superman, threw him over her shoulder like a rescuing firefighter, started climbing the stepladder. Superman's head bent over at an unhealthy angle.

I started to laugh. Christine turned to look at Superman. Then she started to laugh.

Christine climbed back down the two steps she'd ascended. We perched on the edge of an old cardboard refrigerator box in the middle of a big blue dumpster with Superman reclining between us.

We laughed and we laughed, that crazy out of control kind of laughter that hurts your stomach after a while and doesn't happen nearly enough once you're a grown up. When one of us wound down, the other would get us going again.

Christine straightened Superman's head and held it to keep it from flopping over again. "He'll be fine. All he needs is a little bit of duct tape."

I wondered if it was just me or if there are moments in every life when it feels like you've time-traveled into an *I Love Lucy* episode.

I shook my head. "You are so Ethel."

"No way," Christine said. "I'm totally Lucy. Ricky can beat his bongos for me anytime."

"Fred is entirely underrated," I said. "He's much more even keeled. You know, low drama. You can count on him."

"Like John?"

I shrugged. "Maybe a little bit."

"Then why haven't you guys gotten married yet?"

"I don't know, Chris. Maybe because I'm stuck in a freakin' dumpster."

"Don't get testy with me." Christine stood up, threw Superman over her shoulder again, climbed to the top of the stepladder while I held it.

Superman flew over the edge of the dumpster, hit the driveway with barely a thud.

"Okay," Christine said, "roll that go-cart up here. Sean and Sydney will definitely want it someday."

We managed to get the go-cart over the edge of the dumpster without killing ourselves. It made a lot more noise when it hit the driveway than Superman did.

"What else?" I said. "Hurry up. The smell down here is getting to me."

Christine pointed. "How about that big grapevine wreath? Remember, it used to be on the front door?"

"Remember that year the house finches built a nest in it?" I kept one hand on the stepladder and reached for the grapevine wreath with the other. "And we weren't allowed to use that door until the baby birds had all grown up and flown away?"

"And we all started climbing out one of the living room windows instead until Mom caught us?"

"Aww, I forgot that part." I managed to get the grapevine wreath up to Christine. She lobbed it over the side. Then she grabbed on to the edge with both hands, threw her head back, as if she was reenacting that scene from *The Titanic*, only with a dumpster instead of the bow of a boat.

"*Now* what are you doing?" I said.

"Just trying to get some fresh air. Great view from up here. Hey wait, where did that canned ham trailer come from?"

"Dad borrowed it from his friend Ernie. I think he just wanted a little space to himself."

"*What?* You put Dad in a *trailer*?"

"Nobody puts Daddy in a trailer," I said in my best Patrick Swayze in *Dirty Dancing* imitation. "Of course we didn't *put him in a trailer*. The trailer was his idea."

"Don't think I'm not going to go over there and check," Christine said. "As soon as we get out of here."

"Be my guest." I sneezed. "Okay, one more thing and that's it. I have no intention of spending my entire day in a dumpster."

Christine looked around. "How about that old rotary lawnmower? See, it's behind those three Styrofoam coolers and next to the leaded glass window with the broken panes?"

"How about the badminton set over there instead? It looks a lot lighter."

"We already have two badminton sets. And the mower is a piece of Americana. It needs to be preserved for posterity."

"It's covered with rust. Come on, Chris, what are you going to do with it, use it for a doorstop?"

"Maybe I can put it in our garden and find a way to turn it into a planter."

"Genius." I rolled my eyes. "A lawnmower planter. So what, it cuts whatever you plant in it when it gets too long?"

"Come on, wheel it up to me like you did the go-cart. Just watch out for the blades."

"No problem," I said. "But just so you know, you're paying for my tetanus shot if I need one. My health insurance has a ridiculous deductible."

It turned out that a vintage rotary lawnmower was a lot heavier than either of us had anticipated. I could barely lift it up to the first rung on the stepladder.

"Come on," Christine said. "Push it up to the next rung."

I pushed. The lawnmower pushed back and hit the floor of the dumpster, barely missing my toes.

"Fine," Christine said. "We'll do it together."

Climbing a stepladder with another person while pushing a rusty rotary lawnmower up ahead of you requires a certain leap of faith, especially when it's your sister. It takes teamwork. And trust.

Slowly we moved, step-by-step, rung-by-rung, squished so closely together we were almost one person. We held the mower by its wheels, the handle waving back and forth menacingly over our heads. We muscled the heavy metal weight above our heads, propelled the mower over the edge of the dumpster.

"Shit," Christine and I yelled in perfect sibling harmony as the stepladder tipped over.

We heard some loud creaking, and then the dumpster door screeched open.

"Hey," Joe said. "Keep it down in there, will you?"

"Cute," Christine said. "And thanks for opening the door—I just spotted a few more things I can save."

She worked her way over to a big pink plastic flamingo. "Come to mama, Pink."

My old baton sparkled up at me from the depths of the dumpster. I picked it up, twirled it over my head, threw it up in the air, missed.

"I see you haven't lost your touch," Christine said.

"Okay, so I'm a little bit rusty. Being a successful majorette requires constant practice and discipline. You cheerleaders had it so much easier."

"Don't be ridiculous." Christine put the hand not holding the flamingo on her hip. "There's a big difference between dropping a baton and getting dropped by a bunch of cheerleaders who, by the way, did not necessarily have your best interests at heart."

My eyes met John's. He looked away.

I was pretty sure we were still in love, but at this particular moment in time, we didn't seem to like each other very much.

Twenty-two

While Christine was checking up on my father in the trailer, I figured I had just enough time to run in to the house and get back outside again before she missed me. I gave Pebbles some fresh food, changed her water, scooped her litter.

I picked up Sunshine, held her, or possibly him, close. It was harder to think of the tiniest kitten as an it now that it had a name.

S/he actually licked my cheek.

"Hey," I said. "It's like you're a whole new kitten."

Sunshine tried to wiggle out of my hands. I put her/him down on the shelf and s/he toddled right over to the other three kittens.

"Well, that was quick," I said. "I guess you're over me already."

I heard the kitchen door open, pulled the family room door shut behind me, sprinted to the kitchen to head Christine off at the pass.

"Dad already told me," Christine said. "Where are they?"

"How's he doing?" I asked to change the subject.

"He was having a tea party with John's dog and three women. It's a little bit crowded in there, but other than that I'd say he's doing okay. By the way, one of the women said to tell you they'll stop by to check on the cats as soon as they finish their tea."

"Hmm," I said. "Interesting. I wonder what she meant."

"Not falling for it," Christine said. "Come on, I don't have all day here. Take me to them."

Secrets simply did not exist in our family.

"Okay," I whispered as I opened the family room door. "Stay low and sit right down on the couch so you don't freak out Pebbles—that's the mama cat."

For once in her life Christine did as she was told.

Pebbles backed into a corner of the shelf, green eyes wide. The kittens kept frolicking.

"Ohmigod," Christine said. "They are so adorable. Promise me you won't give a kitten to Sean and Sydney, even if they beg. Even if *I* beg."

The bigger ginger and white kitten dive-bombed one of the black and white kittens. The two of them rolled around like little puppies.

Christine's eyes lit up. "Did I find out about them before Carol?"

Christine's need to find out about something, anything, just once, before our all-knowing older sister was so pathetic that I almost lied.

"Sorry," I said. "She guessed."

"Unbelievable," Christine said. "How?"

I shrugged. "She saw the cat carrier and the litter boxes in my car Friday night."

"You're kidding. I walked right by your car twice Friday night, and all I noticed was what a mess it was."

"Thanks," I said. "Siobhan's the only one who's actually seen the kittens though. She helped rescue them."

"That's good," Christine said. "At least I saw them before Carol did."

I picked up Sunshine again, sat on the couch next to Christine. I cuddled the tiny kitten in close. Christine reached over and started scratching it behind the ear.

"Just don't tell anyone else about them for a while, okay?" I said. "I want to give them all a chance to settle in before everybody mobs them."

"Consider it pinkie sworn."

We linked pinkies on it. I yawned. "Sunshine and I had a long night last night. I woke up from a dead sleep and just knew something was really wrong. She, or he, was acting so lethargic and not nursing at all."

"The exact same thing happened when Sean was a newborn. I called Mom in the middle of the night, and she threw a raincoat over her pajamas and came right over. I was so exhausted and Sean wouldn't eat and my nipples felt like they were half chewed off—"

"Eww," I said. "Thank you for that lovely image.

"It was awful. I mean, the nurses at the hospital tell you to make sure the baby's all the way on your breast so you don't get sore, but how do you know what that *means*? Anyway, by that point I had *blisters*, and milk was spraying all over the place because he hadn't nursed in so long. And I was crying and Sean was crying."

I scratched the fur above Sunshine's nose. "What happened?"

"Mom pushed Sean on me like she was trying to jam my breast down his throat and held him there and stroked his head. Maybe he was just waiting for someone to step up and act like they knew what they were doing, but he settled right down and started nursing like a pro."

A tear landed on Sunshine's fur before I realized I was crying.

I sniffed, wiped my eyes with the back of my hand. "I just can't believe that if I ever actually manage to get pregnant, Mom won't be here to do something like that for me. It's like this epic, crushing sadness sitting on my heart that won't ever go away."

"Carol and I will be there for you," Christine said. "I might even get there first."

When I laughed, it came out like a croak.

"Thanks," I said. "I appreciate that. And I'm just so relieved that I figured it out in time to save Sunshine. I know she, or he, is a cat and not a baby, but—"

"There are lots of different ways to mother." Christine tickled Sunshine under the chin. "Furbabies definitely count. And you're pretty much all our kids' favorite aunt. Plus, you're a *teacher*. Talk about getting your mothering in."

I shrugged. "I guess that's true to an extent. Although it's also a job that will eat you alive unless you realize that you're *not* the parent. You give the kids everything you can in the time you have with them, and if you're lucky you can make a difference. And then they go home to the people who have the biggest influence, good, bad, or in between."

"Yeah," Christine said, "but everybody remembers that special teacher, the one that made them feel special. Mine was Miss Miller. You and Carol knew so much more than I did—she was the first teacher who made me feel smart."

I scratched Sunshine behind one ear, then the other. "Preschool students are usually over you once they move on to kindergarten. I think the teachers they always remember come along later."

"Yeah, but you set the stage for all that," Christine said. "That's huge. You're the bridge between home and the whole educational ladder."

"Do me a favor," I said. "And don't use the L word for a while, okay? At least until my bruises fade."

"Ha-ha. Everybody else in the family is going to be so jealous when they find out they missed our dumpster adventure. And that I got to pet her, or him, first."

"This she or he thing is getting old," I said. I held Sunshine up for a quick gender assessment. "I don't see a penis," I sang in no particular tune. "So I guess that makes you a she, Sunshine."

"I've been wondering when you'd finally get your body parts down. Come on, let me hold her. Just for a minute."

"Wait," I said. I got low and brought Sunshine back to the shelf, picked up one of the black and white kittens, backed away carefully. Pebbles kept her eyes on me.

I sat down next to Christine. We petted the kitten until it seemed comfortable and then I held it up. "Another girl."

Christine leaned over to get a good look. "I concur. How about calling her Fiona? That's a great name for a girl cat."

"Sure," I said. "As long as you let me name one of your kids."

"Too late. I'm done. Joe had a vasectomy last year as an anniversary present to me."

"How romantic. Thanks for oversharing that, Chris. I'm amazed it took you so long."

"No problem. Let me know if you want any swelling details."

I held the kitten in close. It started to purr in fits and starts, like the little engine that could. "I think I can, I think I can," I whispered to it.

"So Fiona's totally off the table?" Christine said.

"Actually, I think I should wait and let John help me name the kittens so he doesn't feel left out. Although I have to admit this one sure looks like a Hazel to me."

I changed out Hazel for the other black and white kitten. Christine and I cuddled it, then I held it up.

"Girl," Christine and I said at exactly the same time.

"Owe me a Coke," we both said.

"This one looks a little bit like an Oreo," I said. "Or maybe a petite Orca whale. Not that I'm naming her without John, but Orca's really cute."

"Okay," Christine said. "How about this? If the last kitten is a girl, then you have to give me back my suede jacket you stole, and if it's a boy, you only have to let me borrow it long enough to determine whether it's a fashion go or a fashion no."

"No way," I said. "I'll let you borrow it sometime, but not until I find the box with all my coats in it."

"That's the only coat you have?" Christine said. "Please don't tell anyone we're related."

"No," I said. "It's the only coat I can locate right now. Totally different." I walked over to exchange Orca for the biggest kitten.

Christine and I stroked its ginger and white fur. It started purring right away, strong and sure. I held it up for gender assessment.

"Another female," I said. "Holy girl power. And this one looks like a Delilah, not that I'm naming her. Wow, great odds in this house now. That's Pebbles, the kittens, and me to Dad, John and Horatio. Females rule 6 to 3—I love it."

Christine was looking around the room. "Where's Mom's vase?"

I closed my eyes. "It was an accident. Pebbles was terrified and she accidentally knocked a few things over."

"What else?"

I scrunched my eyes tighter. "Some of the photos hanging over the stairs."

Christine jumped up, headed for the front hallway. When I put Delilah down, Pebbles looked at me and meowed.

I grabbed the empty food bowl. "Coming right up."

Christine was sorting through the pictures on the hallway table.

"Sorry," I said. "I'll have all the glass replaced. I think the pictures are fine."

"Stuff happens," Christine said. "But when you put them back up, do you think you can move Joe's and my wedding photo up to the top row?"

Twenty-three

Christine had taken off in Joe's truck, Superman and Pink the flamingo riding shotgun. She was supposed to be sharing some of our dumpster diving treasures with the rest of the family, but I had a sneaking suspicion that pretty much everything would end up in Christine and Joe's garage. At least until my other siblings found out and decided to stake a claim on their share.

I'd just popped a frozen ziti and sausage casserole in the oven. Technically it belonged to my father, since it was casserole pay from the Bark & Roll Forever ladies. But my plan was to plate some up for him and deliver it to the trailer as a little peace offering. And then John and I could dig into the rest before we overdosed on microwaved leftover pizza, which was starting to seem like a distinct possibility.

I heard a knock on the kitchen door, opened it to find the Bark & Roll Forever ladies. They were dressed for work in hot pink company T-shirts, black spandex leggings with hot pink racing stripes, and the kind of white Skechers sneakers that had memory foam insoles. Their hair still ranged from salt and pepper to sterling silver to snow white, but all three of them had big pink streaks down one side today.

I stepped back. They walked into the kitchen single file.

"Betty Ann," the first one said.

"Marilyn," the second one said.

"Doris," the third one said.

"Of course," I said, though I had to admit they all still kind of blurred together as BettyAnnMarilynDoris. I resisted a kneejerk urge to explain that I wasn't planning to eat my father's casserole paycheck on him. Or at least not the whole thing.

"Sarah," I added in case they'd have a hard time picking me out of a lineup as well. "How's my dad doing out there in trailerville?"

They laughed. "Actually," Doris said, "I think he was just about to declare his intentions to Betty Ann, but he can't quite give up the hope that he might have a shot at dating all three of us."

I smiled. "Sounds about right."

"Let's see those felines Billy Boy told us have taken over his house," Marilyn said.

They waited while I got another dish of cat food ready, then followed me to the family room. We stopped in the doorway. Pebbles backed into a corner of the bookshelf, eyes wide.

"We're going to step away for a moment," Betty Ann said, "so you can give the queen her food. Then put a pillow from the sofa in that pretty carved box and tuck it up on one of the top shelves. Take a seat on the sofa and we'll meet you there."

I followed Betty Ann's instructions. Pebbles chowed down as soon as I gave her the food. I stuffed a faded green chenille cushion into the bottom of Ethan's carved wooden box. When I stood on my tiptoes on the lower shelf, Pebbles backed into the corner again. I managed to get the box up to the second highest shelf.

As the Bark & Roll Forever ladies joined me on the couch, Pebbles worked her way up to the box and disappeared inside.

"Perfectly done," Betty Ann said. "Let her decide when and if and how quickly she wants to come closer. The box will give the queen a place to get away and feel safe. A room of her own, if you will. I don't know how all this man cave hoopla got started—women are the ones in serious need of a chick coup. Or maybe a diva den."

Marilyn shook her head. "When my kids were little, I used to dump a tub of Legos on the playroom floor and lock myself in the bathroom. We had a long corded harvest gold telephone hanging on the wall next to the toilet. I'd sit on the toilet and paint my toenails and blow on them while they dried as I talked to a friend who was going just as stir crazy as I was."

"I used to lie on my back on the floor in my bathrobe for most of the day," Doris said, "while my kids stuck kitchen utensils in my hair. And then an hour before my late husband got home, I'd feed the kids and put them to bed. Then I'd throw on a dress and lipstick and pearls, mix a pitcher of martinis, and pretend I'd looked like that all day."

All four kittens started climbing Carol's rolled-up comforter as if they were scaling Mount Everest. The biggest kitten, Delilah, led the way.

"Let the games begin," Marilyn said. "A cardboard box might work as a playpen to keep them contained for a little while, but once they get moving, they'll be all kinds of trouble. You're going to have to start keeping the door to this room shut when you're not right here. And you might want to think about ordering cord covers and cabinet latches."

"Really?" I said.

"Really," Betty Ann said. "Okay, stay low and hand those babies over to us while you tell the whole rescue story."

"All of them?" I said. "Are you sure Pebbles is going to be okay with that?"

"She'll be fine," Doris said. "She might even appreciate us taking them off her hands for a bit so she can get a nap in without being mauled."

I handed each of the Bark & Roll Forever ladies a kitten, kept Sunshine for myself. Pebbles stayed hidden in her box.

"Hand me those cat wipes," Betty Ann said. "These kitties sure could use a spit and a polish."

We wiped our kittens down while I told the story of the rescue, and the ladies nodded along. Then I told them Sunshine's story.

"Well done," Marilyn said. "They can go downhill fast at this age."

"Thanks," I said. "How old do you think they are anyway?"

All three women started trying to get the kitten they were holding to open its mouth. I copied them, felt Sunshine's little kitten teeth as if I were trying to read Braille.

"I'm going to guess around five to six weeks," Doris said.

"I'd say closer to seven or eight," Marilyn said. "See what the vet thinks when you bring them all in for their shots."

"When am I supposed to do that?" I asked. "And do I bring them one at a time or all of them together?" I was so not equipped to handle all this.

"Relax," Betty Ann said. "Let them settle in first. We'll give you the phone number of a mobile vet, too. It might be worth it to have her make a house call, given that you've got five of them. But they all look healthy so there's no rush."

I nodded, wished I'd thought to bring a notebook in so I could write this all down.

"And don't worry about Horatio and your dad," Doris said. "They're both just a couple of big ol' pussycats themselves. Let Pebbles and the kittens get used to them through a closed door for a while, and before you know it they'll all be one pack."

"Eventually," Marilyn said, "the kittens will convince Horatio he's a cat, and they'll all start head-butting to mark each other as their territory."

Even though she was talking about Horatio, I liked the image of my father on his hands and knees, as if he were giving pony rides to his grandchildren, head-butting with the kittens.

More questions flooded in. "How about using the litter box? When will they be ready? And what's the best way to go about introducing them to it?"

Betty Ann stood up, walked over to the small litter box, put Delilah down in it.

"She peed!" I yelled. I couldn't believe it.

We all clapped.

I put two fingers in my mouth and let out a Hurlihy family whistle, a toned down version so I didn't freak out the kittens.

"Isn't that developmentally advanced to be using the litter box so early?" I asked. I knew I probably sounded like one of those parents who swore up and down to me at a parent-teacher conference that their child had started singing opera at four months and walking shortly thereafter, but I didn't care.

Marilyn nodded. "It's a mark of true feline genius."

"It sure is," Doris said. "I think we're looking at a litter box prodigy."

Betty Ann traded Delilah for Hazel. Hazel sniffed Delilah's pee and then peed on top of it.

"Another Kitty Einstein," Marilyn said.

"You have no idea how proud I am," I said. "Okay, what about solid food? And what kind should I be feeding them? And what should I be feeding Pebbles?"

"They'll start tasting Pebbles' food, "Doris said. "And then you can take it from there. Keep the food bowl shallow and get ready for a mess. Wet food only. Cats are obligate carnivores, which means they thrive on a grain-free canned diet and prefer small meals throughout the day if you can do it. Don't give them dry food—the water content is too low and the carbohydrate content is too high."

"As for cat food brands," Marilyn said, "it can get very confusing. High end and grocery store brands might both have some varieties that are great and some to avoid. A good place to do your homework is CatInfo.org."

"I'm all over it," I said.

"Let Pebbles nurse for as long as she's willing," Betty Ann says. "When she starts to howl in the middle of the night, you'll know she's in heat again, and you'd better have her spayed before she manages to get out and you've got another litter of kittens on your hands."

"I have to admit," I said. "This is all a little bit overwhelming."

"Imagine how the queen feels," Doris said. "Every new mother is overwhelmed. But you just keep putting one foot in front of the other and figure it out as you go."

"The kittens will need to be spayed or neutered, too, of course," Marilyn said.

"Fixed animals are healthier and live longer than unfixed animals," Doris said.

"Most vets recommend any time after eight weeks and before six months for sterilization," Marilyn said. "Are they males or females?"

"All girls," I said proudly, as if I had something to do with it.

The three women picked up the kittens they were holding to double-check my diagnosis.

"Male," Betty Ann said.

"Male," Doris said.

"My three sons," Marilyn said.

Betty Ann traded kittens with me. She held up Sunshine. "Plus one."

"Seriously?" I said. "Four boys? My sister Christine seemed so sure they were girls."

I'd been brought up just Catholic enough that throwing my sister under the bus was immediately followed by the need to confess. "Actually, they looked a little bit like girls to me, too."

I lowered my voice. "As in I didn't see a penis."

"Essentially at this age, you're looking for an absence as opposed to a presence," Marilyn said.

"One way to tell," Doris said, "is that the distance between the anus and the penis of a male kitten is significantly greater than the distance between the anus and the vulva of a young female kitten."

I giggled. "It sounds like one of those word problems I sucked at in high school. You know, if the distance between the anus and the penis is X, and the speed you're traveling is Y, how long will it take you to get to where you're going?"

Everybody laughed.

John took a step into the family room.

"All finished out there?" I said.

"But then again," Betty Ann said at the same time, "your misjudgment might have come down to this: how much penis were you expecting to find?"

John turned around.

"Wait," I said. "That wasn't what it sounded like."

He kept walking.

CHAPTER

Twenty-four

"Oops," I said.

The ladies started to laugh. Not in a mean way, but more like how crazy is life, when you can't tell a girl kitten from a boy kitten, and even random snippets of innocent conversation can come out sounding like the punch line of a bad joke.

John and I would laugh about this later, too. I mean, it was funny. Or at least funnyish.

"Well, on that note," Doris said once we'd settled down. "I've got a little boxer to see about a walk in ten minutes."

"Canine or human?" I said.

"Time will tell," Doris said.

"We charge double for walking humans," Marilyn said. "They're a lot more aggravation than animals are."

"I should get back to check on our boarders," Betty Ann said. "Besides our usual pooches, we've got everything from a pair of guinea pigs to a pot-bellied pig who showed up with her own stroller."

One by one, they handed over the kittens and I put them back on the lower shelf. Then I walked the Bark & Roll Forever ladies to the front door.

"Thanks so much for all your help," I said.

"You know where to find us if you need anything," Betty Ann said as she handed me a business card. I took a moment to hope my dad would start dating Betty Ann, or at least one of them, so I could hang out with them more.

I stood on the porch, shivering a little as I watched them all climb into a bumblebee-yellow jeep with a sign on the side that said Bark 'n' Roll Forever. I waved. They backed out of the driveway with a *beep beep a beep beep, beep beep.*

When I walked into the kitchen, the cozy smell of casserole hit me like a hug.

John was wearing two ancient oven mitts and taking it out of the oven.

"Thanks," I said. "I was just going to check to see if it was done."

John shut the oven door. He walked over to the kitchen door, balanced the casserole against the wood trim with one hand, turned the doorknob.

"Where are you going with that?" I said. Too late, I realized my tone could have been a tad less confrontational.

He elbowed the door open. A gust of cold wind blew into the kitchen.

"My plan," he said without turning around, "is to see if I can trade it for my dog."

I shut the kitchen door behind him, perhaps harder than was technically necessary. The least he could have done was to leave some of the casserole behind for our dinner. Especially since I'd done all the hard work of warming it up.

I considered catching up to John, walking across the yard with him to the trailer. But John and my father were perfectly capable of working this out themselves. And it wouldn't be the worst thing in the world if Horatio spent another night out there with my dad. Pebbles and the kittens could have a little more elbowroom to settle in. There'd be plenty of time for us all to become one big happy pack down the road.

I was exhausted. John was exhausted. I couldn't wait to spend a nice quiet night with my head on a fluffy pillow instead of on the edge of a bookshelf. After a good night's sleep, John and I would be back in the zone again. Renovations were supposed to be stressful, and when you factored in that we were renovating my family house, not to mention that we'd simultaneously rescued Pebbles and the kittens, it was amazing that we were doing as well as we were. We'd be fine.

Without really planning it, I put the suede jacket on, grabbed the flashlight from the hallway table, flipped on the outside light. It was almost dark out already, and the nip in the air had turned into a full bite. I ran the flashlight beam back and forth along the space between the boards. I knew this checking under the porch for kittens thing was getting a little bit out of control, but I couldn't seem to help myself.

Headlights lit up the driveway as Carol's minivan crunched over the crushed mussel shells. Siobhan jumped out, strolled toward me with that long-legged gait you don't appreciate until you get to be my age and see your lanky teenage self in an old photo.

"You finished your term paper," I yelled.

She held her arms up in the air in a V for victory.

"Ohmigod," she said when she got closer. "I'm so glad you're still looking for them. I kept waking up all night last night worried that we'd somehow missed a kitten."

"Me, too," I said. "I'm afraid it's going to get to the point that I'll never be able to walk over this porch again without checking. I wonder if they have a twelve-step program for obsessive-compulsive kitten hunters."

"If they do, my mom would know about it. She keeps emailing me all these links. I think she thinks if she can find the right group, or program, or book, or something, she can keep me out of trouble until I get to college and she won't have to find out about it."

"I don't know how mothers do it," I said. "I'm not even sure I'll be capable of keeping Pebbles and the kittens out of trouble."

"Can I see them?"

"Of course." I held out the flashlight. "Just do a quick kitten check first. Your eyes are probably better than mine."

Phantom kittens checked for, we headed for the family room.

"Wow," Siobhan said. "They got bigger just since yesterday."

Pebbles climbed up the shelves to her box.

"Did I make her do that?" Siobhan said.

"It's okay. She's just going up to spend some time up in her throne. Here, sit down on the couch and I'll hand you a couple of kittens."

"Really?" Siobhan sat on the couch. I handed her the kitten formerly known as Hazel and the kitten formerly known as Delilah.

I grabbed Sunshine and Orca and sat down beside her. "So apparently, it's important to hold and play with them as much as possible so they'll be socialized to people."

"Cool." The kittens Siobhan was holding both started nibbling at the ends of her long hair. "Do they have names yet?"

"Well, at first I thought they were girls, but it turns out they're all boys." I pointed to my kittens. "This is Sunshine and this is Orca, but I don't think Hazel and Delilah are going to work very well as names for boys."

Siobhan put her kittens down on her lap, then dangled a lock of her hair in front of them. The big ginger and white kitten took a swipe at it with one paw. "What about Catsby for this one? You know, like the cat version of *The Great Gatsby*. I might even be able to get extra credit if I tell my English teacher about it."

"That's good," I said. "Hey, have you ever watched that old show *Laverne and Shirley?*"

"Yeah, it's on Hulu."

"Well, I just noticed that the black and white kitten you're holding has the exact same hairline as Squiggy."

Siobhan turned the kitten around so she could get a good look. "Squiggy could work."

"We should probably let John help us name them," I said.

"Whatever," Siobhan said. "As long as you don't change Catsby."

We put the kittens down on the floor, let them toddle around for a while. Then I got out the toys Polly and Ethan had brought for them. Siobhan dangled the feather toy. The Great Catsby stalked it like a pro.

My stomach growled. "Do you want something to eat? I thought I had a casserole, but I can microwave some never ending leftover pizza for you."

"Thanks, but I better go home for dinner. If I don't eat in front of my mom, she starts to think I'm anorexic. And if I go to the bathroom after I finish eating, she thinks I'm bulimic. And if my phone rings, she thinks Jeremy and I are back together."

"Oh, Vonny," I said. When Siobhan was Maeve's age I'd called her Vonny, and every once in a while it still slipped out. "It's got to be so hard for both you and your mom. I'm sure she thinks if she'd been paying more attention, you wouldn't have—"

"Embarrassed her by getting pregnant? I mean, she probably missed booking a few sweet sixteen parties because of me."

As usual, Siobhan's teenage radar was spot on. Carol had her own event planning business, and in a little town like Marshbury, word getting out about a pregnant seventeen-year-old daughter had probably cost her just that.

"Listen," I said. "Your parents love you. I love you. Our whole crazy family loves you. And the thing to remember is that we're all doing the best we can. And we know you are, too."

. . . . .

After Siobhan went home, I just sat on the couch in the family room for a while. I pictured John and my dad each holding one end of Horatio right about now and having a tug of war with him. I pictured them eating the whole delicious baked ziti and sausage casserole without saving any for me.

Then I pictured John moving into the trailer, sleeping on the vinyl dinette that converted to a surprisingly comfortable second bed. He'd peer over the pom-pom trimmed café curtains and through the louvered windows across the yard at the house every morning when he woke up. And he'd wonder what the hell he'd been thinking.

I pictured myself as a crazy cat lady, living with Pebbles and her four sons in this great big old house. I scooped a hell of a lot of litter, but other than that, it wasn't a half bad life.

I shook my head to clear it. Nothing was wrong. My father was doing his own thing. John would be back any moment, probably even with the rest of the casserole. Because that's the kind of guy he was, even when he was a little bit annoyed.

Pebbles came down from her throne and meowed. I got her some more cat food. Sat on the couch again.

I thought about throwing in a load of laundry. I thought about planning tomorrow's school day. Instead I dug up the remote from between two couch cushions, flipped through the channels until I found *My Cat From Hell*. I carried the kittens all over to the couch so they could watch it with me.

Pebbles walked over to use the litter box, then sauntered right out of the family room. Apparently I was kitty sitting again.

"Have fun," I said. "And don't forget, I get time and a half after midnight."

The couple in the first *My Cat From Hell* episode was trying to get their cat to behave by giving it a time out. This worked well with preschoolers, but apparently with cats, not so much.

"Good to know," I said to the kittens after Jackson got the couple squared away.

Another cat had become morbidly obese, gorging on everything from fried peanut butter and banana sandwiches to donuts.

"Can you believe that?" I said. "I mean, who gives donuts to a cat?"

Jackson not only got the food addict cat straightened out, but he helped the woman who owned it break through her denial about her own unhealthy eating habits, too. A third cat owner called her cat Bastard, and wondered why he acted like one. Jackson took care of that, too.

I loved that Jackson Galaxy carried his cat toys in a guitar case. His tattoos would take a little bit of getting used to, but the man knew how to talk about cats. No way would he walk out the door with a casserole he hadn't even put in the oven to begin with. No way would he bring his dog right home, when it had a perfectly good place to stay for a little while. He'd wait to be sure that the recently rescued cats had healed from their trauma first.

Jackson knew how to tell it like it was, too. *The cat's not a jerk*, he'd say, *it's bored*, the implication being that the humans were the ones being jerks.

I binged on episode after episode. And then it hit me: the only reason the cats were having behavior issues was that the humans in their lives were a mess. As soon as Jackson fixed the relationship between the humans, he could help them help the cat.

It was a lot like being a preschool teacher. The kids did the best they could given the parents they had to work with. Help the parents and you could help the kids.

I kept watching. I learned some more about feral cats. I learned about therapy cats. I learned about special needs cats. I learned that cats don't really try to climb into the crib and steal a baby's breath—it's an

old wives tale. I learned just how many couples used
their cats as pawns in their own power struggles.

After a few more episodes, I didn't even need
Jackson Galaxy to make a house call. If John's and my
relationship was in a good place, we'd be able to figure
out what was best for the animals in our lives.

And if John ever came back from my father's friend
Ernie's canned ham trailer, preferably with the rest of
the casserole, I planned to tell him just that.

Twenty-five

When my alarm went off, I didn't even hit the snooze button. I jumped right in the shower, dried my hair fast, grabbed some clothes from the clean laundry pile on top of my bureau.

Last night, after the *My Cat From Hell* episodes started to become one big blur, I'd eaten a piece of pizza that was on its last legs and called it a night. I'd been sound asleep when John finally came to bed, whenever that was.

I looked over at him now as I pulled on some barely wrinkled black pants, tried to decide whether he was still asleep or just pretending to be. I flashed back to the last year or so of being married to Kevin, when one of us would almost always stay in bed until the other left for work, one more way of not dealing with our crumbling marriage.

"Love you," I said in case John could hear me. "Have a great day."

I fed Pebbles while the coffee was brewing, then picked up each kitten, one by one, for a cuddle. By the time I scooped the litter, I was running late. I washed my hands, opened the fridge only to find it casserole-less. Grabbed a handful of almonds, washed them down with my final gulps of coffee.

I found a piece of paper, scribbled a quick note:

J—

I'll come home at lunch to check on the cats, but in the meantime can you feed Pebbles every time she meows? And also keep the family room door closed. Unless maybe you want to work in there today so you can keep an eye on the kittens who, by the way, need to be handled as much as possible?

LOVE YOU and we totally need to talk.

—S

P.S. You do know that penis comment was referring to the kittens, right?

I slid my arms into the suede jacket, found my car keys. Looked around for my big canvas teacher's bag, realized I'd left it in my car for the whole weekend. Circled around to the storage pod and grabbed the wicker basket filled with pinecones I'd left sitting next to it.

I ran to my car, fumbled in the bottom of my bag for my phone. The battery was practically dead, so I plugged it into my car charger, thinking I could at least partially charge it on the way to work. If we had a smooth morning, maybe I could sneak off and give John a fast call to make sure Pebbles and the kittens were doing okay.

As soon as I got to the end of my driveway, a phone message beeped in. I took a quick peek. *Bayberry Preschool*, it said. I pushed Speaker, then Play.

Sarah, my bitch of a boss's voice said. *This is Kate Stone. It's Friday at 4:02 and we have an issue. Be in my office at 7:45 Monday morning.*

Which was three minutes ago.

"Shit, shit, shit," I said.

I pushed the speed limit as much as I dared as I drove to Bayberry, fighting the urge to beep at a school bus in front of me that was stopping at practically every freakin' corner. I mean, couldn't these kids walk a few blocks and consolidate to make everybody's commute more efficient?

My tires screeched a tiny bit as I made the right into the long school driveway. I checked my big teacher watch as I cruised past the totem pole made of brightly colored clay fish.

"Shit, shit, shit," I said again as I drove past the row of painted plywood cutouts of teddy bears.

"What are *you* looking at?" I said as I ran past the boxwood sheared in the shape of ducks that edged the walkway to the Cape Cod shingled building.

I said hello as I breezed by the school receptionist, knocked on Kate Stone's door, opened it the nanosecond I heard *come in.*

I gave the wicker basket of pinecones I was carrying a little swing. "A tisket, a tasket, a green and yellow basket," I sang to break the ice. As soon as it came out of my mouth, I realized it was a really dumb thing to do.

Kate Stone and Polly both stared at me.

"Sorry," I said. "I had a very intense cat rescue over the weekend and we're also heavy into renovating our new old house and as a result I didn't check my phone for messages until I got into the car to leave for school this morning. I'd actually be slightly early if you factored out this meeting, which as I said, I didn't know anything about until moments ago. All by way of saying, I sincerely apologize for being late."

My bitch of a boss's face was expressionless. "Sit down, Sarah. Polly, you may go to your classroom—it's not fair to you to have to listen to this twice."

I sat down, put my canvas teacher's bag on the floor beside me, my wicker basket of pinecones on my lap. Reconsidered and put the basket on the floor, too. Looked down at my lap. My semi-wrinkly black pants were now covered in a combination of dust from the wicker basket and short strands of kitten fur. My fringed suede jacket was looking just orangey enough in this light to make the call that it was a distinct fashion don't.

I put the wicker basket back on my lap.

Polly stood up, rested her hand lightly on my shoulder as she walked by.

"I'll get right to the point," Kate Stone said, as if I'd imagined any other possibility. "Tiffany Swift has asked to have her son Gulliver moved to another classroom."

I blew out a puff of air. "Because she's chronically late to pick up her son, and I finally sent him to childcare. Which I should have done ages ago."

Kate Stone picked up a tiny wooden rake and scraped a circle in the sand of the miniature zen garden on her desktop. "According to Mrs. Swift, you had Polly bring Gulliver to childcare so that you could leave school early. I believe her exact words were 'to get a jump start on your weekend.' She also said that you were speeding as you left the premises and almost hit her as she turned the corner."

"What? Are you kidding me? That's a complete lie. I wasn't speeding—she was."

The miniature zen garden might be working for my bitch of a boss, but it was having the opposite effect on me. I wanted to grab it and fling it across the room like a Frisbee.

Kate Stone put the rake down and moved three tiny stones to make a triangle in the middle of the circle. "Your contractual hours are eight to four, Sarah. Did you or did you not leave school early on Friday?"

Nights. Weekends. All that personal time spent on materials preparation. Hours and hours spent coming up with fresh ideas. Parent-teacher conferences. Phone calls. Continuing education workshops. Pre-planning. Post-planning. Emails. Notes. Phone calls. Shopping with my own money to buy the things our paltry classroom budget didn't cover. A teacher's contractual hours were barely the tip of the iceberg.

Kate Stone knew all this. And she didn't care.

"Yes," I said. "I did."

"Don't let it happen again. Particularly on a Friday. Unless you inform the office in advance that you're using your allocated personal time. Also, in the interests of full disclosure, Mrs. Swift's underlying issue is that she questions whether you and Polly are appropriate role models for Gulliver. Two young single teachers—"

"Young," I said. "How sweet of her."

My bitch of a boss didn't crack a smile. "One pregnant, one living in sin."

"Oh, come on, it's not like Polly and I weren't both married at one point. Clearly we can *do* it. And my boyfriend and I just moved in together. My father lives with us, for goodness sakes. Okay, he's staying in a trailer in the backyard right now, but still."

"Your personal lives are none of her business. The school her son attends is. I've refused her request for a switch for Gulliver. She'll be observing in your classroom this morning. Our open door policy has helped make Bayberry Preschool the resounding success we are. Transparency is key to our parents appreciating the wonderful work we do here."

"This morning?" I said. "Really?"

. . . . .

A good preschool teacher can think fast. I zipped in to our classroom, opened the supply cabinet tucked into a little alcove at the back of the room. I stared at its contents as I scrolled through the years of classroom activities stored in my memory banks.

I squirted blobs of acrylic paint in Thanksgiving colors on a paper plate. Then I dipped one end of Q-tip after Q-tip in the paint, spread them all out on paper towels so they'd dry quickly.

Before I knew it the students started to arrive. While Polly greeted them and got them settled in with individual work, I dusted off the pinecones, arranged one for each student, plus two more for Polly and me, on a cute plastic turkey tray. I broke out the googly eyes and the glue sticks. I found some orange construction paper, put it on the shelf next to the tray of pinecones.

"Okay, your turn," I said to Polly. "One of your brilliant turkey faces cut out of orange construction paper and glue-gunned to the big end of each pinecone."

"Got it," Polly said.

Polly went to work while I greeted the rest of our students as they trickled into our classroom. Mondays can be tough on preschoolers, not to mention their teachers, after the weekend break in routine. Hunter came in rubbing his eyes as if he could use a nap already.

I helped Hunter hang his backpack on his hook, roll out a mat, choose a letter matching activity. I complimented Jaden's new haircut. I convinced Kiera to take off her new faux fur jacket, wondered if it came in my size, and if so whether or not I could afford it.

Morgan was so excited to see me again after the weekend that she threw her arms around my legs in a bear hug, and for a moment I remembered why I loved my job.

When I looked up, Gulliver and his mom were walking through the doorway.

"Gulliver," I said. "Happy Monday." I nodded at his mother, grabbed a kiddie chair for her. It took all my willpower not to set it up facing the corner. Instead I put it against a wall where she'd get a good view but stay out of our way.

"Have a seat," I said.

Tiffany Swift didn't make eye contact.

CHAPTER

Twenty-six

I did a headcount to make sure all the students had arrived.

I sidled up to Polly. "Okay, let's razzle dazzle."

We walked around the room, both of us making peace signs with both hands.

"Circle time," I sang.

I stood next to Polly and held my breath that the kids would find their places without a single *dumb fuck* or *fire fuck*. I mean, with my luck Gulliver's mom would tell my bitch of a boss I'd assigned them as vocabulary words.

The students found their places without a swear word. I looked skyward, nodded a quick thank you.

"Just repeat whatever I sing," I whispered to Polly.

I grabbed a mini pumpkin off the shelf. Polly and I took our places on the circle.

"I am thankful," I sang to the tune of "Frère Jacques."

"I am thankful," Polly sang.

"Yes, I am," I sang.

"Yes, I am," Polly repeated.

"A pumpkin I am passing."

"A pumpkin I am passing."

"Around the room."

"Around the room."

By the second time through, even our youngest students were singing along with Polly.

I held up the tiny pumpkin like a magic orb. "I'm thankful for all the wonderful students in this classroom who learn so much every day."

I passed the pumpkin to Griffin. He started to stuff it down his pants. I gripped his wrist gently, redirected the pumpkin.

"I'm thankful . . ." I coached.

"I'm thankful," Griffin said, "that after I go poop I get a cookie."

Violet reached over and grabbed the pumpkin from Griffin. "I'm thankful for our coconut tree in Maui."

Violet passed the pumpkin to Depp.

"You're the coolest of love, pumpkin," Depp said.

"I'm thankful that I can draw a circagle," Celine said.

"I don't like this pumpkin," Pandora said. "I like rare white pumpkins."

"This is the baddest thankful day of my whole life," Hunter said.

Polly wiggled in next to Hunter to get things back on track. "I'm thankful for the leaves on the trees and the sun in the sky and every single day I get to spend at Bayberry Preschool."

Polly passed the pumpkin to Gulliver.

"My mommy said the F word this morning," Gulliver said.

Tiffany Swift looked up from checking her Fitbit.

"Okay then," I said. I jumped to my feet, collected the pumpkin from Gulliver, stood in the middle of the circle and held it up over my head. "I'm thankful that we have some fun new work to do right now."

I grabbed the turkey tray from the supply alcove. I handed Polly the paper cup filled with googly eyes, and she passed out two to each student. I followed right behind her with glue sticks. As Polly gave the kids pinecones, they went to work gluing the googly eyes to the construction paper turkey faces.

I ran back to get the Q-tips, did a couple of quick fingertip tests to make sure the paint was dry. I gathered the Q-tips together, popped them into a wide-mouth jar.

I kept the jar beside me, glued googly eyes on my own pinecone. Waited until the kids had finished and Polly had collected the glue sticks.

I held up the painted Q-tips. "These are our turkey feathers."

I stuffed three Q-tips with their painted tips showing into the little spaces in my pinecone. Then I held up the pinecone for everyone to see.

"My turkey has three feathers," I said.

The trick to a successful preschool activity is to keep it moving, so I jumped up, started passing out random numbers of Q-tips to each student. Polly jumped up, too, grabbed some Q-tips, and started going around the circle in the opposite direction.

The kids began poking their Q-tip feathers into their pinecone turkeys.

"My turkey has four feathers," Harper yelled.

Hunter stuck his turkey feather in his ear. By the time Polly redirected his hand back to his turkey, he had a bright red streak from ear to chin. Apparently the paint wasn't quite as quick drying as it claimed to be.

Griffin saw Hunter sticking a turkey feather in his ear, so he stuck one of his turkey feathers in *his* ear. I got to him so quickly that the Q-tip only left a barely noticeable ring of brown in one ear.

"One, two, three," Polly said as she pointed at each Q-tip. "Hunter's turkey has three feathers."

"My turkey has six feathers," Ember said.

"My turkey has four feathers," Josiah said.

"My turkey has ear wax," Pandora said. "And it's disgusting."

"My turkey has five feathers," Annie said.

"My turkey has six . . . fucking . . . feathers," Gulliver said. And then he turned and hurled his pinecone turkey at his mother.

. . . . .

Tiffany Swift and I sat on chairs across the desk from my bitch of a boss. Kate Stone's desk was made from a massive freeform slab of redwood still edged with rough bark. The top of the desk had been polyurethaned until it was so shiny that Gulliver's mother could probably see the insignificant couple of paint spots on her white exercise top. I mean, come on, who wears white to a preschool?

My stomach growled. *Missing my lunch break is not okay*, I wanted to shout, maybe with a foot stomp for emphasis. I wondered if Tiffany Swift had been sitting in Kate Stone's office since she'd stormed out of my classroom, waiting for me to have a break so I could be summoned. Or if she'd run out to take a quick yoga class or get her nails done while I was working my butt off in her son's classroom.

From the center of my bitch of a boss's desk, Gulliver's pinecone turkey stared up at me with crooked googly eyes.

"Sarah," Kate Stone said. "Would you like to begin?" She adjusted one sleeve of her dog poop brown batik tunic, rested her folded hands on her shiny power desktop.

I cleared my throat. "Well, the good news is that Gulliver's got a great arm. No worries at all about his large motor coordination. I'd say he's in the top percentile when it comes to developmental markers." I couldn't seem to stop myself. "He'll be throwing the opening pitch at a Red Sox game before you know it."

"This is a brand new yoga top," Gulliver's mother said. "Quality exercise wear doesn't come cheap."

"Alcohol," I said. "Soak a cotton ball in it and just keep dabbing and dabbing at the paint."

She side-eyed my dust and kitten fur-decorated pants as if I hadn't a prayer of ever grasping her standards. In my defense, I'd brought a lint roller in to school at the start of the school year, but I'd repurposed it by covering it with bubble wrap and letting the kids use it to roll paint—it made awesome polka dots.

"Rubbing alcohol," I clarified, "as opposed to, say, vodka." Which I had to admit I could use a shot of right about now. "And just to file it away for future reference, an unpeeled cucumber does a great job of erasing crayon marks from walls."

"Actually," Tiffany Swift said. "I'll have my new yoga top professionally cleaned and send the receipt to the school for reimbursement."

I wished I'd thought of that. The truth was that every year I'd swear to only wear certain clothes to school. And then every year the day would come that I was out of clean clothes and so I'd rotate in another outfit. By the end of the school year, most of my clothing would be dotted with paint or glue or Play-Doh and even the occasional errant googly eye. Maybe the teachers could lobby for a dry cleaning budget in our next contract. Or even Plexiglas body armor that could be hosed off at the end of the day.

I tuned back in to Tiffany Swift, moved from fantasizing about a dry cleaning budget to trying to decide whether her yoga top was a size zero or some kind of negative number. Missing lunch was clearly not an issue for her, since there was no way in hell she ever ate it.

"Q-tips are not okay," she was saying. She flipped her heavily highlighted hair for emphasis.

"Excuse me?" I said.

"Nothing smaller than an elbow should ever go in a child's ear," Gulliver's mother said.

By this point in my career, I'd thought I'd dealt with every category of crazy parent, but I had to admit this was my first Q-tip Nazi. I mean, of all the issues in all the world, Gulliver's mom wanted to eradicate *Q-tips* from the classroom?

I realized everybody was waiting for me to say something.

"Right," I said. "Which is why we were putting the Q-tips in the pinecones and *not* in our ears. Manipulating Q-tips helps build fine motor dexterity, a very important part of our work as well as a precursor to handwriting."

"Feathers would have been a better choice," she said.

"Feathers," I said as I tucked my hands under my thighs so I wouldn't inadvertently punch her out. "Feathers are so much fun, and we use them quite often in our classroom activities. We're always careful to use responsibly sourced feathers colored with non-toxic, non-hazardous dye. And I sometimes even collect feathers on the beach. On my own personal time, of course."

Tiffany Swift looked at Kate Stone. "Feathers," she said, "can carry a variety of mites and bacteria."

No shit, Sherlock," I restrained myself from saying. It wasn't easy.

I stayed in my chair, even though it might have been more appropriate to climb up on my bitch of a boss's ginormous desk and tap dance while I spoke, maybe a couple of kick ball changes followed by a quick shuffle off to Buffalo. "Which is why found feathers are carefully sterilized before classroom use. They're put in a 250-degree oven, placing the feathers four inches apart on a cookie sheet, which allows the hot air to circulate around each feather until it's completely sterile. The entire process takes precisely two-and-a-half hours, at which point the feathers are removed, cooled, and placed in Ziploc bags."

So there, I wanted to add. *Tell me how to do my job instead of doing yours. I mean, can't you see why Gulliver is acting out? Can't you see how angry he is?*

Tiffany Swift and I both stared at Kate Stone.

Kate Stone looked at Tiffany Swift. "Is Gulliver having any issues at home we should know about?"

She shook her head.

Kate Stone looked at me. "How about in the class-room?"

You mean, I wanted to say, *besides hurling himself off the dismissal bench when his mother's late, swearing at her, and throwing a pinecone at her? Gee, not that I've noticed.*

I ventured a careful step into dangerous waters. "Children thrive on consistency and predictability in routine. And they often act out with the adults they love most when they can't articulate their feelings, and also when it gets them the attention they crave—"

Tiffany Swift crossed her arms over her chest. "He's perfectly fine at home."

My stomach growled again, loud and angry.

"Okay then." I looked at my big teacher watch. "Excuse me, but my lunch break is over."

CHAPTER

Twenty-seven

There's a certain way teachers talk to other teachers when they're out on the playground with their students. They stand side-by-side as they watch the kids and barely move their lips.

"Who are you supposed to be in that jacket anyway?" Lorna said. "Annie Oakley?"

"You guessed it," I said. "My spurs are in my car. And it's a good thing, because I might have been tempted to use them in that meeting."

Lorna put her hands on her hips. "I cannot believe Tiffany Swift had the balls to call me over the weekend to try to get her kid in my class. I will kill whoever gave her my cell number."

"Take him," I said. "No skin off my back."

"No way," Lorna said. "I told her that half my class is trying to get into your class so she should thank her lucky stars that her son has you."

"Thanks," I said. "This job sucks."

"Oh, please," Lorna said. "This is nothing. Remember the year that lunatic dad parked in the fire lane while he went off to play tennis with the mother of another student in his kid's class, and when the firefighters showed up because we had a fire drill scheduled, they had his car towed. And when the lunatic dad finally showed up again after playing tennis and who knows what else, he totally freaked out about how incompetent we all were, and we had to call the police on him? Man, that guy could swear."

"I forgot about him," I said.

"And remember," Lorna said, "that mom who wanted the whole school to learn Spanish because she was planning a trip to Barcelona? And the one that asked me to call another mother and force her to invite her kid to a pool party? Oh, oh, and how about that micromanaging father who used to call you every day after school to try to trick you into telling him his kid was gifted?"

"You're scaring me," Ethan said.

"No worries," Lorna said. "You'll probably just get the bored moms who want to sleep with you."

"Thanks," Ethan said.

"I'm not sure I can take it anymore," I said.

"Oh, honey," Gloria said. "We have so many great parents. The ones who ask us what we need, who write those beautiful letters to us about the difference we've made in their child's life, who give us gift certificates we actually want to use. It's just that you start to forget about them when you run into the awful ones."

"You're such a Pollyanna," Lorna said.

"Thanks, sweetie," Gloria said. "I love you, too."

My stomach growled again. "Does anyone have any food?"

Lorna reached into her pocket, handed me a mini Snickers.

"And let's not forget the perks of the job," I said. "If I'm still hungry after this feast, I can always eat a handful of goldfish from the snack shelf."

"Look on the bright side," Lorna said. "There's a big nor'easter heading this way tomorrow night. If it doesn't blow out to sea, maybe we'll luck out and get a storm day or two out of it."

. . . . .

Tiffany Swift was actually first in line to pick up Gulliver, maybe because she'd been hanging around for most, if not all, of the school day trying to make me look bad.

I stood beside our dismissal bench with the kids and stared straight ahead while Polly put Gulliver in the car. I listened to the chatter of the full-day students. Violet told the other kids they were all invited to her birthday party. Hunter had finally woken up just in time to go home and was trying to balance his backpack on his head.

They were sweet and well behaved, tired from a busy day of learning. But the thrill was gone for me.

Ember made circles with her index fingers and thumbs, held them in front of her eyes, peered through the holes. "I spy with my little eye, something that begins with C."

"Car," Pandora said.

"Cock-a-doodle-do," Hunter said.

"Cat," Millicent said.

I sighed. My heart actually hurt as I thought about Pebbles and the kittens. I hoped they were okay. I wondered if the kittens would look bigger when I saw them again. I wondered if they missed me. I hadn't had a moment to give John a quick call, or even to send him a text. I hoped he'd remembered to give Pebbles fresh water when he fed her.

"You can come to my birthday party," Violet said as I opened the back door of her mammoth SUV.

"Absolutely," Violet's mother said. "We'll put you right to work."

My eyes teared up, even though I knew it was really stupid. I pictured myself at Violet's birthday party in their fancy schmancy house, sweeping the floor like Cinderella. I blinked back the tears, smiled a fake smile, turned my head away as I shut the car door.

Eventually Polly and I finished escorting the rest of our students to their cars. We started weaving our way back to our classroom.

"Sarah," Kate Stone said as I passed her. "Please stop by my office when you're ready to leave."

I've been ready to leave since I got here today didn't seem like the smartest thing to say, so I just nodded.

"Sarah," a familiar voice said beside me. I pretended not to hear it.

My wasband's wife put her hand on the shoulder of my fringed jacket. "Dress up day in your classroom? Let me guess, you're Pocahontas?"

"Not now," I said.

Nikki Senior circled around until she was right in my face.

"Sarah?" Polly said.

"I'll meet you inside," I said.

" *What?* " I said to Nikki.

She looked around to make sure no one was listening. "Tiffany Something or Other has been calling the other mothers and saying all sorts of nasty things about you. Let's see, basically you don't know what you're doing and you send your students to childcare anytime you feel like it. There might have been more, but she was going on and on so I tuned her out after a while."

I closed my eyes to make my wasband's wife go away. When I opened them she was still standing there.

She smiled one of those obnoxious radiant pregnant smiles. "I just wanted you to know that I stuck up for you. I told her Big Kevin used to be married to you and even he thinks you're a great teacher."

She put one hand on her baby bump. "Oh, and how's it going with the house? Did you and John end up getting one of my contractors, or do you need me to find some more names for you?"

"Excuse me," I said.

Polly and I put the shelves in order, straightened out the books and fluffed the pillows in our reading boat, filled the filtered water pitcher in our tiny refrigerator, turned all but two chairs upside down on the tables. Finally we sat across from the table from each other on the two remaining kiddie chairs.

"You okay?" Polly said.

"I just don't get it," I said. "I mean, what possesses a person to repeat the bad things someone says about you? And act like they're doing you a favor."

Polly shrugged. "Who knows. Maybe it's a pathetic attempt to get in your good graces. You know, like this person doesn't like you but, hey, be my friend, because *I* like you. Or maybe it's a kind of putting you down to lift herself up."

"Getting pregnant by my wasband while he was still married to me wasn't enough?"

"Clearly she's got some boundary issues," Polly said.

"Ya think?" I turned to a fresh page in our class notebook. "Let's just do this. Okay, three good things that happened today."

"We survived it," Polly said.

I slid the notebook in her direction. *Survived it,* she wrote.

She slid the notebook back to me.

"I've got nothing," I said.

. . . . .

As soon as I was sitting across the desk from her, Kate Stone stood up. She flipped to a fresh white sheet on a big pad of paper sitting on an easel in the corner of her office. She uncapped a marker with her teeth, flipped the marker around, put the cap on the non-business side without taking it out of her mouth.

Possible Solutions, she wrote in annoying orange at the stop of the page.

My bitch of a boss looked at me.

I looked at my bitch of a boss.

She tapped the marker on the page. "Sarah? Shall we brainstorm?"

Let's not and say we did, I wanted to say just like my friends and I used to back in high school. Brainstorming was depressing, draining, demoralizing. Because brainstorming was a total sham. The reality was that my bitch of a boss just wanted to make me jump through hoops until I said whatever it was she was waiting for me to say.

"Fine," I said. "I've got two possible solutions. Put her kid in another classroom. Or tell her that I'm the teacher and she needs to respect that and stop bad-mouthing me to the other parents, or you'll put her kid in another classroom."

Kate Stone capped the orange marker again, put it on the ledge of the easel, sat back down at her desk.

"Perhaps," she said, "we could start a notebook that Gulliver carries back and forth between home and school. Mrs. Swift can voice any questions or concerns in writing. You can write a short daily report. I'll sign off on it once a week. You'll schedule a follow-up meeting just before the holiday break. I'll sit in as an impartial observer."

"An impartial observer," I repeated.

"Essentially that's my job," my bitch of a boss said.

"And here I thought your job was to have your teachers' backs."

A long beat of silence passed. "Or perhaps," she said, "a daily email exchange would be more efficient all around."

My stomach growled. Kate Stone's phone rang three times and went to voicemail. Out in the hallway, someone laughed as if she didn't have a care in the world.

"I'm not a rookie teacher," I said, "and I'm not a slacker. I know what I'm doing in my classroom, and I give my heart and my soul to this place. I won't have my time wasted by a mother who wants to blame me instead of giving her son what he needs."

Kate Stone reached for her mini zen garden.

When I pushed my chair back, it made the exact scraping sound of fingernails on a blackboard.

I looked at my watch. "It's seven minutes to four. And I'm leaving anyway. Feel free to dock my pay. Feel free to fire me."

I took a deep breath. "I mean, really, make my freakin' day."

Twenty-eight

I couldn't wait to get home, to see Pebbles and the kittens, to throw my arms around John and tell him how much I loved him. To curl up on the couch with the whole gang and tell them all about my horrible day. What had Hunter called it—the baddest thankful day of my life.

After we'd spent some quality time with the cats and I'd finished venting, John would make a pot of tea to go with his sympathy. Or better yet, we'd open a bottle of what my father called John's fancy pants wine, which I'd started hiding under the sink while we kept decoy bottles of more pedestrian wine in plain sight on the kitchen counter for my father.

John would pour and we'd hold up our glasses. I'd borrow Depp's line for a toast and say, "You're the coolest of love, pumpkin." And John would laugh and I'd laugh and we'd clink glasses and before we knew it we'd be back in the zone again.

I had so much to be thankful for. I wasn't going to let Tiffany Swift get to me. Or my wasband's wife. Or my bitch of a boss.

Maybe the teaching thing had simply run its course. I loved the kids, I really did. But I wasn't sure I had it in me to deal with their parents anymore. Maybe I could finish the year, take some time off. Maybe I could even get the Bark & Roll Forever ladies to hire me while I figured out my next chapter. Though first I'd have to remember to ask them if dealing with animal parents was as exhausting as dealing with human parents.

As soon as I had a sip, or maybe two, of wine, I'd put a casserole in the oven. John and I would stroll to the garage to see the amazing progress Joe had made on the renovation in just one day, two if you counted demo day. When the casserole was hot and bubbly, I'd plate up a generous serving and bring it out to my father, who would have completely forgotten he was mad at me. I'd tell him we'd make plans to introduce Horatio to Pebbles and the kittens in a day or two, and my dad would say he and Horatio were just hunky dory out in the trailer and there was no rush, no rush at all.

John and I would have a romantic casual dinner in the family room, our plates balanced on our laps, as we alternated between watching the cats and watching the news. With luck, the nor'easter would be barreling right at Marshbury and I wouldn't even have to work a full week. Maybe it would be a record-breaking storm, bringing down massive numbers of trees, which would in turn pull down power lines all over the place. It was a little bit early in the season for a major snowstorm, but some serious wind and ice would be nice. Maybe it would take a whole week to get the electricity restored.

When we were kids, our bag of tricks included all sorts of things to increase the chances that school would be cancelled, usually via a blizzard, though any natural disaster would do as far as we were concerned. Flush three ice cubes down the toilet. Wear your pajamas inside out and backward. Put a penny on the porch. Sleep with a sock on one foot and not the other. Put a white crayon on the windowsill. Open the freezer and yell *snow day* at the top of your lungs. And of course do your homework, which in a Murphy's Law kind of way guaranteed you'd wake up in the morning only to find out you could have waited an entire extra day to finish it.

My trusty Civic crunched over the mussel shell driveway. I hiked my teacher bag up over my shoulder, stopped on the front porch for a quick kitten check before the dwindling daylight completely disappeared, opened the heavy oak door.

I went right for the family room. Pebbles was stretched out on the lowest shelf, and all the kittens including Sunshine were nursing away.

"Hey, babies," I said. "I missed you all so much." I picked up Pebbles' empty food bowl and her water bowl. "Be right back."

John was sitting at the kitchen table hunkered over his laptop.

"I hope your day was better than mine," I said. "Sorry I didn't get a chance to call. And thanks for feeding Pebbles."

"It didn't appear that I had a choice," John said without looking up.

My stomach overreacted as if I'd been kicked. I resisted the urge to lean back against the kitchen wall, slide down until I was sitting on the cracked linoleum floor, cry the tears I'd been mostly holding in all day.

I put the repurposed cereal bowls I was holding in the kitchen sink, squirted some dish detergent in them.

"Can you please put those in the dishwasher?" John said.

"I'm letting them soak." I found two clean cereal bowls, opened a can of cat food.

John stood up, crossed behind me to the kitchen sink, emptied the soapy water out of the cereal bowls, rinsed them, crossed behind me again and loaded them into the dishwasher.

A horrifying vision came to me, in full Technicolor. I was standing at the playground with Lorna and the other teachers, watching the kids.

You're kidding, Lorna said, barely moving her lips. *You broke up. Why?*

I'm not sure, I said, barely moving my lips. *But I think it had something to do with cereal bowls.*

You're scaring me, Ethan said.

Oh, sweetie, Gloria said. *It's always the little things.*

On the one hand, immediate retreat until whatever this was blew over seemed like my best option. On the other hand, if I didn't get something besides a handful of almonds and a mini Snickers into my stomach, I was afraid I wouldn't be able to resist dipping into the Fancy Feast. I opened the freezer, pulled out the top casserole, put it in the oven.

From the depth of my teacher's bag where I'd dumped it on the kitchen floor, my cell phone jingled. I rummaged for my phone, found a text from my sister Christine.

Will u tell Joe to stop and pick up some milk on his way home? He's not answering his phone.

"What time did Joe leave?" I asked John.

"He never showed," John said to his laptop.

"Really? Maybe he has to wait for the building permit. Did you call him?"

John didn't look up. "No, I didn't call him. He's your brother-in-law. This is how these guys make a living. They take on too many jobs and start them all and then they leave everybody hanging."

Not here, I texted Christine. I grabbed my phone charger off the counter, tucked it under one arm along with my phone so my hands were free to carry Pebbles' food and water. I fed Pebbles. Plugged the charger into a wall socket in the family room, plugged my phone into the charger.

I sat for a moment on the couch in the family room staring straight ahead. Then I went back to the kitchen, opened a bottle of decoy wine, poured myself a glass. Thought for another moment. Got out another glass, filled it for John, left it on the counter.

"Here you go," I said. "If you don't want it, you can just put it in the fucking dishwasher."

. . . . .

I picked up Sunshine and Orca, carried them over to the family room couch, got them settled on my lap. I petted one with each hand, long strokes down soft kitten fur. Sunshine started purring almost immediately. Orca closed his eyes for a quick catnap.

Catsby and Squiggy scaled my sister Carol's old comforter with no problem at all and toddled right for us. I scooped them up and added them to the cat pile on my lap. Pebbles stretched, walked over to her litter box and peed, headed for the doorway.

"Watch out for that grouchy guy out there," I said.

I might have spent the whole night in the family room cuddling kittens. But when you're starving to death, the smell of creamy macaroni and cheese bubbling away in the other room is impossible to resist.

I waited for Pebbles to come back from her jaunt around the house. Then I put the kittens back on their shelf. "Okay, everybody," I said. "I'm going to go out there to get some dinner, and I'm not going to say anything else I'll regret. No matter what." I picked up Pebbles' food dish to get her a refill.

The glass of wine I'd poured for John was still sitting on the kitchen counter. Beside the bottle I'd opened was an open bottle of John's fancy pants wine.

John was still typing away, a glass of wine beside his laptop.

"Sorry the wine I opened wasn't up to your standards," I said. I poured it back into the bottle dramatically. About a third of it ended up on the kitchen counter.

"I figured I might as well drink it before your father does," John said.

I pulled the cork out of John's wine, wrote JERK and the date in permanent marker, shoved the cork back in the bottle.

I opened the oven door, slammed it shut again. "What is your problem? Is this about Horatio? I mean, I was hoping to give Pebbles and the kittens another day or two to adjust before we introduced them to one another, but if it's that big a deal to you, why don't you just bring him in right now instead of taking my head off?"

When John looked up his eyes were flat. "I did some research. All five of the cats need to be seen by a vet before Horatio can be around them. They need rabies shots, deworming treatments, flea and tick medicine. Am I supposed to take on all that, too? On top of calling your brother-in-law to talk him into showing up for work? And feeding Pebbles? And cooking meals on the off chance that we're going to eat something besides casseroles ever again. And picking up everything you leave all over the house? Let me point out that just because I'm working remote doesn't mean I'm not working."

We stared at each other.

"Anything else you'd care to dump on me?" I said.

"How many of them are you planning to keep?"

"What?"

"How. Many. Of the cats. Are you planning to keep?"

"All of them," I said. "Of course."

We stared at each other some more.

"We can't split up a *family*," I said. "And what if we gave one away and the new owners didn't give it enough attention? Or let it out and it got hit by a car. I mean, we can't control that unless we keep them. It's like that old Chinese proverb that if you save someone's life, you're responsible for them."

"That's not even a real proverb," John said. "They made it up on an old *Kung Fu* episode."

"Really? Anyway, it doesn't matter. Pebbles and the kittens are our responsibility, our gift, a little miracle the universe left under the front porch for us."

I grabbed a potholder, took the casserole out of the oven. Put a heaping spoonful on a plate. Added a second heaping spoonful, because if you're going to be depressed you might as well have plenty of comfort food.

Then I re-poured the decoy wine back into the glass John had rejected, because if you're going to overeat homemade mac and cheese you might as well bring that second glass of wine into the family room. Just in case you need it. Because you're certainly not coming back to the kitchen again.

John closed his laptop. "If you've had enough of that casserole, I'm going to take the rest out to the trailer so I can spend some time with my dog."

"Knock yourself out," I said.

As soon as John and the casserole left, I stomped upstairs, grabbed my pillow off our bed. I pulled one of the ancient blue and brown madras bedspreads from one of the bottom bunks in my brothers' old room. I clomped downstairs again and threw them on the family room couch.

Pebbles looked at me through anxious green eyes.

"Don't worry," I said. "I won't take up much space and I won't snore."

I sat on the edge of the couch and called my brother-in-law's cell. It went right to voicemail. "Hi, Joe," I said after the beep. "It's Sarah. So it's Monday and we didn't see you today, and I'm just checking to make sure you're going to be working here tomorrow. If not, can you give John a call and let him know when to expect you? His number's 781-555-8890 if you don't already have it. Thanks. Oh, and if you get this before Chris reaches you, can you stop and pick up some milk on the way home?"

I dug in my purse until I found the card the Bark & Roll Forever ladies had given me, picked up my phone, still attached to the charger. I left a message on their voicemail asking for the name and number of the mobile vet they'd mentioned and also saying I'd like to hire them to come over and feed Pebbles mid-morning and again after lunch for the rest of the week, unless the storm was bad enough that school was cancelled, starting tomorrow if they could do it.

Even though he mostly drove the pink ice cream truck for them, I wondered if the ladies would assign the job to my father, which might actually help him warm up to the idea of the kittens. It would be like its own little ecosystem: I pay the Bark & Roll Forever ladies to feed the cats, they hire my father to do it and pay him in casseroles, I eat the casseroles.

Which reminded me that I still hadn't eaten. I circled back out to the empty kitchen, grabbed my plate of mac and cheese and my bonus glass of wine.

I woofed down my dinner in the family room, barely tasting it, as I thought about all the things that can go wrong in your life and how often you don't see them coming.

Twenty-nine

When I woke up, my first clue that I'd spent the night on the family room couch was my stiff neck. My second clue was the fact that I was still wearing yesterday's school clothes.

Last night I'd flipped back and forth between *My Cat From Hell* and the weather channel. I'd gone from watching Jackson catify a condo for a couple of high energy foster cats to watching an ambidextrous meteorologist in a tight wrap dress and seriously spray-tanned legs point with both hands and talk about deepening low pressure off the eastern seaboard. After that, Jackson had featured an adorable cat with no front legs and a huge Instagram following. Then the same meteorologist was still pointing with both hands

but had moved on to predicting wind gusts near 60
miles per hour, serious flooding, coastal erosion.

I'd fallen asleep with the remote clutched in one
hand. I must have set my cellphone alarm at some
point, because it went off. I rubbed my stiff neck. I tiptoed up the stairs, grabbed a towel and some clothes,
tiptoed back down and took a shower in the downstairs
bathroom. It was almost like having my own small
garden level apartment.

I got Pebbles and the kittens squared away, stood
beside my car and looked up. Horizontal bands of
reddish pink lit up the sky as the sun rose. "Red sky in
the morning, sailor's warning," I said.

The moon was visible, too, an almost full circle with
a ring of light around it. "When the halo rings the
moon or sun, rain's approaching on the run," I added.

My weather poetry recitation complete, I swung by
Morning Glories for a takeout cup of coffee and breakfast sandwich, then looped down by the harbor. Camera
crews, Boston and national, were already staking out
their claims on the town pier.

Marshbury wasn't famous in any other way, but
hurricane, blizzard, or nor'easter, you could always
count on the meteorologists and their people showing
up. Marshbury had a beautiful sheltered harbor, and
just a few blocks away, there were plenty of crumbling
seawalls and streets guaranteed to flood in a camera-
worthy way. Not to mention lots of locals who made a
point of happening to stroll by to give pithy statements
about the resiliency of New Englanders.

I circled back around and pulled into the parking lot of Marshbury Provisions. The bread shelf was empty already, as was the small condom area tucked between the vitamins and sunscreen. The bacon shelf had been completely wiped out, and the milk and egg shelves weren't far behind.

The snow shovels were going fast, too, sales spurred on by a hand-lettered sign that read *Limit One Per Customer*. I grabbed one of the last cases of bottled water. The batteries were pretty well picked over, but I wasn't sure what kind of batteries the flashlight in the front hallway took anyway. If worse came to worse and we lost electricity, we had to have some old candles somewhere.

I was here for the cat food. I gave my neck a quick massage, filled my shopping cart with can after can, making my best guesses and vowing to do my cat food research before my next trip. Picked up a few new cat toys. Grabbed the last two bags of cat litter. Took a moment to resent the cat-less storm hoarders who'd probably bought up all the rest of the cat litter to sprinkle on their icy walkways so they didn't slip and fall.

John ordered Horatio's food online by the case so Horatio was all set. I considered buying some food for John and my dad and me, too. But if it needed to be re-frigerated and I swung back to the house to drop it off first, I'd be late for school. Plus we really should eat up the rest of those casseroles to keep them from going bad if we lost power. And really, no matter what John said, I couldn't for the life of me imagine why anyone would want to cook when you had perfectly delicious casseroles in the freezer. I tossed some nuts and granola bars and a couple cans of tuna fish in the cart for backup.

As I rolled my cart to the end of one of the long register lines, all around me people were buzzing about the wicked bad storm on the way.

I reversed direction and made one more loop around the store. Lucked out and found graham crackers, marshmallows and Hershey bars so John and I could make s'mores in the fireplace.

Because there's nothing like a wicked bad storm to make you remember what love looks like.

· · · · ·

Bayberry Preschool was crackling with storm excitement. My bitch of a boss had made the call already: *No School Wednesday*, a huge sign said as I pulled into the school drive. Smaller letters below it read *Call the no-school number for updates on the rest of the week.*

"Woo-hoo." Lorna high-fived me in the teachers' room. "This better not be nor'easter hype. I hate when they exaggerate storms just to mess with us."

I put a pod in the coffee machine, pushed the brew button. "School's already cancelled for tomorrow, so at this point it doesn't matter. I'm just glad I didn't quit. It would really suck to miss a no school day."

Lorna grabbed her mail from her teacher mailbox cubby. "You can't quit. Then I'd have to quit. Well, actually I probably wouldn't quit. I'd try to get my hands on your classroom since it has better windows, but in spirit I'd quit."

"Thanks," I said. "In spirit I appreciate that." I pulled some papers out of my mailbox. At the top of the pile was a printed email from Tiffany Swift. *FYI*, was scrawled across the top in Kate Stones unmistakable handwriting, followed by her initials.

To: K_Stone@ bayberrypreschool.edu
From: Tiffany108087@ gmail.com
Subject: Classroom Cleanliness

I'll be keeping Gulliver home from school today. He woke up this morning with a sore throat and I'm very concerned that he picked it up at school. Please confirm that his teachers are fully cleaning and sanitizing all toys and other surfaces at the end of each day.

"Seriously?" I said. In that moment I understood restaurant servers who made a point of spitting on people's food after they gave them a hard time. I was a professional, so I'd never actually sneeze into a child's backpack, but if Tiffany Swift left her yoga bag hanging around, I had to admit I'd be totally tempted.

I scrawled my response across the bottom of the email:

FYI, rest assured our classroom is completely germ free. We even soak the books in bleach and water at the end of each day and hang them out to dry overnight.

I initialed it and shoved the note into Kate Stone's mailbox.

. . . . .

"Snow, snow, snow, snow," Jaden chanted as he jumped up and down in the reading boat.

Kiera had staked out a window, watching for the first sign of anything wet.

Josiah refused to take off his mittens and hat.

"Wow," Polly said. "I can't believe how wound up they all are."

"It's always like this," I said. "I have to admit I kind of feel that way myself. There's nothing like the energy of a storm on its way."

When Polly ran her hand through her hair, silver streaks glittered like tinsel. "I'd probably be a little more excited if the house I'm renting wasn't right on the ocean. I ran into my next door neighbor this morning, and she said everybody on the street just opens all their doors on the first floor and the waves wash in one side and out the other."

I laughed. Then I took another look at Polly. Her freckles jumped out against her even paler than usual skin. "Hey, if you get worried and decide you don't want to ride it out, you can come stay with us—we've got plenty of room."

"Thanks." She put one hand on her baby bump. "I'm sure I'll be fine. But I have to admit I'm really wishing I'd learned how to swim."

Griffin had climbed into the reading boat with Jaden. "Snow, snow, snow, snow," they chanted together as they jumped.

"Let's get this show on the road," I said. "Circle time," I sang. Polly and I walked around the room making double peace signs.

"My mommy said it's only going to rain," Hunter said from his place on the circle.

Juliette elbowed him. "My mommy said it's going to snish. That's slush and snow smushed together."

Hunter elbowed her back. "My mommy said those weather people don't know what the hell they're talking about."

I sat down at my place, cleared my throat. "Can you say nor'easter?"

"Nor'easter," everybody yelled.

"Nor'easters," I said, "happen in the eastern part of the United States, usually between October and April, when we have lots of moisture and cold in the air. A nor'easter is named for the winds that blow up the coast. Warm air from the gulf stream collides with cold arctic air, and it circles around and around and around."

"And then bam!" I clapped my hands. "It's stormtastic!"

Everybody clapped their hands. "Stormtastic!" they yelled like preschool parrots.

I jumped up, jogged to our little fridge and opened the freezer, grabbed some more things from the supply shelf, jogged back to the circle.

"And here's the recipe to make sure we have a super stormtastic nor'easter." I put a big bowl in the middle of the circle.

I popped the ice cubes out of the tray and they pinged as they hit the metal bowl. I added three white crayons and two gray crayons, a pitcher full of water, a handful of cotton balls.

The kids watched with wide eyes.

I stirred the contents with a wooden spoon. "Double, double, no toil, no trouble," I said as I gave a silent apology to Shakespeare. "Abracadabra, wind blow and storm bubble."

I nodded at Polly. She walked around the circle with a paper cup full of pennies and gave one to each of us.

I squeezed my penny in my fist and scrunched my eyes shut. "I'm wishing for happy lazy days in a toasty warm house."

My penny splashed when I threw it into the bowl.

"I'm wishing for rain," Hunter said as he threw his penny in.

"I'm snishing for wish," Juliette said. "I mean wishing for snish."

"Snow, snow, snow, snow," Jaden chanted.

"Snow, snow, snow, snow," Griffin chanted.

"I'm wishing for a house with no leaks," Polly said.

Once we all had a turn making a wish and throwing in a penny, I moved the storm bowl safely out of the way.

"And now," I said, "it's time for us to do our special magic storm dance, which is also known as . . ."

I paused dramatically.

"Freeze dancing!"

The kids cheered. I broke out my storm music and we rocked out to Foreigner's "Cold as Ice" and "Riders on the Storm" by The Doors. We boogied to The Bangles' version of Simon & Garfunkel's "A Hazy Shade of Winter."

We jumped around the room. We hopped on one foot and then the other. We twisted and swam and wiggled our butts. I danced close enough to the CD player to hit the pause button and stop the music so the kids had to freeze when they were least expecting it.

But mostly I kept them dancing. Kept all of us dancing. Until our cheeks were pink and we'd broken a sweat. Until Polly looked a little less nervous about the storm.

And until I remembered that everything, even an approaching nor'easter, is more fun when you share it with a roomful of three-, four-, and five-year-olds.

CHAPTER

Thirty

"No school tomorrow," I shouted as I walked into the kitchen. I put this morning's Marshbury Provisions bags on the kitchen counter, let my school bag fall to the floor.

John didn't say anything.

I did an about face, walked down the hallway to the family room.

"No school tomorrow," I said.

Pebbles meowed.

"Thank you," I said. "I'm excited about it, too." I scooped up her repurposed cereal bowls, circled back to the kitchen.

I dumped the bowls in the sink, reconsidered and stuck them in the dishwasher. This seemed like a fair compromise. I wasn't leaving the dishes soaking in the sink, which it didn't take Nancy Drew to figure out drove John crazy. But I certainly wasn't going to wash them first either. I mean, what is the point of using the dishwasher if you've already washed everything by hand? Life needed to be streamlined, not made more complicated by adding unnecessary steps.

John looked up from his laptop. "Joe didn't show today either."

"I left a message on his phone yesterday," I said. "I'll leave another one."

John was still looking at me. "Why did you hire Bark & Roll Forever to feed Pebbles without telling me?"

"Because you appeared to object to feeding her?"

"Did you ever stop to think that me being right here while someone else was feeding her would make me look like an idiot?"

I was pretty sure that acting like an idiot was the only thing that was making John look like an idiot, but I didn't think this was necessarily the best time to tell him that.

"A heads up would have been nice," John said. "I could have worked at Starbucks."

I crossed my arms over my chest. "It's hard to give someone a heads up when you're sleeping on opposite floors of the house."

On the kitchen table across from John, I spotted an invoice from Bark & Roll Forever and a business card from the mobile vet. I rummaged for my phone, called Bark & Roll Forever and left a message that school was cancelled tomorrow. I grabbed the card, made an appointment for the mobile vet to do a home checkup for Pebbles and the kittens.

"Tuesday at 4:30," I repeated. "Thanks. See you then."

I filled new food and water bowls for Pebbles. I had to admit the family room was calling out to me like a sanctuary.

"When were you going to tell me about the scratches on my The Addams Family pinball machine?" John said.

"Oh shit," I said. "I forgot all about that."

"You forgot."

"Sorry," I said. "It was right after I shut Pebbles in the house. She was terrified. She wasn't trying to hurt it—I think she just wanted to claw her way inside to hide out with Morticia and Gomez."

"Do you have any idea how valuable that pinball machine is, how long it took me to restore it?"

I put the cereal bowls back down on the kitchen counter. "I said I was sorry. I'll find someone to fix the glass. Or you can pick someone to fix it and I'll pay for it."

"That's not the point."

I picked up the bowls again. "What is the point? I mean, other than the fact that suddenly you don't like me anymore."

"I can't live like this. I mean, one minute I have a dog and the next minute I don't. One minute we're supposed to be trying to have a baby and the next minute we're going to have cats instead."

"*What* are you talking about? Wait, let me just bring these in to Pebbles. I'll be right back."

Pebbles gave me *a what took you so long* look and dug right into her food. I picked up each of the kittens in turn for a quick cuddle. A part of me wanted to get back to John so we could work things out. Another part of me wanted to stay right here. Cats made so much more sense than boyfriends. What was wrong with John anyway? Did he have some kind of mysterious infection that was changing his personality? Or had he always been like this and I just hadn't noticed it until we moved in together? If I had a choice, I'd probably go with the infection, since at least it would be curable.

"Okay, kitties," I said. "I'll be back. Wish me luck."

John was typing away on his laptop.

I started putting the cat food away.

I stopped a few cans in, turned and leaned back, my hands braced against the counter.

John closed his laptop.

"What was that thing you said about having cats instead of a baby?" I said.

John took off his glasses, rubbed his eyes, put his glasses back on. "I was trying to bring some semblance of organization to the cardboard boxes that are piled all over the house, and I found the box with your coats in it."

"When was this?"

John shrugged. "A couple days ago, I guess."

I realized I was still wearing the fringed suede jacket. "You knew where my coats were and you let me go to school wearing *this?*"

I took off the jacket, threw it over the back of a kitchen chair. I watched John resist the urge to get up and hang it in the front closet.

John shut his laptop. "Why didn't you tell me you'd stopped using that digital ovulation test?"

"What?"

"It was in the box with your coats, test sticks scattered everywhere."

"Oh," I said. "Your point?"

John put his elbows on the table, scratched his head with both hands. "My point is that I thought we were actively trying to get pregnant."

"The thing about *we*," I said, "is that I'm the one who has to pee on the sticks."

"I realize that."

"It's not that easy to remember to do it. Especially when there's a lot going on. Like there has been since we moved in here."

"Pee on the sticks, don't pee on the sticks. But don't leave me out here hanging, thinking any minute you're going to tell me you've hit those fertile days and this time around it might actually happen."

"I guess I didn't really think about that," I said.

"We made a commitment. We had a *plan*. If you decide you want to have cats instead of a baby, don't you think you owe it to me to let me know?"

"Where are you getting that? Cats and babies don't have anything to do with one another."

John shook his head. "Of course they do. You're mothering them all."

"Oh, please. Like Horatio isn't your spoiled little baby boy. I mean, do you know how left out that makes me feel sometimes?"

"I thought we worked through all that," John said. "Horatio accepts you as a pack member now. At least he did the last time I saw him."

I blew out a puff of air. "This is a really stupid conversation. How about this? I jump back in with the test sticks on the fifth day of my next cycle. And until then, we can hang out, have a nice storm together." I wiggled my eyebrows. "Maybe even have some fun, non-goal-oriented sex just so we don't get rusty."

"I'm going to take a ride to Tampa," John said. Like it was right around the corner and not on the opposite end of the country. Like he was just going out to get a gallon of milk or a bottle of fancy pants wine.

"What do you mean?" I said.

John shifted in his chair. "Your father can make his own call, but I don't want Horatio staying out there in that little trailer during a nor'easter."

"So? Bring Horatio over here. We'll shut the family room door. I mean, what are the kittens going to do, break out and pin him down and give him rabies?"

"I haven't seen my parents in a while. They're a little bit disappointed I won't be coming down for Thanksgiving. So we can have turkey Lean Cuisines and cranberry juice, and you know, catch up."

John tried for a laugh, but it went flat.

"Basically I can work anywhere," he said. "I'm remote."

"You sure are," I said. "And I don't know what to do about it."

He looked over at the kitchen clock.

"You can't leave," I said. "It's supposed to be a really bad storm. The highways might even be closed."

"It's not going to hit for a few hours and it's heading straight for New England. If I get out now—"

"If you get out now."

"It'll be calm as can be in the South. I found a pet friendly hotel right off 95 in North Carolina that has good reviews and is pretty close to midway."

"Wait," I said. "You planned this? It's premeditated?"

I leaned sideways, saw John's rolling suitcase on the other side of his legs. "You're *packed*?"

"I told you—"

"No," I said. "You packed and then you told me. There's a huge difference."

John unzipped the front flap of his suitcase, slid his laptop in, zipped it back up again. "I need a break. I can't breathe. Cats come. Dogs go. Somebody's always stopping over."

"Nobody's stopping over. Not even my father, and he's supposed to be living here."

The old pine trestle table creaked when John pushed off on it. He stood up. Our eyes met. His kept moving.

"Aren't you worried about leaving me alone in the storm?" I tried. I wasn't proud of it, but it was the only thing I could think of.

"Right. The minute the first drop of precipitation falls, your family will start circling around you like a wagon train."

I bit my tongue so I wouldn't say *I hate you*, even though I thought there was a distinct possibility that it was true.

"Fine," I said. "Go."

John's suitcase made a definitive click when he extended the handle. "I'll call you."

"Don't bother."

He took a step toward me.

"And don't even think about kissing me goodbye."

He shrugged, rolled his suitcase across the linoleum. Walked out the same door Pebbles had walked in.

I waited until he'd pulled it shut behind him, then I opened the door again.

"I was going to make storm s'mores," I yelled.

Thirty-one

As soon as John and Horatio were gone, I put on the fringed suede jacket again and stepped out on the front porch to search for kittens. I needed something to do besides cry, and it was all I could come up with on short notice.

The wind was barely blowing, a few dry leaves skating across the porch. All this anticipation and upheaval would probably just amount to weather hyperbole. Tomorrow the meteorologists who'd made the forecast and the administrators who'd cancelled school would look like fools.

John had just been waiting for an excuse to get out.

I knelt down and aimed the flashlight between the porch boards. I didn't really expect to find another kitten, but it was soothing to run a beam of light back and forth along straight lines when the rest of my world seemed to be zigging and zagging and spiraling all over the place.

When my fingers started going numb, I went back inside. I thought I might be hungry somewhere underneath the ache that started in my heart and radiated out from there. But I wasn't sure I had the energy to carry a casserole from the refrigerator to the oven.

I considered starting a fire in the family room fireplace, roasting a marshmallow on a stick I cut myself from a tree with a kitchen knife, eating a solitary s'more for dinner. But building a fire in the fireplace for just one person seemed heartbreakingly sad, and I also wasn't sure whether or not a roaring fire would frighten Pebbles and the kittens.

I opened the graham crackers, broke one in half. Put the two squares beside each other on a big dinner plate. Tore open the marshmallows, placed one on a graham cracker square. Unwrapped the Hershey bar, broke off a piece and put it on the other graham cracker square. I put the plate in the microwave, set it on high for 15 seconds.

The marshmallow puffed up like magic. The chocolate melted. The graham cracker halves got perfectly soft. I flipped both sides together and made a sandwich, ate the whole thing before it had a chance to get cold again.

Just as I was finishing the last bite of my third s'more, somebody knocked on the kitchen door. Great. John was coming back to apologize. He'd find me with chocolate and marshmallow dribbling down my chin and my stomach puffed out like a microwaved marshmallow.

My brother Michael stuck his head into the kitchen. I saw my mother's hazel eyes and crooked smile, the way I always did when he took me by surprise.

"Did I get you at a bad time?" he said.

"Actually you may have saved me from overdosing." I pointed to the ingredients. "You know, death by s'mores."

"S'mores? Awesome. I haven't had a s'more in forever."

Mother Teresa, his St. Bernard, pushed past him.

"Wait," I said. I nudged Mother Teresa and Michael back out to the patio, pulled the door shut behind me.

"Whoa," I said. "It's really starting to get cold. Listen, we rescued a mother cat and her kittens from under the front porch and—"

"Yeah, Dad just told me. Actually Carol told me before that. And Chris might have mentioned it, too."

I leaned over to scratch Mother Teresa's chest. "What a good girl." She wagged her tail in agreement. "Anyway, they haven't been seen by a vet yet, so you probably shouldn't bring Mother Teresa inside until after Tuesday."

"We'll take our chances," Michael said. "You should see some of the fleabags we run into at the golf course." Michael's favorite place to walk Mother Teresa was the Marshbury Municipal Golf Course. He collected stray golf balls there, too, even though he didn't golf. This didn't go over so well with his wife Phoebe, but I understood the charm. It occurred to me that stockpiling golf balls you didn't have a use for might be a second cousin to looking for nonexistent kittens.

Michael held the kitchen door for Mother Teresa and me.

"Kittens or s'mores?" I said.

"That's a tough one. How about a quick s'more and then the kittens?"

I gave Mother Teresa a couple of Horatio's treats from the jar on the counter, microwaved a s'more for Michael.

They both chowed down. "That was crazy good," Michael said. "I had no idea you could make s'mores in the microwave."

"Neither did I till I tried it. Apparently I have culinary potential after all."

"Annie and Lanie will be all over it."

I smiled. "They must be excited about having a storm day."

"Yeah, they're trying to finish all their homework so they get the rest of the week off, too. And they're wearing their clothes inside out and walking around with only one shoe and one sock on."

I considered taking off a sock and a shoe, decided it could wait for later. I led the way to the family room.

"Sit," Michael said. Mother Teresa sat in the doorway.

Pebbles hissed, climbed the shelves to her throne, disappeared inside.

Catsby hissed, then scaled Carol's comforter and started toddling over to us, the other kittens hot on his heels.

"Down," Michael said. Mother Teresa lowered herself to the floor. Her tail thumped against the hardwood.

"Stay," Michael said. The kittens approached. Squiggy explored Mother Teresa's fur. Sunshine and Orca started chewing on it.

Catsby hissed and biffed at Mother Teresa with one paw. Mother Teresa started licking Catsby with her long St. Bernard tongue.

"Look," I said. "She's grooming him."

"She does that to Annie and Lanie, too. It really saves them time in the morning."

"Ha." I sat down on the couch, kept an eye on the kittens.

Michael sat down next to me. "So Dad told me John took his dog back and high-tailed it to Florida."

"Relationships," I said, "are ridiculously hard. I mean, who even invented them anyway?"

"Don't look at me," Michael said. "I've got no right to give relationship advice in any way, shape, or form. And if anything slips out, let me warn you that you should probably ignore it."

"But you and Phoebe are doing okay, right?"

"Yeah, mostly. I mean, I'm not going to tell you that every day's a walk on the beach. We still fight, same as we always did. But I think we're in a good patch. If I didn't just jinx us by saying that."

Mother Teresa was licking the four kittens, dividing her time equally between them. Sunshine wiggled under Mother Teresa's armpit and started trying to nurse.

"John," I said, "didn't want Horatio to come in the house until Pebbles and the kittens had been checked out by a vet."

"Phoebe would have said the same thing. She worries about those things. I don't. I want everybody to loosen up and have some fun. She wants us to have clean clothes and structure and more rules."

I sighed.

"Maybe," Michael said, "that old saw about how opposites attract is true. When it works, it's a good thing and Phoebe and I balance each other out. When it doesn't work, we drive each other right up the wall."

"The wall is considerably closer than Tampa," I said.

Michael leaned back in the couch, laced his fingers together and put them behind his head. "If you want me to jump on a plane with you, just say the word. I owe you one."

"You sure do," I said.

Michael and Phoebe's marriage had hit a bumpy stretch last summer, and Phoebe had taken off with Annie and Lanie to Savannah, where she'd grown up and where her parents still lived. When Michael realized they might not be coming back, he'd freaked out and decided to go after them. Long story short, I'd gone with him for his own protection. Carol and our dad had tagged along for reinforcement.

"We might have to bring Christine with us this time," Michael said. "She still hasn't shut up about us leaving her out the last time."

"Thanks for the offer," I said, "but I think I'm going to stay here and grow into my spinsterhood, maybe rent out rooms to Dad's girlfriends to make ends meet."

"There's a thought," Michael said. "Speaking of Dad's girlfriends, I just met one over at the trailer. At least I think it was a girlfriend. She was dropping off some chocolate chip cookies to make sure he survived the storm."

"Great," I said. "As long as he's got cookies, I won't have to worry about the canned ham trailer blowing over in a nor'easter."

Michael shook his head. "I stopped by there first to try to talk him into coming back to the house at least till the worst of the storm is over. Carol made me flip a coin with her and I lost."

"What'd he say?"

Michael ran one hand through his hair the way our dad always did. "Don't be a blatherskite, Mikey Boy," he said, sounding exactly like our father. "I camped outside during the Blizzard of '78 just for the lark of it."

"He did not," I said. "Mom would never have let him."

"I think he actually believes his own blarney though. He also said the safest place to be in a nor'easter is a canned ham trailer. If lightning strikes, it just travels around and around the metal."

"Great," I said. "What was the girlfriend like?"

"Young."

"How young?" I said. "I mean, too young?"

Michael shrugged. "I'm pretty sure Dad's definition of too young is when her sneakers still light up."

I laughed.

"Although he doesn't appear to have any objection to older women either," Michael said, "so I'd have to say he's pretty much an equal opportunity dater. Oh, I almost forgot. Apparently the woman with the cookies lives next door to your old Kevin and his new wife. She told me to tell you Nikki says hi."

I blew out a puff of air. "This is the thing about small town living that sucks. You can get divorced, but you can never really get rid of anybody. It's like every mistake you've ever made just keeps hanging around to haunt you."

Michael stretched, stood up. "Dad was right, you know. Kevin was never on his best day good enough for you. But John might be worth trying to hang on to."

CHAPTER

Thirty-two

After Michael and Mother Teresa left, I threw myself wholeheartedly into becoming a pity party animal. Pebbles and the kittens were the perfect pity party guests. They had no problem at all letting me wallow. They never once told me to get over it.

I fed Pebbles again. The kittens curled up on the couch with me. Alternating *My Cat From Hell* episodes with storm coverage didn't seem quite pathetic enough, so I scrolled through the television offerings until I came to *The Addams Family*, not the TV show from the '60s but the '90s movie starring Angelica Huston and Raúl Juliá.

I watched the whole thing, feeling vaguely connected to John, or at least to his scratched pinball machine. I wondered if the movie would be playing again when John and Horatio got to their hotel in North Carolina, if they'd watch it, if it would make John think of me. MC Hammer's "Addam's Groove" video in the movie made me remember the Break It Down contractor. When Morticia tried her hand at being a preschool teacher, I couldn't help giving her some seriously needed tips. When Gomez hit golf balls from his roof, I filed it away to mention to my brother Michael as something to consider with his own golf ball collection when the weather got better.

Somewhere along the way, I realized that *The Addams Family* was a movie about the importance of family, and love. That they're all that really count, and it doesn't matter whether your family consists of a disembodied hand with a job as a courier, and a brother who gets amnesia after being lost for 25 years in the Bermuda Triangle, and kids who ask whether the Girl Scout cookies are made out of real Girl Scouts. Or slightly less quirky companions like the ones in my own life.

At the end of the movie, everything finally got worked out, and Morticia told Gomez she was pregnant.

I cuddled the kittens and cried like a baby.

. . . . .

My ringing phone woke me from a dead sleep. At first I thought it was my alarm warning me to hurry up or I'd be late for school. I opened my scratchy, puffy eyes. The family room TV was off but the lights were on.

I found my phone lodged between the sofa cushions, remembered putting the kittens back on their shelf and then sitting with my phone clutched pathetically in one hand, resisting the urge to call John.

"Hello," I croaked as my muddled brain tried to focus on the time and the caller ID at the same time. The time check won out: 9:13 PM. Even my stint as a pity party animal was an epic fail.

"Sarah, it's Ethan. I'm at Polly's house and she needs to get out fast. It's flooding here already and high tide is still a couple hours away. She doesn't have that much stuff but, well, the bed of my truck isn't covered and her car isn't that big. Maybe—"

"I'll be right there," I said. I gave Pebbles a quick bowl of food, threw on somebody's old boots and the suede jacket, grabbed a box of extra-large trash bags from under the kitchen sink.

No matter how many you've been through, you always forget how quickly a nor'easter comes on. I had to fight to open the kitchen door against the wind. Icy rain stung my face. The suede fringe hit the arms of my jacket again and again, like so many tiny whips. Even a mile or so from the ocean, I could smell the salt water, even taste it.

I held the box of trash bags in front of my face for cover. I stepped over a heavy-duty power cord that connected the canned ham trailer to the house like an umbilical cord.

My father opened the door to the trailer as soon as I banged on it.

I stepped inside fast. "Listen, Dad, I need to help someone evacuate and my car's not big enough. Can we take the ice cream truck?"

"I knew you'd show up when you needed me, Sarry girl," my father said.

A pink ice cream truck is not the first vehicle you think about driving in a major storm, but it was heavy and low to the ground, so at least I was pretty sure we wouldn't blow off the road or flip over. My dad drove and I played co-pilot, keeping an eye out for tree limbs blocking the streets, the ice cream truck playing "Turkey in the Straw" in that distinctive melodic chime of ice cream trucks everywhere.

Main Street was flooding already and blocked by a trio of sawhorses. An electronic highway sign sat on blocks in front of the sawhorses, flashing *Wicked Bad Nor'eastah. Get Off the Road. Now.*

"Damn rubberneckers," my father said. "What are they thinking driving around in this kind of weather?"

We cut inland and looped through some neighborhoods, worked our way back toward the ocean. After each pass of the wipers, we'd get a glimpse of the road, and then a deluge of icy rain would obscure it again.

Under the streetlights, we could see someone rowing a boat carrying people down the middle of Fourth Avenue. Two rescuers wearing orange dive gear were sitting in the back of a big military-style vehicle.

My dad slowed almost to a stop. "Well, will you lookee there. It's one of those amphetamine vehicles."

"Amphibious, Dad. Look, I think they're rescuing that news crew."

Sure enough, a female meteorologist wearing a zip-up parka with the station's logo and cute polka dot rain boots climbed out of the boat and splashed through the thigh high water over to a waiting Marshbury police SUV. A camera guy climbed out right behind her, the storm jacket covering his camera matching their twin parkas.

The pink ice cream truck started to play "Let it Snow."

"I don't like to rush the seasons," my dad said, "but the ladies insisted on adding this one to the rotation. What the hey, it's their casseroles."

"That's the spirit," I said. "And if you have to have Christmas music before Thanksgiving, this is the weather for it."

My father and I sang along as we splashed up the road, the windshield wipers keeping time like a metronome.

"Your mother would have loved this," my father said.

"I was just thinking that."

"We used to throw you kiddos in the back of the station wagon as soon as the wind began to howl, head straight to the beach."

"Yeah," I said. "I mean, why worry? If one of us kids blew out to sea, you'd still have five left."

The ice cream truck started to rock as we turned on to Polly's street. Slush splatted the windshield. I took a moment to wonder how much water it took for an ice cream truck to start hydroplaning. When the wipers made their next arc, we saw power lines dangling low, shaking in the wind.

We passed two cars parked at the side of the road, water mostly covering their tires.

"It's this one," I said. "On the left."

My dad put on his blinker, splashed into Polly's driveway.

We heard a massive crash, and then the ocean surged between Polly's house and her next-door neighbor's, heading right for us.

"There are worse things in life than not being able to afford waterfront," I said just before the wave hit.

When the wave splashed over the windshield, it was like being inside a saltwater carwash. My father put the ice cream truck into park. We waited until the wave headed back in the direction of the ocean, trailing sand and rocks and seaweed across the driveway of Polly's rental.

I reached for the garbage bags. My father turned off the headlights.

We stepped into bone-chilling calf-high water. The wind whipped my hair over my eyes. Icy salty water found its way into my nose, my ears. But the sound was the worst, like gazillions of sheets flapping in the wind, so loud it actually hurt.

Just as we heard another big wave hit, Ethan opened the front door for us.

Polly screamed.

A heavy unseen object bounced off one of the metal hurricane shutters on the waterside of the house.

Polly screamed again. "Come on, I don't need anything else. Let's just go."

"Relax, dollface," my father said. "We'll have you out of here in a jiffy."

I knew Polly had rented the beach house furnished. It looked like most of the stuff she'd brought with her was already piled up near the front door.

I shook out big black garbage bags, handed them to Ethan and my dad, kept one for myself.

"Okay," I said. "We're going room to room. Polly, just point if it's yours and one of us will grab it."

In no particular order, we filled garbage bags with books and clothes and shampoo and towels and the baby stuff our teacher friend Gloria had handed down to Polly. We closed them with twist ties and piled them by the front door.

Ethan and I ripped head and arm holes in four more bags, and we all put them on over our coats like rain ponchos.

The lights flickered, went out, came back on.

"Okay," I said. "Let's cram this stuff into all three vehicles and drive to our house while we still can."

"If you don't mind storing my stuff at your house," Polly said, "you can drop me off at the storm shelter. My neighbor said they set up cots in the high school gym for the people who evacuate."

"Don't be ridiculous," I said. "There's no way you can stay at a school when we've got a storm day tomorrow—it's like an oxymoron. We've got plenty of room."

A wave broke, followed immediately by the sound of splintering wood. Polly screamed. Water sprayed in through the side door.

My father put a beefy paw on Polly's shoulder.

"You," he said, "look like a little lady who could use a ride in an ice cream truck."

Tears streamed down Polly's cheeks.

I drove Polly's car, Polly and my dad taking the lead in the ice cream truck, Ethan bringing up the rear in his truck.

Just once, as our storm caravan splashed its way through the stormy streets of Marshbury, the wind stopped gusting long enough for me to sing along with the faint strains of "It's a Small World After All."

Thirty-three

On our laps we balanced plates piled high with four-cheese seafood lasagna from the casserole collection. Neither Pebbles nor the kittens seemed the least bit bothered by the massive fire in the fireplace.

"This is amazing," I said. "Why would anyone in their right mind ever cook again?"

My father took another sip of John's fancy pants wine. "'Outside,'" he said as he leaned back in his old recliner, "'are the storms and strangers: We/Oh, close, safe and warm sleep I and she, I/and she.'"

"Browning?" I said.

"Good girl," my father said. "The apple doesn't fall far from the strudel, as I've been wont to say."

I took another sip of John's fancy pants wine, too. I mean, after all, my father had already opened it. The

first thing he'd done once we'd taken off our garbage
bag ponchos was to pull out a bottle of it from its
hiding place under the kitchen sink. When the bottle
was finished, I'd write NOR'EASTER and the date and
put the cork in the bowl.

Polly sipped her milk, put her glass back on the
coffee table. The wind rattled the old windowpanes.
The lights flickered here and there. Pebbles had come
down from her throne and was stretched out on the
lowest shelf with the kittens, who were nursing away.
My dad had turned on the record player and Dean
Martin was softly crooning "Memories Are Made of
This" once again.

"I think this is the warmest, coziest, safest house
I've ever been in," Polly said. "Thank you again for
rescuing me. All my neighbors seemed so brave, I guess
I thought I should be able to ride out the storm."

"My speculation is they'll be tucking their tails
between their legs by the next high tide," my father
said. "You simply used your noggin' and made the call a
wee bit early."

"Yeah," Polly said. "Like when the first wave
exploded over the seawall."

"I think," I said, "there's a distinct possibility that
we might have overdone that storm dance in school
today."

"Juliette's mommy was right though," Polly said.
"It's definitely snishing out there."

A branch cracked somewhere outside. A thud
followed. The lights flickered but held.

"And where, pray tell, was that young man of yours off to in such a hurry?" my father said to Polly.

"Back to his girlfriend," Polly said.

Polly turned to me. "Not that it's any of my business, but where's John?"

"He took his dog to Tampa to visit his parents," I said.

"If I might offer you gals a wee bit of advice it would be this," my father said. "You'll never plow a field by turning it over in your mind."

"Thanks, Dad," I said. "Polly and I feel better already. So what about you, you're not going back out to the trailer tonight, are you?"

My father put his empty plate on the coffee table. "I only run into trouble over there if I try to use the coffee maker and the toaster at the same time." He picked up his wine glass. "But I do believe I'll hunker down here for the night just in case you need anything."

"I don't mind sleeping on the couch," Polly said.

"Enough with that stuff," I said. I stood, picked up my father's plate, slid it under my own, reached a hand out for Polly's plate. "Stay right there. I'm just going to make up my sister Carol's old room for you."

Since the kittens were using Carol's old comforter, I grabbed another madras bedspread from one of my brothers' old bunk beds. I found fresh sheets and a pillowcase in the hallway linen closet, fluffed up Carol's old pillow, turned on the bedside lamp. I could totally do the Suzy Homemaker thing when I focused. As my final welcoming touch, I taped the sign that said STOP! KEEP OUT! to her bedroom door.

I ran back downstairs and started opening the drawers of the dining room sideboard, searching for candles. In the third drawer, sitting on top of a platter, I found four big pillar candles that smelled like cinnamon.

I pulled out three. Hidden behind them were the long brass keys that locked the bedrooms from either the inside or the outside.

"Woo-hoo," I said. "We have privacy."

I gathered the keys, tucked the candles in the crook of one arm. Swung by the kitchen to find three books of matches in case the lights went out overnight.

When I walked into the family room, Dean Martin was singing "That's Amore."

My father was holding Polly's hand and circling her around in time to the music as he sang along with Dean. "When the moon hits your eye like a big pizza pie. That's amore."

Polly looked up at him, a big grin on her face.

"Dad," I said. "Don't even think about it."

. . . . .

Polly and I were each cuddling two kittens in our lap. We'd finished putting every white crayon I could find on the windowsill. Our clothes were on inside out, and we each had one shoe and sock on and one off.

My father was stretched out in his recliner, remote in hand, flipping through the channels. He stopped at some storm coverage—massive waves were crashing over a huge seawall that had broken into pieces.

"Wow," I said. "It looks like a gigantic cement jigsaw puzzle."

The camera cut to a line of houses, decks dangling, staircases ripped off. A window box filled with burgundy and gold chrysanthemums had landed on top of a perfectly intact blue and white striped awning.

"Ohmigod," Polly said. "I think the house without the staircase is mine."

"Never underestimate the power of the sea," my father said. "She's as deadly as she is spectacular." I waited for him to launch into a long-winded story to impress Polly, about his former boat or the time he was appointed Marshall of the Marshbury Blessing of the Fleet.

"Why don't you pass one of those little furballs over this way," he said instead.

I handed Catsby to him, then turned back to Polly. "Once the storm settles down, I'll drive you over there so you can see what kind of shape it's in."

"Thanks," Polly said. "But I am never setting foot in that place again. If I have to lose my deposit, I'll deal with it."

"You'll get your money back," my father said. "I'll give that landlord of yours a good talking to if I have to."

"I appreciate that," Polly said. "I'll start looking for a new place right away, but if I'm getting in your way, let me know and I'll try to figure something out."

"You absolutely will not look for a new place," I said. "You can stay here. At least until the baby's born or you can't take us anymore, whichever comes first."

"The pleasure would be all ours," my father said.

Polly started to cry, deep ragged sobs shaking the kittens on her lap.

"There, there, darlin'," my father said. "We're not that dreadful to live with."

Polly started to laugh, then she cried some more, then she laughed again. "Sorry," she said. "Hormones."

"We'll have none of that talk under this roof, young lady," my father said.

"Wait," Polly said. "What about John? I mean, don't you think you should ask him if he minds if I stay here for a while?"

"John can stay in Tampa if he doesn't like it," I said. "It's a nonnegotiable."

"There's always the trailer," my father said.

"For him or for me?" Polly said.

We all laughed. And then I fed Pebbles again and put the leftover casserole in the oven for lunch.

The day stretched on and on, long and luxurious.

"How about a little game of Monopoly?" my father said at one point.

So we played Monopoly at the kitchen table. My father charmed Polly and flattered me and then took all our money.

The call came in just as I was about to declare bankruptcy. I ran to the family room, grabbed my phone. Listened for a moment, then screamed at the top of my lungs.

I ran back to the kitchen. "That was the teachers' phone chain. Power's out in about half the town, including Bayberry, there are limbs all over the roads, the temperature's dropping, there's black ice everywhere, and one more flood tide coming in. No school for the rest of the week!"

Polly and I cheered, jumped around the room like we were our own students, except that Polly kept one hand on her baby bump.

"Well," Polly said. "I guess we can put our other shoe and sock back on now."

"Oh, wait," I said. "I have to call the next person on the phone chain."

I dialed my phone.

Polly's phone rang.

"Hello," she said.

"No school for the rest of the week!" I yelled.

Thirty-four

As the wind whistled and the panes rattled, I tossed and turned in the vast expanse of a half-empty king-sized bed. I also couldn't seem to stop flipping over the old proverb my father had dispensed like a prescription: *You'll never plow a field by turning it over in your mind.*

Okay, the field had to be flooded and frozen by now. So, what? Let the field lie fallow for the winter and plow it in the spring? Dig up some old skates and go ice skating on it? Think about something else? Tell my father to keep his proverbs to himself? And what was the field anyway? This house? My classroom? John and me? All of the above?

It was almost dawn when what my father may or may not have been saying hit me. That the thing about life is just about everything is solvable. But the trick is that you have to be willing to roll up your sleeves and do the work.

Ugh. I hated that.

I sighed. Flipped over again, untangled the sheets that were now strangling my legs. Sighed some more. What was so wrong with waiting to be saved? I mean, did I have to do *everything*? Couldn't I hang around whining and complaining and pity partying until somebody showed up to fix my life?

Apparently not. So the way it looked was that I had two extra days to fritter away or to make the most of. Two bonus days that I could theoretically use to get everything back on track.

I allowed myself one more sigh, then I kicked off the covers. I tiptoed downstairs, poked my head into the family room.

Pebbles was eating her breakfast.

My dad was sitting in his recliner, all four kittens in his lap.

"I thought I smelled coffee," I said.

"When you get to be my age, Carol, you don't sleep the way you used to."

"Sarah," I said. "Listen, Dad. Just for the record, Polly's pregnant and single. She's my teaching assistant at school. She's my age. My point being that the last thing she needs is a man in her life right now, especially one who's too old for her and has a slight tendency to be a womanizer."

My father started scratching Sunshine under his chin. "I couldn't agree more, darlin', I couldn't agree

more. Our Miss Polly is one choice bit of calico, and I'll
have you know that I've made it my mission to protect
her. Why else would I have left a perfectly comfortable
canned ham trailer?"

"I need caffeine for this day," I said.

I drank my coffee at the old pine trestle table. I
watched the kitchen clock until I was sure Christine
was awake, found my cellphone.

"What's wrong?" she said by way of answering.

"What's wrong," I said, "is that your husband hasn't
shown up for work since the day he and John did the
demolition on the garage."

"Well, he's got a lot going on. And I may have
pressured him a tiny bit to take the job."

"But you did," I said. "So now you've got to pressure
him a whole bunch more until he finishes it. I expect to
see and hear him this morning."

"The roads are iced over and half the town is
without power."

"We've got plenty over here. And if we lose power,
Joe can figure something out. Or borrow a generator if
he doesn't have one. I mean, what would the Property
Brothers do? What did carpenters do before electricity?
What did *Jesus* do?"

Christine didn't say anything.

"Come on, Chris. He can put in four full days,
preferably with a full crew, before his other clients
even miss him. I'm not kidding here. If Dad's man cavern isn't finished by Thanksgiving, Joe's going to be in
the oven with the turkey. And you'll be basting both of

them. Because Thanksgiving dinner will be at *your* house."

"Fine," Christine said before she hung up on me.

It took me a little bit longer to work up to emailing Tiffany Swift, but I did it.

Dear Tiffany,

I hope Gulliver's sore throat is all better and this email finds you both enjoying the storm days! Polly and I are just thrilled to have the extra time to do another deep cleaning of our classroom.

We've also decided to institute a new program, and I'd like to congratulate you on being chosen as our first official Wonder Parent. If you can find time in your busy schedule to come in about half an hour before dismissal on Monday with something (book/project/activity) you'd like to share with the full-day students, we'd really appreciate it.

Until then, have a stormtastic time!

Warmly,
Sarah Hurlihy

After that I got a little bit bogged down. The nor'easter was blowing back out to sea almost as quickly as it had blown in, but it would take time to clean up the aftermath. I scrolled through the local news sites—Logan Airport had two runways de-iced already, but tons of people, many who'd been camping out all night, were waiting to be rebooked after their flights had been cancelled.

I pulled up a discount flight-booking site, typed in airports and dates.

"Are you kidding me?" I said when I saw how much it would cost. When I went straight to an airline website, it cost even more.

I went back to the original site, typed the same information in again. The cost for the exact same flights had gone up by two hundred dollars.

"Cookies are for eating," I yelled to the kitchen walls. "Not for ripping people off."

"Keep it down to a dull roar out there," my father yelled. "The felines and I are trying to relax."

Polly came into the kitchen, dressed in yoga pants and a sweatshirt and wearing fuzzy slippers. "That was the best sleep I've had in months," she said. "Maybe forever."

"Great," I said. "Can I borrow your laptop?"

"Of course," Polly said. "I'll go get it."

My father lumbered in, Pebbles' empty dish in his hand. "And I'll rustle you up some pancakes, little lady."

"You know how to make pancakes?" I said.

Ten minutes later, the kitchen was a mess, Polly had her pancakes, and I had a round trip ticket.

. . . . .

I threw myself into a storm of activity. I washed the sheets and pillowcases. I picked up my dirty clothes from the floor and washed those, too. I threw my high school Lollipops away and emptied the trash. I cleared off the top of my dresser and hung things up or put them away in one of the drawers.

After that I went on a hunt for the box with my coats. I found it in the front parlor, tucked in the doorway across from John's two pinball machines. I dragged the box to the front hallway, hung my coats and jackets in the front hallway.

I gathered up all the test sticks and grabbed the digital ovulation monitor, clomped up the stairs with them, left them on top of my clean dresser where I wouldn't miss them.

When I went in to check on Pebbles and the kittens, Polly was stretched out on the family room couch reading a book.

"Where's my dad?" I said.

Polly smiled. "Out in the garage supervising the building of his man cavern."

I shook my head. "That'll keep my brother-in-law working as fast as he can if anything will. Hey, are you sure you're okay with me taking off?"

"Absolutely," Polly said. "You totally need to do this. Your dad and I can take care of Pebbles and the kittens. Your dad even said he'll change the litter since I'm not supposed to."

"My dad?" I said. "Change litter?"

"And anything else you remember that has to be done while you're gone, just call."

"Thanks," I said. "I really appreciate it."

Orca was trying to climb the couch. I gave him a boost, and he headed right for Polly and curled up on the open pages of her book. Catsby dug his tiny claws into the couch and started working his way up from the floor. Squiggy and Sunshine were right behind him.

"I really appreciate you letting me stay here," Polly said. "I can't tell you how grateful I am."

"Listen," I said. "If my father gets on your nerves, or if he asks you to marry him or anything like that, tell him to knock it off and call me immediately. I'll leave my sister Carol's number for you, too. She'll kick his butt."

"Don't be silly. Your dad's adorable." Polly shook her head. "Why don't they make men like that anymore?"

I wandered around the house for a while. I turned on the TV, flipped through the channels. Tiffany Swift emailed me a lengthy itinerary of her Wonder Parent plans, and I emailed her a short thank you. I played with the kittens. I fed Pebbles.

I carried my laptop up to my frighteningly clean room. I curled up on the bed. I composed and tweaked and deleted and started again. And again. Finally I sent a text to John.

Slightly self-destructive but well-meaning divorced woman of a certain age seeks renewed relationship with remarkable if recently remote man she's lost touch with. Please consider meeting me at the Tampa International Airport baggage claim at 12:55 tomorrow— American Flight 20153. I'll be wearing a single red rose.

Thirty-five

Pebbles looked up from her pre-dawn feeding.

"You'll be fine, sweetie," I said. "I won't be gone long."

The fairies gazed out at me through her emerald eyes and wished me luck.

Even though I had to leave at 3 AM to be sure I made the 6:05 AM flight to Tampa, I knew my brother Michael would have given me a ride to Logan Airport. My sister Christine might have even tagged along just so she wouldn't miss an adventure and mostly so she could one-up Carol. Christine would have wanted to ride shotgun to the airport, but I would have bumped her out of the front seat and told her she could ride shotgun on the way home.

But I needed to do this alone. The driving was a little dicey getting out to the highway, but after that it was fine. I pulled into long term parking at Logan, left my newly found winter parka in the trunk of my Civic and put on a lightweight jacket.

The good thing about flying early is that the day's flights haven't had a chance to get backed up too much yet. There were still a few bedraggled people wandering around the airport, which might have been storm-related, or maybe they always looked like that. I did a quick check for those flower vending machines I'd once seen at the airport in Las Vegas, but I didn't find any. What is wrong with the world that you can still get your shoes shined at an airport, but you can't buy flowers?

I had a three-hour layover in Charlotte, which made me feel like I should start walking to Tampa to get some exercise in and have the pilot pick me up along the way. Instead I walked the terminal, checked for flowers, came up empty. But I did meet up with an awesome therapy dog named Tucker, who was wearing a blue and yellow vest that said "Pet Me." His owner told me Tucker was one of a rotating group of volunteer therapy dogs at the Charlotte airport whose job is to make travelers feel less stressed about traveling.

Traveling was the only part of this trip I wasn't stressed about, but it was nice to get those doggie kisses anyway.

Much like a Girl Scout, a good preschool teacher is always prepared. So I grabbed a cup of coffee at Starbucks, commandeered one of the white rocking chairs perched in a long row in the middle of the atrium. I rolled my carryon over beside me. I unzipped the front flap and pulled out a sheet of red tissue paper, a green pipe cleaner, and a pair of TSA-compliant nail scissors.

And I made the red rose I'd promised.

· · · · ·

In a movie, John and I would spot each other across the crowded Tampa terminal. Our eyes would meet, hold. Time would freeze. And then we'd run. He'd scoop me up and spin me around as if we were ballroom dancers. I'd bend my knees, one pointed toe a little lower than the other, and dazzle him with my smile while he was dazzling me with his.

Real life is more awkward.

John didn't see me until I was standing right behind him.

"Hey," I said.

He turned around. His Heath Bar eyes went to the tissue paper rose I'd tucked behind one ear.

"Nice rose," he said.

"Thanks," I said.

We hugged clumsily, the tissue paper rose rustling in my ear when he grazed it.

He reached for my carryon.

"Listen," I said.

"Wait," he said. "Let's go somewhere first."

I turned on the radio while John drove over Tampa Bay. The Beatles were singing "When I'm Sixty-Four." It seemed like a good oldies omen, but I also had to admit the lyrics contained more questions than answers. And it was a song to sing along to, at the top of our lungs. It made me sad to miss it.

We drove to the end of a causeway in Dunedin. A big sign appeared to our left: Honeymoon Island State Park.

"Well, that's encouraging," I said.

"Wait till you see this place," John said. He paid the admission, drove down a road flanked with dune grass. We passed the dog park and John parked his car near the nature center. I twisted my tissue paper rose around his rearview mirror.

It was a gorgeous beach. Unspoiled. Turquoise water. Sugar white sand. Tidal pools and rugged trees on the inland side. We walked and walked the long arc of the beach, stopping to pick up a shell here and there, or to get a closer look at a piece of coral or one of the huge sponges that dotted the sand. We saw ospreys and a great blue heron and oystercatchers and plovers and sandpipers and terns, and lots of other birds we couldn't identify.

A gang of laughing gulls flew over us, doing what they do best, their shrill raucous calls unmistakable.

"I think," John yelled over the roar of waves and the wind, "they're telling us to lighten up."

"Excellent advice," I yelled.

We took a ferry ride across Hurricane Pass to Caladesi Island, dolphins frolicking beside us, a manatee floating majestically as we docked. We bought some bottled water, cut behind the ranger station and found the start of the nature trail.

The trail was sheltered and shady, and we were ready to talk.

"It was big of you to fly down here," John said.

"It certainly was," I said.

He laughed, put his arm around my shoulders.

A single shell was sitting in the exact center of the white sand path. I bent down and picked it up. It was a solid shell, heavy for its size, a shiny twirl of salmon pink turning to orangey brown, a single point at the bottom, multiple spires on top.

"I'm not used to having a lot of people around," John said. "And I like things to be neat and, you know, uncluttered."

I nodded. "I'm okay with criticism, as long as you dole it out one thing at a time. But I don't think it's fair when you save it up and throw it at me all at once."

John nodded.

"I think," I said, "we need to assume that we're both doing the best we can. And that we'll get better at it."

We came to another shell, exactly the same kind, all by itself in the exact center of the path. I stopped, picked it up. It was like the beachy version of following a trail of breadcrumbs.

"Working remote," John said, "isn't as easy as I thought it would be. There's no separation."

I took a sip of my water. "What about working out in the trailer?"

"Your dad's back in the house?"

"He most certainly is. And Joe and his crew are cranking away on his man cavern, you'll be happy to hear, and I think he'll be moved in there before we know it. So maybe you could borrow the trailer, or rent it, and if that doesn't work, maybe we could try to find another one and you could write it off as a business expense."

"That's a great idea. I've always wanted a canned ham trailer."

"See," I said. "The sky's the limit."

I bent down, picked up another shell in the center of the path. I was really starting to understand my brother Michael's golf ball addiction.

"A couple of things though," I said. "I've given it a lot of thought and I want to keep Pebbles and all the kittens. You should have seen Mother Teresa with them—it was awesome. They'll all be one big pack with Horatio before we know it."

We walked in silence for a while. The trail looped around. We came to another shell and I picked up that one, too.

"Okay," John said. "But if we're going to go big in the animal department, then I'd like to raise the possibility of another dog. You know, to balance things out."

"Deal," I said. "As long as it's cat friendly. Okay, here's the big one. Polly's house got hit by the storm and she's moved in with us. Probably until after her baby is born."

John didn't say anything.

"But," I said, "the good news is I found the keys that lock the bedrooms."

We walked. I picked up another shell. We walked some more.

"Listen," I said. "I know the next few months aren't going to be easy, and I know you like tidy. But life isn't like that. It's not all orderly. Shit happens. Stuff gets packed away in boxes. Cats get born under your porch. Assistant teachers you really like get pregnant and need some support, and you have to do it, because you can and because that's who you are. And sometimes in life you get off track. And then you have to get back on again."

"I might be a little bit more hesitant about some of this," John said, "but I've spent the last two days watching TV with my parents and Horatio and explaining to them what just happened. Explaining to my parents, that is—Horatio already gets it. And by the way, just so it doesn't take you by surprise when you meet them, my parents only eat on television tables, and my mother still insists on cutting up my meals into little squares."

"Sorry," I said. "I don't do crazy families."

I picked up one more shell just before the trail ended. John and I cut across a grassy area toward the ferry dock. I stopped at a big wooden Shells of Caladesi display stand. I held up one of the shells and tried to match it to the labeled shells under the glass.

"*Strombus pugilus*," I said. "They're fighting conch shells. Oh, wow, I think somebody must have left them for us, to help us get back on track."

"Interesting thought," John said. "But that doesn't mean we have to take all those shells home with us, does it?"

"Seashells are not clutter," I said, "but I'm willing to compromise. How about we keep one shell and put the others back on the trail for the next couple that needs some good fighting juju?"

John sighed. "Fine."

We looped through the trail again, left the fighting conch shells for the next fighting couple that came along. Because I was pretty sure there wasn't a single couple out there that couldn't use some extra help during the rocky stretches.

I threw my water bottle in a trash barrel, kept the cap. I rummaged in my purse for a marker, drew a little heart and the date on the bottle cap, held it up for John to see.

He reached for me. When we kissed, it felt like home, and as if we were fueling up for whatever life blew in our direction next.

. . . .

Be the first to hear about the next book in the Must Love Dogs series and stay in the loop for giveaways and insider extras at ClaireCook.com/newsletter/.

Sarah's Red Tissue Paper Rose

(Because you never know when you might need one)

1 sheet red tissue paper
1 green pipe cleaner
1 pair scissors (blades no longer than four inches if you're flying)
1 pencil

1) Fold tissue paper in half. Fold in half a second time. Fold in half a third time.

2) Cut the largest circle you can, going through all layers, and remembering to keep it loose rather than perfect, because that's the way nature is and that's the way life is.

3) Keeping the tissue paper circles stacked, roll them all around a pencil. Move the pencil up and down and side to side to curl the petals.

4) Roll one circle into a cone shape. Wrap a second circle around the first one, starting it down from the top a bit. Do the same thing with the next three petals, moving each one down a little.

5) Wrap only about a quarter of the final three circles around the cone, leaving the rest of the tissue paper flat so that the last three pieces reach all the way around.

6) Twist the pipe cleaner around the bottom of the rose. Give the rose a good fluff and tuck it behind your ear.

Claire

Thank you so much for reading *Must Love Dogs: Who Let the Cats In?*, Book 5 of the *Must Love Dogs* series! If you enjoyed it, I hope you'll take a moment to tell a friend or leave a short review online. I really appreciate your support!

As I write this, I'm just about to turn my attention to a new adventure for the three women of *The Wildwater Walking Club*. So just in case you haven't read the original novel, I've included an excerpt for you.

Happy Reading!

Excerpt
The Wildwater Walking Club

DAY 1
132 steps

On the day I became redundant, I began to walk.
Okay, not right away. First I lay in bed and savored the
sound of the alarm not going off. I'd been hearing that
stupid beep at the same ridiculous time pretty much
every weekday morning for the entire eighteen years
I'd worked at Balancing Act Shoes.

I stretched decadently and let out a loud,
self-indulgent sigh. I pictured the zillion-count
Egyptian cotton sheets I'd finally get around to buying.

I'd pull them up to my chin to create a cozy cocoon, then wiggle down into the feather bed I'd buy, too, a big, fluffy one made with feathers from wildly exotic free-range birds.

I'd once had a pair of peacock earrings that came with a note saying, "Since peacocks lose their feathers naturally, no peacocks were harmed in the making of these earrings." I'd always meant to look that up to see if it was a marketing ploy or if it was actually true. If so, then maybe I could find a peacock feather comforter. Though I suppose what would be the point of using peacock feathers in a comforter if you couldn't see them? Perhaps I could invent a see-through comforter that let the iridescent blues and greens shimmer through. Though I guess first I'd need to come up with a zillion-count see-through Egyptian cotton.

I closed my eyes. I flipped over onto my back and opened them again. I stared up at a serious crack, which I liked to think of as the Mason-Dixon Line of my ceiling. My seventh-grade history teacher would be proud she'd made that one stick.

I rolled over, then back again. I kicked off my ordinary covers. On the first morning I could finally sleep in, I seemed to be more awake than I'd been at this hour in decades. Go figure.

After a long, leisurely shower, a bowl of cereal, and an online check of the news and weather, I called Michael on his cell at 8:45 A.M. It rang twice, then cut off abruptly without going to voice mail.

So I sent him an email. "Call me when you can," it said.

A nanosecond later my email bounced back: "Returned Mail: Permanent Fatal Errors."

I dialed his office number. At least that voice mail picked up. "Hi, it's me," I said. "I seem to be having technical difficulties reaching you. But the good news is I have all the time in the world now. Anyway, call me when you get this." I laughed what I hoped was the perfect laugh, light and sexy. "Unless, of course, you're trying to get rid of me."

By 11 A.M., I'd watched enough morning TV to last me a lifetime, and I still hadn't heard back from him. I tried to remember if we had specific plans for that night. Michael worked for the buyout company, Olympus, so we'd had to keep things on the down low. I mean, it wasn't that big a deal. I was leaving anyway, and he'd be right behind me, so it was just a matter of time.

After the initial army of auditors had stopped acting like nothing was going on, when everybody with half a brain knew something was obviously up at Balancing Act, Michael had been one of the first Olympus managers to come aboard. He was handsome, but not too, and exactly my age, which gave us an immediate bond in an industry that more and more was comprised of iPod-wearing recent college grads. Some of them had become friends, at least work friends, but they were still essentially children.

Michael and I had commonality, both current and past. I was a Senior Manager of Brand Identity for

Balancing Act. He was a Senior Brand Communications Manager for Olympus. Potato, potahto. The athletic shoe industry is market-driven rather than product-driven, which means, basically, that even though we don't actually need a two-hundred-dollar pair of sneakers, we can be convinced that we do. Fads can be created, predicted, or at least quickly reacted to, and in a nutshell, that's how Michael and I both spent our days.

But even more important, we'd both danced to Van Morrison's "Moondance," gotten high to the Eagles' "Witchy Woman," made love to "Sweet Baby James" back when James Taylor had hair. Maybe not with each other, but still, we had the generational connection of parallel experiences, coupled with your basic boomer's urge to do something new, fast, while there was still time.

One of the first things he said to me was, "It's business, baby."

We were sitting in the employee cafeteria, and I felt a little jolt when he called me *baby*. He had rich chocolate eyes and a full head of shiny brown hair without a strand of gray, which meant he probably dyed it, but who was I to talk.

"Of course, it's business," I said. I gave my own recently camouflaged hair a little flip and added, "Baby."

He laughed. He had gorgeous white teeth, probably veneers, but so what.

"What's your off-the-record recommendation?" I asked.

He leaned forward over the button-shaped table that separated us, and the arms of his suit jacket gripped his biceps. I caught the sharp, spicy smell of his cologne. Some kind of citrus and maybe a hint of sandalwood, but also something retro. Patchouli?

"The first deal," he said, "is always the best."

"So grab the VRIF and run?" I asked, partly to show off my new vocabulary. Balancing Act employees, even senior managers like me, didn't find out we'd become the latest Olympus acquisition until the day it went public. Since then, the buzz had been that the way to go was to take your package during the VRIF or Voluntary Reductions in Force phase. Olympus was all about looking for redundancies and establishing synergies, code for getting rid of the departments that overlapped.

Right now, the packages were pretty generous. I could coast along for eighteen months at full base salary, plus medical and dental. They were even throwing in outplacement services to help me figure out what to do with the rest of my life. The only thing missing was a grief counselor. And maybe a good masseuse. By the time we got to the Involuntary Reductions in Force phase, aka the IRIF, who knew what I'd be looking at.

Michael glanced over his shoulder, then back into my eyes. "Here's the thing, Noreen. Or do you prefer Nora?"

"Nora," I said, even though no one had ever called me that until this very moment. I'd been called Nor, Norry, Reeny, Beany, NoreanyBeany, even String-

Beany, though I had to admit that one was a few years and pounds ago. Mostly it was just plain Noreen. Michael's baby reeled me in, but I swallowed his *Nora* hook, line, and sinker.

I forced myself to focus. "Wall Street," he was saying, "will expect some performance from the synergy created by combining companies. The way to get performance is to streamline numbers, to create efficiencies. Human resources, finance, operations, marketing—lots of overlap. Ergo . . ."

I raised my eyebrows. "Ergo?" I teased.

He raised his eyebrows to match mine, and even though it would be another two weeks before we ended up in bed together, I think we both knew right then it was only a matter of time.

I leaned my elbows on the table. "So, what?" I said. "I leave so you can have my job?"

"Off the record," he said, "I'll probably be right behind you. I mean, take my job, please. You'd be doing me a favor. I'm just waiting till they offer the VRIF package to the Olympus employees they've brought in."

"Seriously?" I said. "You really think you'll take it? And do what?"

He laced his fingers together behind his head and arched back in his chair. "Let's see. First off, I think I'd light a bonfire and burn up all my suits and ties. Then I'd chill for a while. Maybe buy a van, find me a good woman, drive cross-country." He smiled. "Then look around for a partner, someone to start a small business with."

At eleven-thirty, I called Michael's cell again. The second ring cut off midway, once more without going to voice mail. I waited, then pushed Redial. This time it cut off almost as soon as it started ringing. I sent another email. It bounced back with the same fatal message. I called his office number, but when that voice mail picked up, I just hung up.

I was seriously creeped out by now. I thought about calling someone else at work to see if maybe there was a logical explanation, like everybody in the whole building was having both cell service and mail server problems, but I couldn't seem to make myself do it.

I thought some more, then threw on a pair of slimming black pants and a coral V-neck top over a lightly padded, modified pushup bra pitched as a cutting-edge scientific undergarment breakthrough in subtle enhancement. A little figure-flattering never hurt, even if it was hyperbole, and if nothing else, the coral worked well with my pale skin and dark hair. The last time I'd worn it, Michael had said I looked hot. Smoking hot, come to think of it, though that was probably an overstatement, too.

The midday drive into Boston was a lot shorter without the commuter congestion. Who knew that unemployment would be the best way to beat the traffic? Still, I had plenty of time to get a plan. I'd simply pretend I'd left one of my favorite sweaters behind and wanted to grab it before someone ran off with it. And I was in the neighborhood anyway because I was meeting a friend for lunch. And I just thought I'd poke my head in and say *Hi, Michael.* And he'd say he was just thinking about me, trying to remember if we had plans for dinner. I'd tilt my head and tell him if he was lucky, maybe I'd even consider cooking for him. And he'd smile and make a crack about maybe it would be safer to get takeout.

The main lot was packed, but eventually I found a parking spot. I reached into my glove compartment for the lanyard that held my employee badge, slipped it over my head, and made for the front entrance.

When the revolving door spilled me out into the lobby, I held up my badge for the uniformed guard.

He waved his handheld scanner over the laminated bar code like a wand.

I headed for the elevators, the way I had a million times before.

"Ma'am?" he said.

I turned. He held up his scanner. I held out my badge again.

This time I watched. When the laser light hit the bar code, it flashed red instead of the customary green.

We looked at each other. This was the grouchy guard, the one who never said a word and always looked like he wished he were anywhere but here. I found myself wishing I'd tried a little harder to befriend him.

I laughed. "Well, I guess it didn't take them long to get over me." I gave my hair a toss. "Lucky me, I took a buyout. I just need a minute to run up and grab something I forgot." He didn't say anything, so I added, "A sweater. A cardigan. Black, with some nice seaming around the buttons. I'll be back before you even start to miss me."

"Sorry, ma'am, I can't let you do that. Orders."

I blew out a gust of air. "Just call up," I said. "Sixth floor." I held out my card again so he could read my name.

He ran his finger down a list on a clipboard. "Sorry, ma'am. You're on the No Admittance List."

"You're not serious," I said, though it was pretty obvious that he was.

I waited. He looked up again. I met his eyes and couldn't find even a trace of sympathy in them, so I tried to look extra pathetic, which by that point I didn't really even have to fake.

"Maybe you can call somebody and ask them to bring it down," he said finally. "On your cell phone," he added.

"Unbelievable," I said. I stomped across the lobby so I could have some privacy. Since I hadn't really left a sweater behind, I decided to just cut to the chase and call Michael's cell. Half a ring and it went dead.

There is always that exact moment when the last shreds of denial slip away and your reality check bounces. I closed my eyes. Eventually, I opened them again. I called his office number. "You piece of shit," I whispered to his voice mail.

I stood there for a minute, scratching my scalp with both hands. Hard, as if I might somehow dig my way to a good idea. When that didn't happen, I walked out, without even a glance at the guard. I kept my head up high as I walked across the parking lot, in case someone was watching from one of the windows. I found my car and climbed back into it.

Just as I was getting ready to pull out onto the access road, I caught the purple-and-white-striped Balancing Act Employee Store awning out of the corner of my eye. I banged a right and pulled into a parking space right in front of it.

I stopped at the first circular display I came to and grabbed a pair of our, I mean *their*, newest shoe, the Walk On By, in a size 8½. It was strictly a women's model, positioned as the shoe every woman needed to walk herself away from the things that were holding her back and toward the next exciting phase of her life. *Shed the Outgrown. Embrace Your Next Horizon. Walk On By.*

Even though I'd been part of the team to fabricate this hook out of thin air, I still wanted to believe in the possibility. I handed the box to the woman at the register. I held up my badge. I held my breath.

Her scanner flashed green, and she rattled off a price that was a full 50 percent off retail.

"Wait," I said. I ran back to the display, grabbing all the Walk On Bys in my size. Then I sprinted around the room, scooping up whatever I could find in an 8½. Dream Walker. *(You'll Swear You're Walking on Clouds.)* Step Litely. *(Do These Sneakers Make Me Look Thin?)* Feng Shuoe. *(New Sneakers for a New Age.)* I didn't stop until I'd built a tower of shoeboxes on the counter.

"Take a buyout?" the woman asked as she rang me up.

I nodded.

I gave her my credit card, and she handed me a bright purple pedometer. "On the house," she said. "It's the least Balancing Act can do for you."

"Thanks," I said. I hooked it onto my waistband, and that's when I started to walk.

DAY 2
54 steps

UGH.

DAY 3
28 steps

SO THIS IS ROCK BOTTOM.

DAY 4
17 steps

NO, THIS IS.

Keep reading! Download your copy of The Wildwater Walking Club or order the paperback online. Stay in the loop for Noreen, Tess and Rosie's next adventure at ClaireCook.com.

Acknowledgments

I'm so grateful to my incredible readers for giving me the gift of my writing career. Thank you for cheering me on, sharing my books with your friends and family, and making me feel that we're all in this together.

A big thank you to my Facebook and Twitter followers for jumping in to be my research assistants time and again. The details you share are always fun, fascinating, and really helpful.

Ginormous thanks to Ken Harvey, Jack and Pam Kramer, and Beth Hoffman for helping me make this a better book. Your support means everything. Another big thank you to Sharon and Ali Duran for perfectly timed enthusiasm.

A huge thank you to Pebbles for giving birth to kittens under the porch. All five of you stole our hearts and walked right into this book.

Thanks and more thanks to Jake, Garet, and Kaden for always being there when I need you.

ABOUT CLAIRE

I wrote my first novel in my minivan at 45. At 50, I walked the red carpet at the Hollywood premiere of the adaptation of my second novel, *Must Love Dogs*, starring Diane Lane and John Cusack. I'm now the *New York Times* bestselling author of 16 books. If you have a buried dream, take it from me, it is NEVER too late!

I've reinvented myself once again by turning *Must Love Dogs* into a series and writing my first nonfiction books, *Never Too Late: Your Roadmap to Reinvention (without getting lost along the way)* and *Shine On: How To Grow Awesome Instead of Old*, in which I share everything I've learned on my own journey that might help you in yours.

I've also become a reinvention speaker, so if you know a group that's looking for a fun and inspiring speaker, I hope you'll send them in my direction. Here's the link: http://ClaireCook.com/speaking/. Thanks!

I was born in Virginia, and lived for many years in Scituate, Massachusetts, a beach town between Boston and Cape Cod. My husband and I have moved to the suburbs of Atlanta to be closer to our two adult kids, who actually want us around again!

I have the world's most fabulous readers and I'm forever grateful to all of you for giving me the gift of this career. Shine On!

xxxxxClaire

HANG OUT WITH ME!
ClaireCook.com
Facebook.com/ClaireCookauthorpage
Twitter.com/ClaireCookwrite
Pinterest.com/ClaireCookwrite

Be the first to find out when my next book comes out and stay in the loop for giveaways and insider extras: ClaireCook.com/newsletter.

CPSIA information can be obtained
at www.ICGtesting.com
Printed in the USA
LVHW041521210920
666682LV00003B/648

9 781942 671183